Tiny Acts of
Love

Tiny Acts of

Love

LUCY LAWRIE

BLACK & WHITE PUBLISHING

First published 2014
by Black & White Publishing Ltd
29 Ocean Drive, Edinburgh EH6 6JL

1 3 5 7 9 10 8 6 4 2 14 15 16 17

ISBN: 978 1 84502 721 6

A CIP catalogue record for this book is available from the British Library.

ALBA | CHRUTHACHAIL

Typeset by Iolaire Typesetting, Newtonmore
Printed and bound by Grafica Veneta S. p. A. Italy

For my girls, Emily and Charlotte

Acknowledgements

I want to thank my agent, Joanna Swainson, for her dedication, imagination and unwavering support. Heartfelt thanks also to the team at Black & White Publishing, for believing in my story and bringing it to life.

I am greatly indebted to Anne Fine, for reading the manuscript in its infancy, and for giving me the advice and encouragement I needed to keep going. Thank you to Ute Carbone, Shuna Meade, Dorothy Shamah, Geoffrey Gudgion, Paul Hutchens and Julie Erwin for their thoughtful critiques of the manuscript at various stages. I would have been lost without the friendship, insight and writerly support of Jane Farquharson and Lesley McLaren throughout this process (thanks also for fixing my plot, Jane!). To Arlene Eves, Vicky Watson, and Katherine and Adam West, thank you for so many things, but especially for telling me I could do this.

Thank you to my mum and dad, for all of the love and the stories. And finally, thank you to my husband Colin, and my daughters Emily and Charlotte. This is my love story to you.

1

I'd been awake for eighty-six hours when I realised what my husband had done. We'd just got home from the hospital and he was upstairs holding Sophie so that I could make myself a cup of tea and possibly have a nap.

But by the time I'd inched my way to the kitchen, tea-making seemed too daunting a task – something I'd been used to doing in a previous life, but not now. From the fridge magnets and the Isle of Skye tea towel to the strand of spaghetti dried onto the hob, everything seemed familiar but distant, as though I'd returned to a house I'd lived in a long time ago.

My eye caught the laptop, open on the kitchen table. People were bound to have heard about the birth by now – maybe I should check my emails. Perhaps some words of congratulation would flick a switch, jump-start me, and shake me out of this jittery, twilight world.

To my surprise, I had a hundred and four unread emails, all with identical subject descriptions. I opened up my sent box, a terrible suspicion forming in my mind. The offending communication was right there at the top.

Subject: 48 Stitches Later!

Attachment: sophiebreastfeeding.jpg

She has arrived! Sophie Louise Carlisle, a bouncing baby girl 7lb 5oz. Cassie's waters broke on Monday afternoon (at work!) and we rushed up to the Edinburgh Royal Infirmary in a taxi (taxi driver NOT happy). However, she wasn't dilated enough, so we were

sent home. Contractions started overnight, and when we went
back the next morning, we were rushed up to the delivery suite
where the midwife decided . . .

Unable to read any more, I opened the attachment. It was a
photograph of my top half, naked and white against hospital
sheets. I was frowning in concentration as I tried to coax my
nipple into Sophie's mouth.

It had been sent to every name in my contacts list, including
the following recipients:

1. David Galbraith, Senior Partner, Everfield Chase,
   London office. He'd been the lawyer acting on the
   other side of a multi-million pound joint venture
   called Project Vertigo. I'd been advising on transfer of
   employment issues and for some reason got involved
   in some late-night emailing from my home computer.
2. Everyone else from Everfield Chase who had ever worked
   on Project Vertigo. This ran to dozens of people, including:
   Nadeem Madaan (employment law), Bill Harkness
   (banking), Julie MacDonald (tax), Benjamin Trent
   (property), and Ashley Green (night typing secretary).
3. Doreen King of HM Revenue & Customs – provider
   of guidance in relation to a tax issue that had arisen in
   another corporate transaction.
4. Elliot McCabe, Manager of Braid Hills Funeral Home
   – correspondence concerning Great Auntie Judith's
   funeral.
5. Renato Di Rollo, Reservations desk, Hotel San Romano.
   Holiday booking.
6. Malkie Hamilton. Ex-boyfriend. Oh my God.

'Jonathan!'

He eventually appeared, carrying Sophie snug against him on one forearm, supporting her head in his palm.

'Is it time for your paracetamol?' he asked with a bright smile.

'What . . . *is* this?' I whispered, my hand pointing somewhere in the direction of the screen. The effort of twisting my head to look up at him had dissolved my vision into a field of black swirls.

'What? Let me see.' He peered in closer. 'It's the email I wrote in the hospital – remember, the one I showed you?'

'What? I've never seen this before in my life!'

He paused for a moment, frowning while he considered his response. 'Well, maybe you were a bit . . . out of it . . . at the time . . .'

Scenes from the birth, fragmented and disconnected, surfaced in my mind: Jonathan fiddling with his BlackBerry during the pushing stage, at around the point where I'd reached a calm acceptance that I would never get out of that room alive; Jonathan taking pictures as the midwife hauled a purple, blood-stained Sophie onto my chest for skin-to-skin contact; Jonathan waving the BlackBerry in my face just as the haemorrhaging started . . .

'You needn't look like that, Cassie. You said it was okay.'

'I might very well have done. But I was not of sound mind at the time.'

This lawyerly pronouncement didn't seem to make much of an impression on him. He merely bent his head and kissed Sophie's nose six times. Her arms flew out in a startle reflex. It occurred to me that we'd have to take off the hospital bracelet that still encircled her thin, translucent wrist; she was ours now. I could scarcely believe they'd let us take her home.

'And anyway.' I glared at Jonathan again. 'Then you decided to email it to half the lawyers in the UK?'

'What do you mean?'

'You've managed to send it to all my contacts, which seems to include everybody I've ever sent an email to since I got this account.'

He was quiet for a moment, taking this in. 'Hmmm. You'll need to change your default settings.'

'So it's my fault now?' Rage was bubbling up in the pit of my stomach, but somehow it wasn't reaching as far as my voice, or the part of my brain that formed words. I sat back with a big shuddering sigh.

'Don't you think you might be overreacting? And besides,' he said, narrowing his eyes, 'you're not supposed to do work emails from a personal email account. You know that, Cassie.'

'There were other people on that list too.' I scanned through it again. 'The damp proofing guy, the fish deliverer . . . people who are now going to think I'm mad.'

'So? I hardly think that matters. If you like, I'll send out another email saying it was my fault, and that it wasn't intended to reach them.'

Before I could reply, the doorbell rang, and Jonathan rushed off to answer it. He came back beaming, an enormous bouquet of flowers in his non-Sophie arm.

The cellophane screeched as I tore off the card, making Sophie startle again.

'Congratulations! With best wishes from the Joint Ventures Team at Everfield Chase.'

With a squeal, I tossed the bouquet onto the table. 'For God's sake! It's from bloody Everfield Chase!'

Jonathan seemed delighted. 'You see, Cassie, everyone is going to be happy for you. I hope there were some clients on the list too. It's quite an original marketing tool – you'll certainly stand out in their memories, look at it that way.'

'Yes, I should think the mental image of their employment lawyer naked and breastfeeding in the delivery room will be quite hard to erase.'

'I'm sorry, Cassie-Lassie.' He came over and folded me into a hug with his spare arm. I detached myself and took Sophie from him – a process that took several moments as I eased my hands around her back, working my fingers upwards to support the back of her head. She felt more like a kitten than a baby; a pliant bag of bones. She curled into an upright position against me, nose nodding into my shoulder as she tried to move her head, sensing milk nearby. I stroked the nape of her neck with one finger, lost in the utter softness of her skin.

'Our very own joint venture, Cassie,' said Jonathan, curling his palm around the back of Sophie's head, his eyes looking moist.

And although it was a terrible line, it did make me smile. Because it was his way of saying that Sophie had been born out of our love, because of our love, and would grow up in our love like a little bud unfurling its petals towards the sun.

2

'Cassie.' Jonathan's voice woke me, pulling me up through fathoms of deep dark sleep. I opened my eyes, disorientated.

'Where's Sophie?' I jerked upright.

But there she was, asleep in her Moses basket beside the sofa.

'Oh, she's fine,' I breathed. She stirred at the sound of my voice, twisting her upper body towards me, pulling the plain white babygrow taut over her middle. One of her hands, resting by her cheek, opened and closed. But she didn't wake up.

'Yes, thank the Lord,' said Jonathan. 'You dozed off for ten minutes – and she's still alive!'

'Ten minutes?' Tears of rage sprang to my eyes. 'Why did you wake me?'

'Your phone's been ringing,' said Jonathan. He thrust it towards me. 'You've got five missed calls. I thought it might be important. You were trying to get Helen earlier, weren't you?'

'It's hardly going to be her, is it?' I snapped. 'It'll be the middle of the night in New Zealand.' I still hadn't entirely forgiven my best friend for moving to the other side of the world as soon as I'd got pregnant.

'And anyway,' Jonathan added. 'You don't want to sleep too long or you won't get to sleep tonight.'

I stared at him in incomprehension. 'I won't be *getting* any sleep tonight. She'll want fed every forty-five minutes as usual.'

'Not now we're back home, surely. That was just the hospital unsettling her.'

My phone rang again in my hand and I answered it.

'Cassie?' It was Murray Radcliffe, the managing partner at McKeith's solicitors, the firm where I worked. His barking voice jarred heavily against the peacefulness of the lamplit room. The sound of the phone ringing had woken Sophie and her face crumpled and turned a deeper pink. Jonathan tutted softly and swooped her up into his arms. Why was it that he seemed to know instinctively how to handle her, didn't seem intimidated by her fragility?

'What the *hell* are you playing at?'

Black swirls again; I must have sat up too quickly. I rubbed my eyes with the back of a hand that suddenly seemed to be trembling.

'I've seen your email. The one with the unsavoury pictures. I'm just going into a meeting with marketing to see what we can do by way of damage limitation. Joan's making a list of the clients and firm contacts involved and it doesn't make for comfortable reading, believe me.'

Oh God. 'Yes, I'm sorry about that. There was a bit of a mix-up, I'm afraid, because my husband—'

'It's not just the pictures, Cassie. There's also this: "If our Babycraft teacher can be believed, Sophie will be more demanding and unreasonable than even the most fearsome clients Cassie advises through McKeith's – so don't expect to hear from us for a while!" I mean, you've sent it to the head of RBS, for Christ's sake.'

I stood up, forgetting that this wasn't as straightforward as it used to be, and grimaced as I felt a hot trickle of blood down the inside of my leg. Clutching the crotch of my tracksuit bottoms, I hobbled towards the bathroom.

'But the thing is, you see, that was only a light-hearted comment. Hopefully any clients will realise that. Some people

7

have even emailed back with good wishes and congratulations.'
Not like you, you sociopath. 'Listen, Murray, I'm going to have
to . . .' I'd reached the bathroom and was rifling in the cabinet
for the heavy-duty maternity pads.

'Who has? Who has emailed you with congratulations?'

'Well, no actual clients, admittedly. But definitely people
within the business community. Such as . . . oops . . .' – two
spare cans of deodorant toppled out of the cabinet and rolled
across the tiles – 'such as a very nice funeral director called
Elliot McCabe . . .'

There was a pause. 'Not THE Elliot McCabe?'

'Umm . . .'

'Elliot McCabe, who owns a chain of funeral homes across
Britain and is thinking of expanding into Europe? Elliot
McCabe, the husband of Lorna McCabe, Chief Exec of
Turley Sturrock Holdings? How do you know him?'

'Well, *I* was a client of *his*, last year . . . or rather, my great-
aunt was. I mean, I wasn't, you know . . .'

'And he was *nice* to you, you say? Right, well maybe we can
salvage something from this. We've been trying to approach
him for months but he won't give us the time of day. He's a bit
of an oddball, by all accounts.'

Murray's tone was edging into the conversational now.
Maybe if I could keep him on this train of thought he'd calm
down and I could get off the phone without being fired.

'Really? Why's that?'

'He came up in discussion at the Signet Library do last
week. Apparently there have been all kinds of goings-on
at this Braid Hills funeral home of his. Peculiar stuff. Rich
pickings for us, by the sounds of it. I want you to telephone
him, apologising for the email and introducing yourself on
behalf of the firm. Try and set up a meeting.'

I looked up and saw myself in the mirror on the ba
the bathroom door – a bare-legged creature perched, Gollum-
like, on the loo, tracksuit bottoms abandoned on the blood-
streaked tiles. My hair was stringy and wild, and my face was
grey with heavy smudges under the eyes. I looked like the
victim of a mining accident, just winched to the surface after
being trapped underground for months.

'A meeting? But Murray, there's no way I can—'

'Cassie, I don't need to remind you how important it is to
build up your practice area, get some clients of your own?
It's one of the factors we'll be looking at in the redundancy
exercise. You did get the email about that, I suppose?'

'I would love to be able to take this on, really, but the
problem is—'

'Just do it, Cassie, if you would. I need to get to that meeting
now. Okay? Great. Bye.'

He hung up. I sank my head into my hands and growled,
furious with Murray, and even more so with myself for my
lack of assertiveness. He knew he wasn't allowed to do this
when I was on maternity leave, and he sure as hell knew that
I knew.

'Trouble at work?' asked Jonathan, when I'd sorted myself
out and returned to the living room. 'Oh look, Sophie!
Mummy's brushed her hair.'

'Murray just wants me to speak to a possible new client,' I
mumbled. 'One of the people you emailed. I'll sort it out.'

Jonathan didn't yet know about the redundancy exercise.
I hadn't been able to face thinking or talking about it, on top
of everything else. I couldn't lose my job. It wasn't just that
we needed the money, it was the fact that I'd managed to
negotiate a two and a half day week, to start on my return
from maternity leave. The chances of finding a new job on the

same terms were close to zero. I didn't want full-time nursery for Sophie. The thought made me hollow inside.

I was about to put down the phone when I noticed that there was another missed call listed. I pressed a key to view the number.

'What's the matter?' asked Jonathan.

'Nothing.'

'Why have you gone all red?'

'I haven't,' I said lightly, placing the phone on the seat beside me.

It was strange how something so embedded in the past could reassert itself in the present with no warning, boldly backlit on an LCD display. And even stranger, perhaps, how a set of digits could trigger such a profound, dizzying response from my circulatory system.

It was the number of Malkie Hamilton; my first head-over-heels love; the one who (as it had seemed at the time) got away; and unintended recipient of the email '48 Stitches Later'.

★

Mirroring my own feelings at that moment, Sophie threw up and started crying.

'I'll go and get her changed,' I said, holding out my arms. Apart from anything else, I wanted to evade any further questions.

Walking up the stairs, step by slow, painful step, I felt it again. I'd been trying to ignore it since getting back from hospital, but the house felt odd, off-balance, somehow.

To look at, it was an idyllic house. Painted cream, with Georgian-style windows and a roof of weathered red tiles, set in a mature garden of long lawns and whispering trees. And it was perfectly situated on Ravelston Dykes, a wide avenue on the spine of a hill on the north-west side of the city. Walking along that street was always a pleasure. In September, the sycamore seeds would spin down around you like tiny helicopters. By October, you would be ankle-deep in smoky leaves. Come May, you would be trailing through a pink slush of blossom.

And it was the perfect house for bringing a new baby home. We'd spent months making preparations, first decorating the nursery, a white sunny room facing the garden. We'd put up a border and matching curtains featuring small pink mice. Jonathan had built the cot, the changing table, and a chest of drawers for all her things. I had washed the tiny baby clothes and hung them on the line to dry in the fresh air before ironing them, folding them, and placing them in the drawers. We'd grown fondly used to the sight of our hospital bags standing packed and waiting at the front door. There were three – one for me (Evian spray, lavender oil, three sets of new pyjamas – white, with broderie anglaise detailing), one for the baby (nappies, clothes, tiny organic baby toiletries) and one for Jonathan (swimming trunks, for the birthing pool that was never to be, and a spare t-shirt).

During all these preparations, I'd thought that I'd known her intimately, this creature who'd poked her heels and elbows into me, who'd squirmed and hiccuped her way through the last few months. Jonathan and I had talked to her each night as we'd snuggled up to go to sleep, telling her about our days or what new item we'd bought for the nursery.

But that imaginary baby had gone now, replaced by this little stranger who made rest impossible, and pulled at my insides whenever she was out of my arms.

She'd pulled the house off its axis, too; that was what had

happened. Its centre of gravity had shifted from the rooms at the front – the hall and living room – to the nursery at the back. That was the heavy point, the point where I was standing if I tried to picture the house in my mind. The rest of the house had twisted, realigned itself, and now seemed to stand silent, waiting.

Waiting for what? Some kind of disaster, it felt like. Even climbing up these stairs was an activity fraught with peril. One slip, causing Sophie to lurch out of my arms, and it would all be over; the exhaustion, the confusion, those extravagant eyes and their dark blue gaze that plumbed unimagined depths of me. My throat went tight.

I found I could go no further. I sat down, three steps from the top, and folded my body around her.

'Jonathan!'

I sat calling him, over and over again, for five minutes or ten or maybe an eternity.

He didn't come.

★

'I was on the phone to Stephen!' he protested later that evening, for the hundredth time.

He was washing the dishes while I sat on a kitchen chair piled with cushions. Sophie had fallen asleep on me, and I was reluctant to move.

'He wanted to hear all about his beautiful niece. I spoke to Moira briefly too, but you've got to phone her tomorrow – she wants a blow-by-blow account of the birth.'

I shuddered. 'You mean they didn't get your email? They must be about the only people in the world who didn't. Was it blocked by the US government, or something?'

'You still haven't forgiven me, have you?'

I shrugged.

'Oh Cassie, I'm sorry. I'm an arse, I know. I was just on such a high during the whole birth thing. I wasn't thinking straight.' He shook his head and winced. 'It's not a very good email, is it?'

'There's no way you can . . . recall it, or stop people from opening it, somehow, is there? We have no idea where that picture could end up.'

I looked down at Sophie. So far, the only place she'd fall asleep was in my arms; she seemed to think I was the person most likely to take care of her. 'I don't like the idea of her spinning around cyberspace where anyone can look at her.'

'It's only a picture, Cass. I haven't sold her soul on eBay or anything.'

'It just doesn't seem safe . . . out there.'

'Out where?'

I waved a hand vaguely in the direction of the window.

'She's not out there, sweetheart. She's in here with us – in our house.'

'Yeah, well. There's something not right about this house.'

'What, Cassie?'

How could I explain it? 'There's a sort of gravitational pull, coming from the nursery.'

Jonathan made a faint squeaking noise, in his manful effort not to laugh. 'I think we'll need to cut down on some of that medication you're taking.'

'Yes, the mind-altering paracetamol.'

'Hmm. Or those tricksy iron tablets. But seriously, Cassie, you're tired. I think you should get off to bed. I'll look after Sophie.'

'I don't want to go to bed. I want us to sit down together

13

and watch television.' Maybe we could pretend, for just half an hour, that things were normal again.

'But there's no point in us both staying up.'

'I can't believe what we've done,' I said, shaking my head. 'I can't believe we thought we could just have a baby. We don't know anything about how to look after a baby.'

'Cassie, she's three days old. All she needs is milk, cuddles and sleep.'

'But this doesn't feel like home any more.'

Jonathan sighed. 'Of course this is our home, darling – you, me and Sophie. Everything will be fine.'

Would it be fine? She lay with her cheek against my forearm, her head resting in the crook of my elbow. What if I dropped her onto the tiles below? Would the back of that rounded head, with its soft whorls of hair, cave in like the shell of an egg?

'Jonathan. Help me.'

He tutted softly. 'Give her to me. Go to bed and get some rest. You'll feel better tomorrow.'

I transferred Sophie into his arms and went upstairs. I wanted to cry, but they were heavy tears, trapped somewhere inside, unable to fall. I hadn't been at all prepared for what would happen, giving birth to Sophie. I had walked through a door and found myself in a parallel world. And Jonathan hadn't come with me.

3

Somehow we survived the first week. And after that we even survived three nights of my mother staying. A former nurse, she was prone to spurts of evangelical zeal over health matters, and my pregnancy had sent her into overdrive. She'd spent the last nine months sending me useful articles about drug-free childbirth, organic skin products, the correlation between maternal broccoli intake and foetal development, and the importance of breastfeeding (which was apparently the answer to everything, including global terrorism, climate change, and the world's financial woes). Now she was here in person, I'd had to endure her Sad Face every time I let slip some failing in these respects (the epidural, the Diet Coke addiction, the bottles of formula lined up in the fridge).

On the last day of her stay, Mum and I had breakfast together in the kitchen – scrambled eggs, toast, and a pot of freshly made English breakfast tea, all prepared by Jonathan while he talked nonsense to Sophie in her Moses basket. He was now preparing to give her a 'top and tail' wash, so he'd turned the heating up high, and had gone upstairs to lay out towels, and find the special organic cotton wool he'd ordered online.

'So,' said Mum.

'So.' I could barely bring myself to look at her as she sat there across the table, rosy-cheeked and perfectly coiffed, her size twenty frame smart in black trousers, a pink shirt and pearls. The effect was only slightly marred by the sick-stained muslin cloth draped over her shoulder. Now that Jonathan had left the room, she'd no doubt start talking about Women's Matters. I braced myself for some enquiry about cracked nipples or stitches.

'Jonathan's having a hard old time, dealing with fatherhood, is he?'

I snorted into my cup of tea. '*What?* What are you talking about?'

'His nightmares, of course.'

'What nightmares?'

'Well, I can only *assume* they're nightmares. Unless he normally shouts, "No, Dad, no no, please," at three in the morning.'

He didn't normally mention his father at all, either at three in the morning or at any other time. Pretty much all I knew about him was that he'd died suddenly, when Jonathan was a teenager.

'When was this? I didn't hear anything.'

'But where have you been sleeping? In the nursery, no?'

'I still would have heard him.'

'It's surprising what happens in the brain of a new mother. You'll be tuned in to hear Sophie's cries, but pretty much oblivious to anything else.'

Typical of my mother to presume she knew what went on in my brain.

'Well, so what if he is having bad dreams?' I said. 'It's not surprising. Our sleep has been very erratic since we got home. I'm not going to start reading anything into it.'

'Just keep an eye on it, that's all I'm saying. It's not uncommon for new fathers to struggle with the transition. Becoming a parent can dredge up all sorts of things. I was reading about it the other day in . . . where was it, now? *Practical Parenting*, I think.'

Typical, *typical* Mum. It would be hard to find a person on this earth more at ease with fatherhood than Jonathan. It was *me* who woke up several times a night, wondering if Sophie had died quietly in her cot, *me* who greeted each morning with trepidation, wondering whether I'd be able to keep her alive for another day.

But, to be fair, Mum didn't know any of this – neither, for that matter, did Jonathan. I'd held tightly to my anxieties. Maybe I should try to be more communicative.

'So did you feel kind of thrown in at the deep end, then, when I was born? Like your life was turned upside down?'

There was a little cry from the Moses basket on the floor, and a flurry of wriggling limbs.

'Come on then, bunnykins,' said Mum, swooping over to pick Sophie up. 'There now! There now, itty-bitty peepkins! That's not so bad, is it?'

When she spoke to me it was in her patient voice. 'Well, I think I muddled through reasonably well, in the circumstances.'

'Sorry.' I'd forgotten, for a moment, that different rules applied to Mum. She'd been widowed when I was a baby, when my father had skidded off an icy road one bitter winter's night, on the Swedish island where they'd lived at the time. I'd learned, as a child, not to question her about it, because of the way the atmosphere in the room would thicken instantly, the way she would impart the minimum of information, and then deftly change the subject.

'What's there to be sorry for?' she asked in a sing-song voice, peering wide-eyed into my daughter's face. 'Itty-bitty cutie-kins, what's there to be sorry for?'

She passed Sophie to me. I rubbed her back, marvelling at her smallness, the way one hand could contain the curve of her ribcage.

17

'Why don't you just try one more time, now you're nice and relaxed.'

'Try what?'

'Just see if she'll take a feed. From the breast, I mean.'

'Mum!' I growled. 'She's been on bottles since she was two days old. I hardly think . . .'

'Ah yes, the whole minefield of nipple confusion. But still, I think it's worth . . . oh dear.'

A tear rolled down my face and plopped onto Sophie's back.

Mum reached out an awkward hand and patted me on the arm. 'Don't worry, Cassie, everyone feels a bit overwhelmed at first. Those post-partum hormones are a bugger,' she added in a conspiratorial tone. 'What you need is to meet up with other mums, establish a support network. Did I mention that a lovely girl called Jody phoned yesterday?'

Oh God. 'Did she?'

'I'm so glad you followed my advice and joined a Babycraft antenatal group. So nice to find an organisation that's not afraid to take proper views on things. Jody was phoning to tell you about the next meet-up – it's going to be at the John Lewis café. I wrote down the date for you.'

'Great.'

'Do at least try and sound a bit more enthusiastic, Cassie. It's a wonderful opportunity. The friends you make in your pram-pushing days will be your friends for life. Those who don't have children – like Helen – may well just drift away.'

There wasn't much further she could drift, though, was there? I had a sudden image of her asleep on a beach lilo, drifting towards Antarctica.

'Oh, and somebody else phoned on your mobile while you were in the shower. Elliot McCabe, he called himself . . .

wasn't that the name of the chappie who did Judith's funeral? Anyway, he said he'd got your message and was returning your call, and that in fact there was an employment problem he'd like to discuss with you.'

I'd been thrilled to get his voicemail when I'd phoned. In my short message, I'd apologised for the unsavoury email, thanked him for his congratulations, and said something like, 'Oh, and if there's ever any employment matter I can help with, don't hesitate to give me a shout.' Not exactly the hard sell; he wasn't supposed to phone me back.

'Cassie, for goodness' sake, stop slouching. You'll fall off that chair.'

★

After driving my mother to the airport, we took a trip to the Botanic Gardens to celebrate. Jonathan was keen to visit the pond first, marching ahead purposively with the pram. Once there, he lifted Sophie out, holding her upright to see the ducks and talking animatedly. She didn't seem all that interested. To be fair, she hadn't totally mastered the whole eye-focusing thing yet.

There was a bench just across from the pond, and I parked the pram – laden with three rucksacks of baby equipment – and sat down. An elderly lady sank gently down onto the bench next to me, and commented that it was a beautiful afternoon.

Jonathan paused in his duck monologue to pull Sophie's little crocheted hat down more snugly around her ears. His upper body was curled around her, like nothing else in the world mattered. But he looked at ease, comfortable, in a way that still eluded me. What I felt for her was so sharp, so uncompromising, always threaded through with terror. It bore little resemblance to the rosy maternal glow I'd felt while pregnant – or the easy, companionable bond I'd shared with Jonathan for the last eight years, for that matter.

What was love supposed to look like anyway? I would have answered the question with confidence two weeks ago; not any more.

But I suspected that easy and companionable wouldn't cut it any more, that something was going to have to change between Jonathan and me in this new, post-Sophie world. Everything that had preceded the birth – wedding plans, house-hunting, mini-breaks, candlelit dinners after work – now seemed irrelevant, like games played between strangers. He was no longer just a person I'd met by chance in a dodgy nightclub and subsequently chosen to marry. Now, through some strange alchemy involving Sophie, he was my flesh and blood.

I jumped when my phone rang.

'Hello, Cassie Carlisle here?'

'It's Elliot McCabe here – from Braid Hills Funeral Home. I'm following up from your phone message last week.'

'Oh yes, hello.' I changed my voice, realising with a little rush of shame that I'd answered the phone in lilting, ice cool tones tailored towards an imaginary Malkie – there had been two more missed calls from him in the last week. 'It's nice to speak to you. How can I help?'

'Your email came at a good time, because I was thinking about trying to find an employment lawyer. It's about the Working Time Regulations.'

'Okay,' I said, just about managing to stifle a yawn.

'More specifically, it's about on-call working. Everyone who works at Braid Hills has to do on-call time – we have a rota covering weekends and nights.'

'Nights doing . . . what? Exactly? Sorry.'

'Well, collections. From hospitals, nursing homes, clients' homes. Death is not a nine-to-five business – so we need to be available. But the thing is, one of our employees, a bit of a troublemaker, was mouthing off the other day, saying we weren't complying with the Regulations, and that his human rights were being violated because he was having to do too many call-outs.'

'How many corpses would he normally collect, on an average night?' I asked.

There was a loud gasp, and I turned round to see the old lady staring at me, open-mouthed in disgust. I couldn't move away from the bench, given the pram and the three rucksacks, so I just sort of curled inwards and tried to hide my face behind my non-phone hand.

'Well, there are only a handful each week. I think we'd be fine under the core working time rules. But this particular employee is claiming that his work involves a "special hazard" within the meaning of the legislation.'

'Oh. What kind of hazard?' If an employee's work involved a special hazard, then there were stricter limits on their working hours. I was damned if I could remember what they were, though.

'Dead people. He says he sees dead people.'

'But surely that's . . . I mean, it's . . .' It took me a moment to twig. 'Ah! Do you mean . . . I wonder if you could possibly mean, in a *Sixth Sense* kind of way?'

'Exactly!' said Elliot, sounding relieved. 'It's getting to be a bit of a problem. He's threatening to lodge a written complaint. Twice now he's refused to carry out his duties on the grounds that the deceased person in question has been rude to him. He refuses to use the back stairs or the upstairs meeting room. And he'll only drive one of the hearses, the newest one.'

'Oh dear. How inconvenient.' Why was it that all the loopy cases invariably ended up on my desk?

'And with this whole night-time working thing, he says the unusually high number of ghosts in the premises constitutes a special hazard, because they put him under intense mental strain. I don't want to have to take him off the night rota, but I don't want to face a claim either.'

'Could I give you a call back later today once I've double-checked the regulations?'

'I'd appreciate it if you could give me an answer now. I've got a meeting with him in ten minutes and I want to get this cleared up.'

My instinct was to prevaricate, but Murray Radcliffe's face popped into my mind, red and beaky and furious, like some mad-eyed Punch doll.

'I'm sure it's not a special hazard,' I said firmly.

'Good. Oh, and he wants me to arrange for an exorcism of the premises. Or a blessing or something.' He sighed. 'I'm ninety-nine per cent certain he's taking the piss, but I don't want to fall foul of the law. Is there any legal precedent for this sort of thing?'

'I doubt there'll be any case law authority. But I'm sure an exorcism won't be necessary.'

The old lady huffed, drew her coat around herself and walked off.

'Great. I'll go and give him a flea in his ear. Now, can I get you on this number in case anything else transpires? He may well lodge a written complaint.'

'Of course, that's fine,' I said in a sweet, capable voice. 'I hope the meeting goes well. Thanks for calling.'

As I said goodbye and ended the call I had a sudden urge to throw my mobile phone into the pond. I might actually have done so, had I not entertained a vague fear that this might have electrocuted the ducks.

I hauled the pram and the rucksacks over to Jonathan. 'What would happen if I threw my phone in there?' I asked him. He just gave me a strange look and turned to carry Sophie in the direction of the monkey puzzle trees.

★

That night I dreamed I was in the dock, in front of twelve bewigged judges, accused of professional negligence so dire that criminal charges had been brought.

'An exorcism of the premises was the only reasonable course of action,' said one of the judges. 'Send her down.'

I awoke to the sound of screaming. But it wasn't mine.

'Dad! No, please! No! I'm sorry. Please . . .'

Jonathan was thrashing around in the bed.

'Wake up!' I shook his shoulder gently. 'You're having a nightmare.'

His eyes shot open, and he stared at me for a second. Then he rolled over, dragging most of the sweat-soaked duvet with him, and started snoring.

I lay back on the pillow, exhausted. It was the first night since Sophie's birth that I'd attempted to sleep in my own bed. She'd taken a sudden, intense dislike to her cot, so we'd decided to let her sleep in our room, in her Moses basket. Although she preferred this, she'd still woken me twice already, and now Jonathan was getting in on the act, not to mention nightmares about exorcisms. I inched some of the duvet out of his grasp, and settled down to try and go back to sleep.

But a little wail emanated from the Moses basket beside me. I swung my legs out of bed, and took her through to the nursery for a feed.

Half an hour later, Jonathan appeared. I was sitting with Sophie in the rocking chair, with the laptop balanced on the changing table to one side of me.

'Did you have another nightmare?' I whispered. 'Are you okay? What was it about?'

'What the hell are you doing?'

'Oh, nothing. I had to check the Working Time Regulations about something, and I got a bit . . . distracted.'

'So why are you Googling "male post-natal depression"?' He leaned over and clicked on the history tab. 'Or "repressed childhood memories", or "psychological trauma and sudden death"? God, Cassie. This is just weird.'

'I was just worried about your nightmares—'

He gave a gusty sigh. 'I'm going back to bed.'

'But—'

'Er, Cassie, why have you heated up two bottles?'

'I didn't. That must be an old one.'

'Well, this one's warm.'

I looked down in horror at the bottle lodged in Sophie's mouth, realising it was cool to the touch.

'Oh shit! This is the bottle she had at bedtime and didn't finish! It must be seven or eight hours old!'

The bottle feeding instructions the midwife had grudgingly given us had stipulated that unused feeds must be thrown away within the hour, formula milk being a rich breeding ground for harmful bacteria.

I pulled the bottle out of Sophie's mouth, waking her and making her arms jerk out in a startle reflex. We both started crying.

Two hours and one frantic call to NHS 24 later, we finally got back to bed. We'd been told there was nothing we could do except stay vigilant, and call back if she started vomiting or had any diarrhoea.

'I can't believe it,' I whispered as we settled under the duvet. 'She's only ten days old and I've already poisoned her. It's my job to keep her safe. How do other people manage it?'

'Most people don't try and psychoanalyse their husbands using Wikipedia, in the dark, at three in the morning,' mumbled Jonathan as he rolled away from me. 'And if they do, they usually put their babies down first.'

I turned on to my side to face Sophie. Her breathing was soft and peaceful, but I knew I'd be staying awake to watch her; sleep went against all my instincts. The milk incident had merely underlined what I already knew: that it was a miracle that this little scrap of flesh had lungs that could breathe, and a heart that could beat on its own. And that it might all stop if I wasn't paying attention; watching, praying, willing the miracle to keep going.

4

'Cassie! Oh, it's good to see you!' cried Jonathan's mother, holding out her arms when I opened the front door.

'Hello, Dita!' I felt small in her embrace. Even with her height-disguising stoop, she stood a good head taller than me. She'd flown in from Holland to meet Sophie, who had now survived to the grand age of five weeks, none the worse, it seemed, for the consumption of the bacteria-laden milk that dreadful night.

'The flight was late, sorry,' said Jonathan, sweeping past us with Dita's bags. 'Then we had to wait ages in a taxi queue.'

I ushered her inside, closing the front door against the dark and rain. She unwound her scarf with a satisfied sigh, and I took it, along with her damp coat, and hung them up. I offered her a cup of tea, but she was looking longingly up the stairs, smoothing down her boyishly-cut grey hair with both hands.

'Would you like to have a peek?' Sophie had only just gone down after an hour of crying, but I knew I wouldn't need to ask Dita to be quiet. She winced as she tried to avoid creaking on the stairs, her paddle-like feet treading slowly in their flat shoes.

When we reached the bedroom Dita peered into the Moses basket, sucking in an 'ahh . . .' on the in-breath. She gripped my forearm and her voice emerged as a whisper. 'Cassie . . . she is gorgeous! What a beautiful baby!'

She kissed a finger, leaned over and gently touched Sophie's sleepsuited chest, the place over her heart. Together,

26

we watched the almost imperceptible rise and fall that came with each breath.

Exhausted by all her crying, Sophie didn't wake up, so I took Dita downstairs and we sat around the kitchen table while Jonathan made cheese-on-toast and heated up a tin of tomato soup. I was doubtful whether cheese-on-toast before bed was a good idea, in light of his bad dreams, which were now a regular occurrence – night-time in the Carlisle household was pretty lively now, when you added Sophie's antics and my insomnia into the mix. But his repertoire of meals was narrow to say the least, and it seemed a shame to dampen his enthusiasm.

'So, what is our plan for tomorrow?' asked Dita.

'Hmm, I don't know. I was meant to be meeting the girls from our Babycraft class in John Lewis, but I'm not sure if I'll go. It's so difficult to time it around Sophie's feeds.'

In truth, I hadn't been out of the house since Jonathan had gone back to work the previous week. I'd watched him shave and comb his hair that morning, and put on his grey pinstripe suit, and leave the house to re-enter the world of fund managing – of markets and stock values, of colleagues and targets and breakfast meetings – as though he was setting off for an alien planet.

'What is this Babycraft?' asked Dita.

'*Nutters*,' breathed Jonathan. Absorbed in his culinary endeavours, he didn't look up. He had pulled the cheese-on-toast from under the grill and was in the process of adding five drops of Worcestershire sauce to each piece in its semi-melted state.

'Well,' I continued, 'when we were expecting Sophie, we went to these antenatal classes run by this organisation called Babycraft. They were in somebody's house in Colinton.'

'Ah . . . *interesting*,' said Dita, leaning forwards and putting her elbows on the table. 'Stephen and Moira attended classes like these before they had the twins, I think. What did you have to do?'

'Mostly, it was the teacher telling us what to expect about the birth. She split us into groups and made us write lists.'

'On bloody flip charts!' said Jonathan, red-faced from heat and concentration, slamming the oven door shut as if for emphasis.

'And was she right?' Dita was lovely, the way she was so interested in everything.

'What do you mean, was she right?' I asked.

'Well, I mean, did you know what to expect, when it came to the birth?'

'Kind of. But there wasn't much about what to expect afterwards.'

'The next eighteen years . . .' Dita nodded, understanding completely.

'Anyway, we were sort of encouraged to stay in touch with the other couples.'

'A pretty weird bunch,' Jonathan cut in with a wiggle of his eyebrows and a big sigh.

'The hypno-birthers were pretty weird,' I conceded. 'In the first class we all had to say if we had done anything to prepare for the birth, and they said they were hoping to bring "prisoner of war wisdom" into the process.'

'What?' Dita looked bewildered.

'They had read this memoir of a man who was in a Japanese prisoner of war camp, and he used to pinch his ear whenever the guards made him do something he didn't want to do.'

'Really? Would that help, I wonder?' She frowned and poured another cup of tea.

'The idea was that it would block out the pain,' I said. 'You know, the pain of the birth. They wanted to have a home birth without any artificial pain relief. Except for the ear-pinching thing, and their special songs.'

'Ah. And did it work?'

'She said it did work. But then they were forced to go into hospital for an emergency C-section.'

'Oh, so, not really then.'

'No, not really.'

We watched as Jonathan deftly transferred the cheese-on-toast to our waiting plates. 'Don't worry,' said Dita. 'I'll come with you to John Lewis, if you like, and help you carry Sophie's bags. It will be really nice for you to see all your friends.'

In theory, I thought darkly.

★

The café at John Lewis was like a Dante-esque vision of hell. Dark, raincoated shapes circled around like vultures, poised to swoop down on any shortly-to-be vacated table. Sharp-elbowed old ladies, meeting for their weekly coffee and scone, were the quickest, and the most ruthless. Then there were the legion of the sleep-deprived – the pale, empty-eyed mothers with wailing offspring arching backwards off their hips, trying to manoeuvre enormous 'travel systems' through the crowd with one hand.

We found the Babycraft group comfortably ensconced in a corner – they'd pulled several sofas together so they could all sit round facing one another. When they saw us, there was a flurry of demonstrative hugs and air kisses. They huddled round Sophie and shrieked their congratulations until she started bawling. I jiggled her around while Dita slipped off to get some drinks. After a while the general discussion turned to the merits of different types of pram, but one of the girls, Jody, turned to talk to me.

'Is Sophie only five weeks old? Gosh, she looks a *lot* bigger than that. She's bigger than Vichard and he's seven weeks now!'

Jody must have been thirty-ish, but looked about twelve with her shiny light brown hair and apple red cheeks. To add to the childlike effect, she seemed unable to pronounce her 'r's' properly – which was unfortunate considering she'd named her son Richard.

'Are you feeding her naturally?' She pronounced it 'natuvally'.

I took a deep breath. Not this *again*. I felt tempted to say I'd installed a machine with a robotic arm in Sophie's bedroom to administer her nightly bottles so I didn't have to bother shifting my arse out of bed.

'Actually, she's on formula.'

'Oh, right,' said Jody, her voice dropping to barely above a whisper.

Dita returned to the table with a tray bearing shortbread, and two tall glasses of hot chocolate topped with cream and chocolate flake. *Helen*. We used to disappear off to Negociants each day after nine o'clock lectures, to alleviate our boredom with brioche toast and the creamiest hot chocolate in town.

'Are you okay?' whispered Dita. A tear escaped my right eye, trickled down and hung quivering on my jawline. I laid my cheek against the top of Sophie's head, but more tears escaped and slid into her downy hair.

'What about you?' I said to Jody when my voice was steady again. 'Are you still breastfeeding?'

She snorted. 'I'm producing it quicker than he can drink it! We're having to throw bags of it away, aren't we shnoozums? Our freezer is overflowing with the stuff!' She lifted the spindly, fearful-looking Vichard up to eye level and squashed her nose against his. Suspended in mid-air, he gave a querulous cry. 'Oh, he's hungry,' she said, thrusting him back down onto her lap and pulling up her top.

Shona, one of the other mums, looked across in approval. She was a lawyer too, but a properly grown-up one. She was a litigator who specialised in medical defence cases, and could sometimes be seen on *Scotland Today* giving a statement on behalf of some exonerated medic outside the courthouse.

'You know,' she said leaning forward and raising her eyebrows, 'I didn't realise that any advertising of formula milk for babies under six months has been completely banned. That's a pretty huge statement, isn't it? They must have found some pretty compelling evidence to back that up.'

I wondered who 'they' were . . . a large-bosomed army of Babycraft 'breastfeeding counsellors', perhaps.

'Oh yes, I saw that too,' chipped in Molly, who was one half of the hypno-birthing couple. 'And it was also saying that they wanted to make it so that formula would be kept behind the counter in pharmacies, and you would have to ask for it if you wanted to buy it.'

'Yes, I go to a housing estate in Muirhouse to get mine,' I said. 'I have to knock on the door of this derelict flat and ask for Jimmy, and it gets handed out to me through a hole in the wall, wrapped in a brown paper bag.'

Not a flicker.

'Do you . . . *live* near Muirhouse?' asked Jody, clutching Vichard to her chest, thinking no doubt of *Trainspotting*-style drug dens and playparks littered with used needles.

'It's okay,' I soothed. 'Our house is a clear two miles away.'

Jody nodded distractedly, as though she was picturing the Muirhouse residents chasing us across town, pressing their bottles of formula on us.

'Well there are advantages to formula,' said Molly, trying to be helpful. 'It obviously helps them to get to a good size quickly.' She nodded at Sophie, and I pictured my poor love obese at fourteen, on one of those Channel 4 documentaries about people who are so fat they can't get out of bed.

'I made fifty ice cubes of puréed carrot, and seventy of puréed spinach yesterday!' announced Shona, attempting to rescue the conversation.

She beamed at me, but the only response I could think of was: 'Why?'

'Well,' she said. 'Elgin is seven weeks old now. I want to have plenty of stocks in the freezer, because we may decide to start weaning when he's four or five months. And I'm going back to work soon, so I want to get on top of things.'

How was this possible? I was lucky if I managed to find time to brush my teeth within the course of a day at home with Sophie.

'When do you find the time?' I asked, feeling exhausted just thinking about puréeing vegetables.

'It's simply about having a proper routine in place. We've been following the Bootcamp method. It sounds brutal, but the name's just tongue-in-cheek. It really works – you should try it. Oh, but actually, if you haven't already started it, it might be too late . . . the book says there's only a short window during which babies are receptive to starting the routine. Any attempt to impose a routine outside the window period can actually be damaging to the child. Have you read the book?'

'No,' I whispered. Failure, compounded upon failure.

'But you haven't told us how your birth went!' piped up Molly, to change the subject. Again, she was trying to be kind. Nosy, but kind.

'Oh, it was fine.' Weary beyond belief I went on, knowing they expected details. 'I had an epidural.' Which had worked for the final hour in a twenty-two-hour labour – but I didn't want to go into all that.

'Did you?' said Jody. 'I had an epidural too, but I asked them to let it wear off for the pushing stage. I read that the so-called pain – *the intensity* – of the birth is important for bonding between the mother and baby. It was wonderful. When he was coming out I could feel his little nose, and his little chin, and everything.'

Wincing at this image, I considered how I had selfishly precluded all possibility of bonding with Sophie, by having an epidural.

'Well, that's what happened anyway,' I said. 'We all lived to tell the tale, and that's the main thing. And I got to feel her nose and chin after she had come out, so it was fine.'

Jody looked doubtfully at Sophie. 'And did you really need to have 48 stitches? I got your email . . .'

'No.'

'Oh, so how many stitches did you have?'

I sighed. 'Two.'

I could have sworn that Jody looked disappointed.

'And I didn't feel a thing, obviously, still being under the epidural.' I didn't mention the haemorrhage, didn't want it pounced upon with 'oohs' and 'aahs'.

'I think these epidurals are really a wonderful thing,' said Dita kindly. 'I don't think a natural birth necessarily helps bonding. I think that the opposite can happen sometimes, you know, that the mother is so upset by the trauma of the birth that it also can interrupt the bonding. And anyway, bonding is something that takes place over many months and years. I do not think there is any problem, whatever pain relief a person decides to have.'

There were no dissenting voices and Dita went on, encouraged.

'And also, it means there is no delay with having to give you an anaesthetic, for example, if the doctor is having to put forceps into your vagina.'

There was a sharp, collective intake of breath at this mention of the 'v' word. Molly spilled coffee into her saucer. Jody dropped her gaze to Vichard and sang a very quiet '*la, la-la.*'

Dita looked at me, confused, as well she might. There was a complex code with these girls. You were allowed (and indeed, expected) to share whatever grisly obstetric details you wished as long as you didn't say certain words out loud.

I glanced across to check the clock on the wall, wondering whether we could get away with leaving yet. And that's when I saw my ex-boyfriend, Malkie, joining the end of the queue for the hot food counter.

It wouldn't be him, of course. Nine years after splitting up, I still 'saw' him in the street with alarming regularity. It didn't make my insides lurch anymore (that was just for the first five or six years). It was just a slight quickening, a spike of curiosity. 'Oh, is that Malkie?' I would think, until I realised that it wasn't him. It was never him. Why would it be him? As far as I knew (from a perfunctory email exchange six years ago) he had moved to London, and had been working there ever since.

It had occurred to me that perhaps these appearances meant that he was there in my head all the time, just underneath the level of conscious thought. It had also occurred to me that this seemed pretty incompatible with a happy marriage to someone else. But what could I do? I didn't seek him out; he was just there, flashing into life in the face of a stranger, or in a half-overheard snatch of conversation. Or captured, fleetingly but perfectly, in the stride of a man passing by on the other side of the street. And then he would be gone again, as lost to me as he always was.

It certainly wouldn't be him now, in the John Lewis café on a Wednesday morning. The man at the hot food counter had his back towards me, and could be anybody. But then again, there had been those missed calls that I'd never returned . . . Maybe Malkie had been phoning to let me know he was in Edinburgh.

The man's profile came into view, as he looked up to read the overhead menu board. It made me wonder. But it was the inward flick of his wrist as he looked at his watch that hit home, and sent adrenalin juddering through my body.

Seemingly in slow motion, he turned, placed his tray back on the stack and walked out of the café towards the main shop floor.

'I think Sophie needs changing,' I said, rising to my feet with her pinned against my chest. I felt, rather than saw, the stares of the other mums as I hurried out of the café, minus the changing bag.

Halfway through the furniture department, I stopped and wheeled round, looking across the expanse of mocked-up living rooms. There was no sign of him at all. Whoever it had been, he'd disappeared.

Suddenly light-headed, I teetered backwards and sank onto an orange and purple display sofa. Hearing a little mew, I looked down and remembered Sophie, pressed against my chest, her hair mussed up and damp from my tears, her thin little arms flailing.

Oh God. What kind of mother was I, chasing the ghost of an ex-boyfriend through the furniture department at John Lewis when I was supposed to be exchanging birthing stories with my Babycraft comrades?

'Are you okay, Cassie?' It was Dita, come to check on me.

'Fine. I just felt a bit dizzy.'

She sat down next to me. 'I could do with a bit of air myself. Let's just sit for a minute, shall we? Maybe I could have a little cuddle?' She held out her arms for Sophie.

I watched Dita shushing and patting my daughter, contentedly at ease with her in a way that still eluded me. But it would be fine, I told myself. It was just a question of time and experience. It would take a bit of time to adjust to this new life, with all its strangeness. And my visceral reaction to the Malkie figure was surely just a symptom of this. I'd been living on the edge of my nerves since the moment Sophie had been placed in my arms.

We left soon afterwards, making a detour back to the café to collect our things and make our excuses. Dita was unusually silent as she pushed Sophie's pram through the shopping centre and out to the car park.

'So what did you think of my Babycraft friends, then?' I asked.

She raised her eyebrows, as though trying to think bright thoughts. There was a long pause, followed by a sigh. 'Oh dear.'

'Exactly,' I said, with a sudden rush of affection, linking my spare arm with hers. Thank goodness she was here. My support network, as advocated by Mum, was looking a little ropey. My best friend was in New Zealand; Jonathan, whilst good on the practical side, merely brushed away all my concerns and baby angst; and my attempts to confide in Mum herself had failed. And after today, it was clear that the Babycraft crew were only going to make me feel worse. So Dita would have to be my network of one – until she went back to Holland next week.

'What's this, Cassie?' asked Dita as she loaded the bags into the back of the car. I was strapping Sophie into her car seat.

'What?' I looked over.

She was holding a handful of white petals.

'They were in the changing bag, just inside the top where it was unzipped.'

'That's odd.'

'I suppose they must have fallen in. Maybe we brushed past one of the displays on the shop floor. Oh – was there not a vase of carnations on one of the tables in the furniture department? That'll be it.'

'Hmm. I suppose so.' It was a plausible explanation. Suddenly feeling a crawling sensation at the back of my neck, I turned and looked around the car park. There was nobody around, just cars and concrete pillars. I shivered and pulled my coat around me.

'Come on,' I said. 'Let's go.'

5

So much for our wedding anniversary. Instead of gazing into Jonathan's eyes over a candlelit dinner, I was locked in the bathroom, clutching a McKeith's pad and a biro, and making a list of my worries.

Jonathan had tried to surprise me by booking a table at my favourite restaurant, and he'd even booked a babysitter from an extortionately expensive childcare agency. But I'd had to explain that this was sheer madness – I couldn't even think of leaving Sophie with a complete stranger, and unless he could spirit Dita back from Holland, or my mother from her Swedish island, we wouldn't be going anywhere. He'd taken it well, and said he'd book somewhere for lunch the next day instead, so Sophie could come too. He'd confessed that he fancied an early bed and a good night's sleep, anyway.

I'd smiled, agreeing that it sounded nice, but in truth, the idea of a good night's sleep was just a fantasy. I'd hardly slept at all in the two months since Sophie had been born. The three-hourly feeds and spikes of inexplicable crying would have been manageable on their own, but my own insomnia tore huge holes into already broken nights. The eight-hour blocks of dark, velvety sleep that I'd enjoyed pre-Sophie had fragmented into a series of short, restless naps. Gritty-eyed, brain-buzzing days had become the norm.

And exhaustion, it seemed, was the perfect breeding ground for anxiety. The spores would settle in my mind quietly, drifting in from snatches of news on the radio, doom-laden passages in the Sunday supplements or conversations overheard in the park. It was at night, under darkness, that they would mushroom and bloom. It began with fears that I would accidentally kill Sophie by dropping her down the stairs, pushing her pram in front of a car or letting her suffocate in her cot. The night when I'd nearly poisoned her with old milk had highlighted how easy it was to slip up. The responsibility – what was being asked of me – was so absolute, so uncompromising, and there were so many ways in which I could fail. Scenarios multiplied in my mind, alternative realities lurking behind every aspect of life. Hardest to shake was the fear that I would die, and abandon her. My own empty, post-pregnancy body became a source of dread.

I'd read in a magazine that psychologists encouraged anxious patients to put their worries down on paper. So, sometime after midnight, I'd left my bed and taken refuge in the bathroom. Having completed the exercise, I was now reviewing the list I'd made. It included the following:

1. Possible brain tumour.
   In retrospect it had probably been a mistake to Google 'dizziness symptoms'. Out of the array of devastating conditions to choose from, a brain tumour had seemed one of the more cheerful possibilities. Against this tide of gloom, it was hard to convince myself that it was just tiredness, or my body getting back to normal after the birth, but nevertheless I purchased a bottle of disgusting iron and vitamin 'tonic' and pinned all my hopes on it.

2. Possible early motor neurone disease.
   That morning I had leaned over and picked up a magazine (in fact the same helpful magazine that had suggested listing all my worries) from where it had fallen

39

under the kitchen table. My thumb and forefinger had trembled slightly, resulting in the magazine slipping to the floor. Google beckoned again, and a few clicks later I found myself reading posts on an internet forum for hypochondriacs. One of the hypochondriacs had cautioned the others that weakness between the thumb and forefinger was the first symptom of motor neurone disease. Horrified, I began to picture myself Stephen Hawking-like, paralysed in a wheelchair with a computerised voice, while Jonathan had to give up his job to provide me with twenty-four-hour care. Since then, nasty little twitches had sprung up all over my body, and my legs began to feel weak when I climbed the stairs. My body seemed to be accommodating itself to my worst fears, weakening in response to the terrible knowledge I had gleaned.

3. Possible onset of blindness.

For a few months, I'd been seeing floaty things in front of my eyes whenever I was looking at something against a bright background. The internet (yes, again) assured me these probably were just harmless 'floaters' but that they could occasionally be due to retinal detachment, or in one in every ten million cases, due to a rare but deadly form of eye cancer.

Obviously, I thought, biting my lip and digging my toes into the thick carpet, I should go and see the doctor about all of these symptoms. However, this was a course of action fraught with difficulty. The last time I'd been there I had seen a big notice in the waiting room advising patients that they were only allowed to ask the doctor about one thing in each consultation. Neither did I feel able to make three appointments to discuss each issue separately. Such an attempt would have probably made the appointment-booking computer explode, given the difficulty in arranging just one appointment with a particular doctor. Even if I were to be successful, the appointments would no doubt be so far apart as to span weeks or months. So that would mean I'd have to prioritise which was the most urgent symptom. The responsibility of this choice made me feel even more anxious than the symptoms themselves.

With a sigh, I put a question mark next to each of the health worries, and moved on to the next item in the worry list.

4.   Exorcism – yes or no?

I couldn't do anything about that unless I wanted to go into the office and trawl through endless databases for case reports that probably didn't exist. Another question mark.

And there, at the end of the list, was the final worry. It had emerged from the deepest, darkest part of my mind, but seemed prepared to display itself only in initials.

5.   J & C ? ? ?

I stared at it for a moment before tearing the sheet off the pad, scrunching it into a ball, and going downstairs to put it at the bottom of the kitchen bin.

*

Driving to the restaurant for lunch the next day, the bright spring sunshine glared through the windscreen, and the potentially deadly 'floaters' danced round in my field of vision. Breathing deeply to try and quell my panic, I decided that I should try and share some of my worries with Jonathan.

Maybe that was the way forward. How could I expect our relationship to flourish when there was an entire soap opera of doom going on in my head that he wasn't even aware of?

I gripped the steering wheel firmly and took a few deep breaths. I've always found it easier to talk about difficult subjects whilst driving. I think it has to do with risk perception. The part of my brain that normally scans the conversational road ahead, to identify potential hazards, is kept fully occupied watching the actual road.

'Are you okay?' asked Jonathan. 'What's with the heavy breathing?'

'It would be terrible to go blind, wouldn't it?' I said. But part of me obviously didn't want to go down this road – my tone was conversational, rather than confessional.

There was a long pause while Jonathan considered the question.

'Yes,' he said.

There was silence for a little while, while I negotiated some roadworks and temporary traffic lights. When we were moving steadily once more, I tried again with a more direct approach.

'Lately, I've felt that perhaps my sight may be failing a little.' It was a good way of putting it, I thought. Not too alarmist, but straight to the point.

Jonathan sniggered.

'What?'

'Why are you talking like a person from Victorian times?'

'I'm not. It's just, sometimes I think I can't see very clearly.'

'Hmmm,' said Jonathan. 'Maybe you need stronger glasses. You should go to the opticians.'

'Do you get floaty things in front of your eyes sometimes?'

'No.'

'But just think how awful it would be to go blind. There

would be lots of things you couldn't do.' I tried to think of a salient example. 'I wouldn't be able to measure out the boiled water to make Sophie's milk.'

Jonathan frowned.

'The measurements have to be very exact,' I went on.

'Hmmm. We would have to buy the ready made cartons, I suppose.'

I considered this. 'But even so, it would be terrible, wouldn't it?'

'Yes, Cassie.'

I gave up. 'Maybe we could go to the garden centre on the way back from lunch. We should get that bird feeder thing. It would be nice for Sophie to see the birds.'

'And we need that slug stuff, remember,' he added thoughtfully. 'You know, it's been a while since I've had my eyes tested. And I saw a nice pair of designer frames in the window of Black & Lizars last week. Let's all go and get our eyes tested next weekend.'

'What, Sophie too?' Maybe he had a point. The blindness could be hereditary.

Jonathan didn't say anything. That proved he was worried.

'Can they test their eyes at that age?' I wondered.

'I don't think so,' said Jonathan. 'I think she would need to be a bit older. Maybe . . . two? She wouldn't need to know the alphabet. I think they can use pictures instead of letters.'

'What, like little bottles of milk, getting smaller and smaller?'

'Yes,' he said. 'Or maybe, in Sophie's case, there could be a very small picture of a bath on the bottom line. And if she started thrashing about and screaming, we would know that she could see it.'

'Oh yes, or a tiny picture of the health visitor.'

He was always doing this; making me feel better, against

my will. With all the confidence of an expert surgeon, he would sweep in and perform a sort of anxiety bypass in three minutes flat. I still had the lunch, though. I was going to make him talk.

★

'The Underground? We're going to The Underground?'

After we'd parked the car, Jonathan had led the way down a narrow close into the Cowgate, bringing us to a halt outside the door of the nightclub where we'd met one foggy October night, eight years earlier.

'They've renovated it and reopened it as a sort of bistro,' said Jonathan, holding the door open. 'I found it on the internet last night, and booked a table. Apparently they still use the basement for functions. I thought we could sneak down and have a re-enactment.'

I remembered the cavernous basement, with its black, sweat-soaked walls, and glanced nervously down at Sophie. The place had enjoyed quite a seedy reputation back in the day, though its clientele had been mostly students and young professionals in disguise: law students, medics, teachers, and even, once, an astrophysicist. Not that anybody ever admitted to such status. The thing was to come across as someone a little bit gritty, if not actually dangerous. Even the skeletal DJ, who looked as if he were in the final stages of heroin addiction and was rumoured to live in a squat in one of the dodgiest parts of Muirhouse, turned out, somewhat disappointingly, to be a trainee meteorologist who lived with his parents in a vast Victorian pile in Morningside.

A waitress showed us to our table, then reappeared moments later with two watermelon Bacardi Breezers, which she set down in front of us with just a hint of a raised eyebrow. Jonathan gave me a beaming smile.

'Oh, that's sweet,' I said. On the night we'd met, Jonathan and his friend Gordon had appeared beside Helen and me on the dance floor and presented us with fresh Bacardi Breezers, which were welcome replacements for the warm, nearly empty ones we had been singing into. We'd introduced ourselves, as policewomen, and Jonathan had burst out laughing, immediately guessing not only that we were students, but also that we belonged to the law faculty.

Sophie, obviously not appreciating the Bacardi Breezer reference, was grizzling a bit so we decided we'd better order – lasagne for both of us, the safest-looking option on the menu. It arrived in minutes, its cheese topping anaemically pale.

'Fresh out of the microwave,' commented Jonathan, grinding copious amounts of pepper onto his.

'Never mind,' I said. 'I'm sure it'll be fine.'

'So, I forgot to ask, did you get that case sorted out in the end?' he asked, spreading butter on a hard piece of baguette. 'What was it, the Working Time Regulations? Something to do with ghosts?'

He'd always enjoyed hearing stories about my work, fancying himself as a bit of an armchair lawyer. In pre-Sophie days we used to discuss work – my cases, his fund-managing stories – in the evenings over a glass of wine.

'Hmm,' I began nervously. 'Yes, he's got an employee who claims he's a special case under the Working Time Regulations because he can see ghosts. He wants Elliot to do an exorcism of the premises.' I put down my knife and fork. 'Oh, Jonathan, I'm worried I might have given him the wrong advice. I told him an exorcism wasn't necessary.'

'Of course it isn't necessary,' said Jonathan.

'What if the employee has a nervous breakdown, and sues Elliot? I could be liable.'

'Listen, Cassie, if you were my lawyer and you told me I had to carry out an exorcism, I'd bloody sack you. Now, forget about it.'

'It's your fault, you realise. If you hadn't sent Elliot McCabe and Murray Radcliffe that terrible breastfeeding email—'

'It wasn't a "terrible breastfeeding email", Cassie. It was an email announcing the birth of our daughter.'

Good – now we were on the subject of parenting. It was time to try and get him talking. 'You're still sleep talking, you know,' I ventured. 'You seem to be having nightmares about your dad.'

He shrugged.

'You've never told me much about your dad.'

I could see him stiffen, though he went on picking through the lasagne with his fork.

'What was he like?'

He didn't answer for a while and I wondered if he was actually going to ignore the question. But then he mumbled something in the direction of his plate. 'He was a wonderful dad.'

'Why was he wonderful?'

'I don't know. It's hard to explain. You can't explain someone to another person.' His voice was different than usual, softer and more tentative.

'How did he die?'

He gave me a dark look. 'He went to work one morning, and collapsed from a stroke. We knew it was bad . . . I mean, he didn't regain consciousness, and the doctors weren't hopeful. We stayed with him at the hospital, all day and . . . well, he died during the night. Another stroke.'

46

'It must have been awful.'

'Yup.' The soft tone had gone now.

'Did you have a good relationship?'

'Yes.'

'It must bring it all back, now you're a parent yourself.'

An even darker look came my way. 'Hmm. So how are you feeling about going back to work? Did that nursery confirm Sophie's place?'

I ignored his attempt to derail my line of questioning. 'I suppose it's different for me, because I never really knew my father. So there's nothing to . . . you know . . . dredge up. Apart from, well . . .'

Absence. That's what I wanted to say.

'What is this, Cassie? Dead Dads Club?'

I laid my knife and fork down. I blinked.

'Come on, sweetheart! It's our anniversary! We should be making plans, thinking about . . .'

Sophie interrupted with a gravelly little wail, ending the conversation. From then on, we had to take turns, one of us eating while the other jiggled Sophie around. But the crying intensified to the point where Jonathan had to take Sophie outside to the cobbled street and walk her up and down.

He came back in eventually; Sophie was quiet but looking very grumpy. 'Have you finished?' he said. 'She's got a dirty nappy.'

With an exaggerated sigh, I scraped my chair back and followed them downstairs to the toilets. There was no baby changing room, so we had to change her nappy on the floor of the disabled toilet, on a disposable padded mat I'd packed in the changing bag.

'Yuch. I've got poo on my shirt.' I scrubbed at it with a baby wipe. 'Shall we just go home? I don't think I want dessert.'

'Hang on,' said Jonathan, leading the way out of the toilet and into the wine cellar area, which had been the old nightclub dance floor. 'This must have been the spot . . . right about . . . here.'

He held out his arms. I dumped the changing bag on the floor and went over to him, Sophie wriggling in my arms. He folded us into a hug and held us, his mouth pressed against my hair. He started shimmying around and humming into the side of my head – 'Disco 2000', an old Underground classic.

It hadn't happened quite like this, of course, on that first night. There had been no physical contact at all. After that initial exchange, Jonathan and Gordon had simply remained next to us – the seething mass of bodies all around would have made it difficult to move away even if they'd wanted to – and shouted questions at us over the noise of the music.

'So what are your first impressions?' Jonathan had asked me after a couple of minutes, never one to hang around. 'They say you can tell whether you like someone in the first eleven seconds. So what do you think?'

'I think you look a bit like a hedgehog,' I shouted.

He looked crestfallen, just for a second, quickly recovering with a laugh.

'No, no, I didn't mean you have hedgehog-like *stature*,' I said. 'You must be nearly six foot tall, are you?' I stepped back and looked him up and down. 'No . . . I was thinking of your . . . hair, because it's dark and sticks up a bit at the front. And you have that whole designer stubble thing going on.' Or had he just not bothered to shave? I had a sudden urge to run my hand down the side of his face.

He gave a mischievous smile, and his eyes locked with mine.

'And what about me? What do you think of me?' I was

curious to see myself through his eyes. Would the dark smokiness of the nightclub lend some mysterious allure?

'Hmmm. A Bambi, definitely,' he said decisively.

I could see his point; there were similarities: diminutive stature (though gently rounded all over, in my case) brown eyes, reddish brown hair, slightly upturned nose. About the same level of personal effectiveness, too.

Jonathan and Gordon stood drinking beside us for the rest of the evening, until the club was about to close. There was always a Cinderella moment when the lights went up, leaving everyone blinking and confused and revealing disasters such as smudged mascara and sweat-soaked hair. So just before three Helen and I said we were going to get our coats and disappeared, knowing that if our admirers were keen they would catch up with us again outside.

'That Jonathan one's quite promising,' I said, once we had retrieved our coats and exited into the cold, damp night, taking care to step around a splattered puddle of vomit on the pavement.

'I thought you'd say that.'

'I don't know if he's exactly my type, though.' I paused for a second, then said, as if it had just occurred to me, 'He's nothing like Malkie, for example.'

'No,' said Helen, pondering. 'No. He doesn't look like the edgy, commitment-phobic type. He looks really quite normal.'

'You're right.' I was starting to shiver now. 'I might give him my number, I haven't decided yet.'

I pulled my phone out of my bag and studied it. I was wondering whether to phone a taxi, knowing it could take the best part of an hour to arrive.

However, Jonathan and Gordon had come out of the club and were striding over to us.

'Right, Cassie,' said Jonathan. 'Have you got your mobile there? Can I borrow it a sec?'

I handed it over with no comment, like an audience member obeying the instructions of a stage magician. I was curious to see what would happen next.

Jonathan dialled a number on my phone, and then when his own phone rang he flipped it open, checked the screen, and flipped it shut again. 'Good,' he said with a curt nod. 'I'll call you.'

At that point, two black cabs swung in to the kerb. 'That's yours,' said Jonathan, opening the door and holding it as we climbed in. 'You'll need to tell him the address. I just told the switchboard it would be Morningside.' He shut the door and saluted as the taxi pulled away.

'You were such an arse that night,' I said now, murmuring over the top of Sophie's head into Jonathan's ear. 'You didn't even ask for my phone number, you just took it.'

'Well, I couldn't risk you saying no. I knew from the moment you compared me to a hedgehog that I wanted to marry you.' His hands reached down to squeeze my bottom and his lips moved to my mouth.

'Oi!!! Get out of it, you two!'

We sprang apart, looking round to see where the angry voice was coming from. Slightly light-headed from the Bacardi Breezer, I burst into giggles at the sight of the now-elderly bouncer who had manned the door at The Underground all those years ago. Helen and I had had frequent run-ins with him. Once, when he'd pronounced that we were too drunk to be allowed into the club, we'd threatened him with legal proceedings (I think we'd just come out of an exam in Civil Procedure) and he'd never much cared for us after that.

Now, however, he was furious at my amusement.

'Out!' he barked, pointing to the stairs up to the exit. 'No funny business in here. Yous should be ashamed of yourselves, wi' a wee bairn and a'.'

I could feel Jonathan bristling, deciding whether or not to mount a challenge, but I pulled at his sleeve and he just shook his head and came upstairs with me to pay the bill.

★

Later that night, Jonathan wanted to bath Sophie and do her bedtime bottle – 'Daddy time,' he said firmly, batting me away. Glancing at the clock, I wondered whether I ought to take the chance to phone Helen – I'd been smiling all afternoon at the thought of telling her about The Underground, and seeing the old bouncer. But then I decided it was too early in the morning in New Zealand, so I pulled out my laptop and began an email.

I sat staring at the blank screen for a full five minutes, then shook my head and forced myself to type. How difficult could it be to write an email to your best friend?

Hi Helen,

Guess what we did today – Jonathan and I went to The Underground for a re-enactment of the night we met! We'd been planning to go out last night and have a proper night out for our anniversary, and we'd arranged babysitters and everything, but we ended up cancelling it because we didn't want to leave Sophie. So Jonathan arranged this Underground thing as a surprise for me, and we went at lunchtime so she could come too! The upstairs is an awful bistro thing now, but the downstairs is just the same! We saw that old bouncer, remember the one that used to chuck us out?

I sighed, and sank my head into my hands. What was the point of this?

> Helen, I'm scared. I'm scared about Jonathan and me. It's hard being a mother. I'm terrified all the time. I don't know how other people do it.

But what could I expect her to do about it? She was living in another world now. I clicked on to her Facebook page: 486 Facebook friends, the vast majority of whom I didn't recognise. Her status updates were all about barbecues on the beach, sunsets and amazing seafood. She didn't even look the same – her mousy, shoulder-length bob had been transformed into a sun-kissed blonde crop.

'What're you up to, Cassie-Lassie?' said Jonathan, breezing into the room with a muslin cloth still over his shoulder.

I switched back to my email and deleted the draft.

'Oh, nothing. What DVD are we watching, then?'

He smiled and tossed over the rental box.

'*Penguin Party Two – Adventures on Ice*?'

'Oh no!' he said. 'They've mixed up the boxes. Oh well, this should be right up your street. Are you ready for some scenes of mild peril?'

Jonathan had always found it most amusing, my refusal to watch any film or TV show that might be remotely disturbing. I'd asked him to look out for a newly released comedy starring Julie Walters and Maggie Smith, but this penguin thing sounded even better.

I would be able to settle into my seat knowing that nothing terrible was going to happen. I could be sure that there would be no penguin abuse, no torture, violence or murder. I knew that the lead penguin's best friend was not going to die in a car crash, leaving her with orphaned twin toddlers to bring up (who would otherwise be left at the mercy of penguin social services).

I knew that no penguin was going to decorate the nursery wearing cute maternity dungarees and then fall off the ladder, thereby bringing on a hideous miscarriage. No penguin was going to find any suspicious lumps and have to undergo scans and biopsies and years of grueling chemotherapy ... no, thank you very much. My heartstrings were quite ropey enough without any of that kind of thing.

I often thought how nice it would be if one's own life could be classified and given a rating at the outset, together with a helpful nugget of consumer advice. At least then you would know what to expect. Of course, you would have to hope that you didn't get '*Contains very strong bloody violence and horror*'. But if you could be sure that life would be a nice comforting PG, containing nothing worse than the prospect of mild peril, well then you could just get on with things.

'*Or . . .*' began Jonathan. 'We could go upstairs and act out some scenes of our own . . .'

Even for Jonathan, this was pretty lame. He grabbed my hand and led me up the stairs to the spare bedroom.

★

'It wasn't too soon, was it?' he said, afterwards, lying in bed with his arms around me. 'Are you okay? You seem quiet.'

I kissed him. 'It was lovely.'

But the truth was, I felt strangely unmoved. I felt as if everything had been warmed up, excited, enlivened, working from the outside in, but leaving a small, cold, hollow space somewhere in the middle of me.

Where was it, that elusive part of me that used to glow with warmth and joy, when Jonathan and I were making love, and wholly absorbed in one another? Why didn't I feel that way any more? With a rush of guilt, and terrible fear for the future, I realised I knew the answer.

When Sophie had been born, when she'd fought her way out of my body and into the world, she had taken my heart with her.

6

The cherry blossom came and went, browning drifts washed away by the heavy rains that fell in May. Sunny weather followed in June, though, and I started to actually enjoy those interminable daily treks through the Botanic Gardens. Perhaps I was beginning, coaxed by that little bit of extra warmth and sunshine, to relax into motherhood. My days with Sophie fell into a rhythm; we would have long naps in the morning, lying together on top of my bed, sunlight falling in pale columns across the carpet. It was the only time I could fall asleep easily, soothed by the rhythm of her breathing, all my frets somehow driven into the background by the immediacy of her.

She gained weight, and her little body grew sturdy, her movements more confident. When she learned to sit up unaided, this opened up a whole new world for her. Positioned on her play mat, surrounded by a ring of cushions, she could sit and play with her rattles and squeaky toys while I put on a load of washing or emptied the dishwasher – although she loved my car keys best, or the remote control for the television. Relieved of the frustration of having to be held all the time, or strapped into a bouncy chair, she cried less, smiled more, and charmed everyone.

But when the height of summer came, I went back to work. I'd agreed to this when negotiating my part-time working package, but at that time I'd had no idea how tiny Sophie would still be at five months, how different my outlook would be. I was in no position to object now – it had been impressed upon me that the part-time arrangement was on a trial basis. If it interfered with continuity of client care, I would be expected to phase a return to full-time hours. The prospect of having to work full time in just a few more months, leaving behind forever those sleepy sunlit hours with Sophie, seemed too cruel.

The call came on my third day back. I wasn't doing much work. From my desk in the basement, I could look up through the window and see people hurrying past on the pavement, on the other side of the elegantly wrought cast iron railings. When I wasn't doing that I was closely studying my colleague, the sharp-suited Annabel Masters. She had barely acknowledged me, since I'd arrived back to find my desk piled high with her filing. Perhaps I'd simply fallen below her radar now that I was a mother and part-time worker. All day long, she paced up and down . . . whilst on the phone, whilst talking into her dictaphone, whilst giving the secretaries a brisk, acid-edged ticking-off. She was particularly imperious today, as there was a new work experience student in the office and she was showing off, continually asking him to make coffee or pick up her documents from the printer.

I flinched when the phone rang and hesitated before answering it; what if it was a client on the other end, seeking advice? I had to remind myself that I had been doing this job, perfectly capably, for years. 'Cassie Carlisle?' I said, trying to sound snappy and professional, imagining I was perfectly presented like Annabel. In fact, that morning the hem of my skirt had been hastily repaired using Sellotape and I had polished my boots with a baby wipe whilst trying to fasten Sophie into her car seat. It didn't seem to have worked well, judging from the soapy smears on the leather.

'Cassie, hello. Elliot McCabe here.'

I looked up through the railings again, wishing myself to be anywhere but here. I hadn't heard from Elliot since that day at the Botanic Gardens, although I'd emailed him to say I was coming back to work and to contact me if there was any work he needed doing.

'I was wondering if you could help me – it's that rather delicate matter again, I'm afraid.'

It seemed that all was not well at Braid Hills Funeral Home. Bobby Spencer – the employee who 'saw dead people' – had been observed, on Elliot's new CCTV system, letting himself into the premises in the middle of the night. He had taken a deceased woman out of the storage area, drawn a moustache on her upper lip with a permanent marker, and then left.

'So I'm going to dismiss him, okay, and I just wanted to check that it was all above board.'

'Oh. Well, I'm afraid it's not as simple as that.'

'Look. All I need to know is, can I sack this . . . this *buffoon*, or not?'

'The thing is, once a person has been in employment for twelve months, they have certain rights not to be unfairly dismissed under the . . .'

'No, no, no, no, no, no, no, NO. In our line of work, this sort of thing is completely, utterly unacceptable. The dignity of deceased persons is quite simply paramount. I just can't have him working for me any more.'

'Well, does your company have a disciplinary procedure? Normally in these situations you would need to allow . . .'

'But this is gross misconduct. Pure and simple.'

Why are you bothering me then, if you know it all? 'In my view,' I said carefully, 'the safest course of action would be to follow the appropriate procedures, which would involve giving written warnings and holding a disciplinary hearing before proceeding to dismiss.'

'Fine. A disciplinary hearing. Can you come?'

'What? You want me to be present at the disciplinary hearing. That's not . . .'

'Can you come now, please. I need to get this wrapped up today.'

'Would it not be better to take a little time to—'

'Look, let me be clear. I'm doing this today. I need you to be there. Are you saying you won't come?'

A tall figure loomed up in the doorway: Murray Radcliffe. *Oh Christ.* Was he tapping my phone or something? I stiffened, certain he was about to stride over and snatch it out of my hand. And he was wearing his favourite coat, too – a long, checked, Sherlock Holmes-style affair; maybe he was going to pull me from my chair and quick-march me to the funeral home in person. But he beckoned to Annabel, who grabbed a file off her desk and followed him out.

I slumped back in my chair. 'Okay, Elliot. I'll be there as soon as I can.'

But as soon as I'd put down the phone it rang again. It was the nursery this time.

'Sophie's had two loose nappies, Mrs Carlisle. That means you'll need to come and take her home. Those are the nursery rules and we adhere to them strictly, I'm afraid. If she has a virus of some sort we can't risk her infecting the other children.'

I bit back the urge to say that if Sophie had a virus, she'd almost certainly caught it from nursery in the first place.

I phoned Jonathan but he was out of the office playing golf, and uncontactable, according to his secretary. I phoned the nursery manager again to plead, suggesting that maybe Sophie had just eaten something that disagreed with her and couldn't they just keep her and see how she got on over the next hour or so.

'We don't bend the rules, I'm afraid, Mrs Carlisle. There are emergency care procedures we can put in place if there is no parent available when we need to hand over care of a child; are you telling me that's what you want me to do?'

I told her I'd be there in ten minutes, although I didn't know how I'd manage it. I was furious with myself for not being assertive enough with Elliot, but cancelling our first meeting because of a sick child on my third day back at work? With the firm in the throes of a redundancy exercise? Well, it wasn't an option.

So this is what they mean by juggling, I thought, as I tried Jonathan's mobile for the third time.

★

We took a taxi to the Braid Hills Funeral Home, Sophie, the work experience student and I. The premises were in an old Victorian house situated in a wide avenue in a very genteel part of town.

'Right, Greg,' I said. 'Don't worry, there's nothing to it. Just wheel her round in the pram. She'll go to sleep, I'm sure of it. I won't be too long. Just come in and get me if there's any problem.'

'Well, just remember I have to be back to walk Murray Radcliffe's dog at three,' he said, scowling. I had honestly thought he would prefer this to photocopying and running round after Annabel, but he didn't seem impressed.

As he turned and began to push the pram down the street, there was a horrible moment when he seemed to transform from a McKeith's employee into what he really was – a random teenager I'd only known for five minutes. Why was I letting him walk away with my daughter?

'Greg,' I called after him. He turned, with a look that said 'what now?' It fleetingly crossed my mind whether I should send him to the meeting and do the more important job of minding Sophie myself. Hmm. Not unless I wanted to go back to the office and find my P45 on my desk.

'Just . . . don't go too far.'

Trying to dismiss my fears, I crunched across the gravel courtyard to the entrance, which was located round the side of the building. I rang the buzzer and stood there, waiting for several moments. It was very quiet. An overflow pipe from the first floor dripped gently onto the gravel near my feet.

Inside, the atmosphere was very calm, very hushed. Given Elliot's phone manner, I had expected a corporate-feeling environment. But it felt almost like somebody's house, with a faded red and gold carpet, and granny-ish antique furniture. There was even a grandfather clock.

'How can I help you?' asked the receptionist.

'I'm Cassie Carlisle, here to see Elliot McCabe.' My voice sounded muffled, tiny, swallowed up by heavy furnishings.

'They're in the meeting room, just along the corridor on the left.'

I knocked and went in. An unusually short young man with thick waves of marmalade-coloured hair stood looking out of the window.

'Are you the lawyer?' he asked, though he looked as if he wasn't really interested in the answer. 'Elliot's just gone to photocopy my personnel file.'

I sat at the table to wait. Several minutes passed. I asked Bobby, out of curiosity more than anything else, what made him become an undertaker's assistant.

'I became an assistant *funeral director*,' he said, 'because I know that I'm uniquely suited to the job. Do you know much about the funeral profession?'

It turned out that after doing a degree in anthropology, he'd decided to train as a counsellor. However, after four years of training and providing counselling to students free of charge through the Students' Union, it became clear he wasn't going to be able to earn any kind of living that way, and with eight years' worth of student debt to pay off, he realised he was going to have to find some regular paid work.

'I've been working here a year now. I'm doing my Diploma in Funeral Directing, as well as training in embalming. I can do all this on the job, you see.'

He looked unaccountably cheerful about all this. But then he stopped and leaned forward in his chair. 'But my thing is counselling, really. As a funeral professional I can offer an informal but compassionate listening service to people. Ultimately, my aim is to set up my own funeral firm, with a fully integrated grief counselling practice. To help the bereaved, to share the darkest hours of their lives – that's what I want to do. Actually, what I was made to do.'

I felt, rather emphatically, I would not wish to share the darkest hour of my life with this boy.

Elliot entered the room in a fluster, paper and pens falling as he tried to shake my hand and set everything on the table at once – his arms and legs seemed too long for the rest of him. And he wore the same troubled look now as he had at Great Auntie Judith's funeral – something to do with his sunken eyes, perhaps, peering from beneath wild grey eyebrows. I suggested that he should outline the allegations against Bobby, which he did with barely suppressed rage, enunciating each word in staccato.

'Bobby, do you have anything to say?' he concluded, slapping the file shut.

Something outside the window caught my eye. It was Greg, walking past on the pavement pushing the pram. Each step was being taken with exaggerated slowness and he was frowning in the direction of the building.

I realised that Bobby was waiting for my full attention.

'Sorry,' I said. 'Go on.'

'Well,' he said, 'it was that Madame Boileau.' He spoke as though that in itself was explanation enough. A muscle near the corner of his mouth twitched, but he was composed enough to pronounce the name with an affected French flourish.

'She was my French teacher, at school,' he went on, looking defiantly at Elliot McCabe. 'Fifteen years ago. She made my life a misery. She made me stand on top of my desk and recite verb conjugations, so the whole class would laugh at me. I tried to run away from home. I packed my gym bag, and stole three bananas and a box of Ritz crackers from the kitchen. But Dad was following me in the car, and I only got to the end of the street.' His voice went soft at this point and he paused.

'When Tomasz, the embalmer, brought her into the preparation room the other day, I instantly realised it was her. And I wasn't sorry,' he added darkly.

Elliot jumped in here, and addressed me. 'Tomasz reported that Bobby was humming a song for the rest of the day. A very inappropriate song. It took me a while to decipher it from Tomasz's description, what with the language barrier.'

'Was it this one?' began Bobby. He cleared his throat. 'Ding, dong, the witch is dead, the . . .'

'All RIGHT!' snapped Elliot. He turned to me. 'Do you see what I'm dealing with here?'

'Anyway,' went on Bobby. 'I was provoked. Because when we were in the preparation room she just opened her eyes, all sort of *evil* . . .' He looked at me, as though I might be a sympathetic audience for this bit, and scrunched up his nose. 'And she shook her head and said, "You were always a stupid boy." '

I gave Elliot a sideways glance.

'She raised her eyebrows!' shrieked Bobby. 'I want that on the record! She raised her eyebrows! She doesn't believe me! Write it down!'

'Calm down, Bobby,' said Elliot. 'We're just trying to get the facts straight.'

'And who's that anyway?' He pointed to the window.

Greg had stopped the pram now, and was standing outside the window looking mutinous, arms crossed, feet planted apart. I could faintly hear Sophie's wails, rising in desperation.

'Don't worry,' I said. 'Please just go on. What happened about Madame Boileau?'

'She went back dead again when Tomasz came in. I tried to let it pass, I really did. But I couldn't get it out of my head. So at around two a.m. I decided that I would have to do something about it. I got in my car, and drove to Braid Hills. I just wanted to talk to her, to tell her she couldn't bully me any more . . . You can't let these bullies get away with it, that's what Dad always used to say . . . before he . . . passed away.'

He gave a loud sniff.

'But it was the right thing to do. Don't you see? Because she didn't bother me again after that. Dad was right.' At this point his voice crumpled and he dropped his head into his hands. 'It's just so hard for me sometimes, with my abilities.'

When he looked up again he gave Elliot a sullen look, but

then addressed me. 'I've told him,' he said through gritted teeth, 'that he needs to get this place blessed regularly. To clear them down.'

'Clear what down?'

'The spirits,' he said. 'How am I supposed to get on with my job when they're milling around all the time? Apart from this business with Madame Boileau, who provoked me, of course, I've actually been very restrained.'

'Bobby,' I said. 'Do you want to give us a minute?' He gave me a very unpleasant look and made for the door. In fact, he very nearly fell through it, since the receptionist was in the process of opening it to come in.

'That's your two o'clock for you,' she announced to Elliot, with a sideways glance at Bobby.

'Elliot,' I said when we were alone. 'The cautious approach would be to give a written warning rather than proceed with a summary dismissal. A tribunal might agree that the moustache constitutes gross misconduct, but there's a risk they might just view it as a prank.'

He sank back into his chair with a deep sigh. 'So you're telling me I wouldn't be safe to dismiss him.'

'Yes. But on the other hand . . .' I felt that someone needed to say it. 'Elliot, this guy is taking the piss.'

'Thank you. I appreciate that.'

'I mean, spirits? Come on. Haunting a funeral home? If you give ground on this, where is it going to end?'

'Do you know . . . sometimes I hate working in this business.' As he spoke, his blustery manner seemed to fall away. He looked tired and grey suddenly, the lines on his face more deeply etched.

'To hell with it,' he said finally. 'I'll take the risk. Give him the boot. Madame Boileau didn't deserve that. Nobody does.

If we can't give them a little bit of respect then what the hell are we here for?'

He gathered the papers together and left the room. It struck me that, for some reason, he was too upset to say anything more.

★

I decided I'd better wait for a minute in case Elliot came back – he hadn't said whether I should stay or go. I went over to the window to see if I could see Greg and Sophie. He had lifted her out of the pram and was jiggling her on his knee, sitting on a low stone wall on the opposite side of the road. I waved and motioned to my watch to indicate that I would only be a few more minutes. He gave a sulky nod in return.

It was then that I became aware of peculiar noises coming from the hall outside – Elliot had left the door open. There was a click-clicking sound and what sounded like something heavy bumping against skirting boards.

After a moment, a small white face appeared from behind the door. I felt a little frisson after Bobby's talk of ghosts, but this little girl seemed very much alive – about seven years old, I guessed, with long curly dark red hair and a pointy chin.

'Hello there,' I smiled. 'What's your name?'

The girl frowned. 'Milly Watkinson.'

'Hello, Milly. I'm Cassie.'

She disappeared momentarily, then shuffled into the room backwards on her knees. Her progress was impeded by the fact that she was pulling along two plastic horses who, in turn, were pulling along a white Barbie princess carriage.

'Wow! They're lovely,' I said. 'White ponies are my favourite. And I love the pink ribbons in their manes.'

The girl gave me a suspicious look. 'This one's Pinkie,' she said. 'And this one's Sparkles. He's really naughty.'

'Cool. And who's in the carriage. Is it Barbie?'

Milly pushed out her lower lip and frowned again.

'No. It's Mummy.'

I took another look. Only then did I notice the miniature coffin that had been shoved through the rear window of the carriage at an awkward angle.

At that moment a tall woman swept into the room. 'THERE you are, Milly,' she exclaimed in an American accent, with an exaggerated roll of her eyes.

'They keep you on your toes, don't they?' she smiled.

I murmured assent, but I couldn't formulate much of a response. In fact, it was difficult to take my eyes off her. Her skin was pearlescent over sharp cheekbones. Her hair was just growing in again, by the looks of it; dark, silky baby curls.

'I'm sorry. We've upset you,' she said, glancing down at Milly's playthings and taking in the situation.

I shook my head vigorously, attempting a bright smile. She kneeled down next to her daughter, and picked up Pinkie, absently stroking his mane with one finger.

'The latest thinking is that children should know what to expect, when a funeral is being planned. They should understand what is going to happen, know how we're going to get there, who they're going to see, that sort of thing. It's supposed to help them cope with it all. The only thing is, our Milly here seems to want to go one step further and plan the whole thing!'

'Kids,' I said, with a forced laugh.

'They'll always surprise you, hmm?'

I shook my head and smiled.

'We're making a memory box,' announced Milly in a loud voice, not wanting to be upstaged by her mother.

66

'Really? How lovely.'

'It's got *Jane Eyre* in it, and *The BFG*.'

'Ah – good choices.'

'Our favourite bedtime book, and then one of Mummy's favourite books to read when you're older,' explained her mother in a sing-song voice, as though this was something she'd repeated several times before.

'And Mummy's shampoo.'

All of a sudden, I couldn't say anything at all.

'Come along, Milly, let's get out of this nice lady's way.'

And they crawled out of the room, Milly dragging the carriage, and her mother clip-clopping the horses carefully along the carpet.

I didn't wait for Elliot any more after that. I left, murmuring a hasty goodbye to the receptionist, and burst out on to the street to find my daughter.

But she was nowhere to be seen.

7

They can't have gone far. They can't have gone far. I stood there for a few minutes, scanning the street in both directions until the empty pavements seemed to buckle and bend in front of my eyes.

Maybe Greg had gone into the funeral home looking for me. I went inside to check with the receptionist, but she hadn't seen him. So I began walking up and down the street – a stiff, wooden walk; my legs hardly seemed to be part of me any more. Widening my search to the side streets, I circled further and further out, all the time listening out for footsteps or the sound of Sophie's crying. But there was nobody around, in this quiet residential neighbourhood in the middle of the afternoon. The only person I saw was an elderly man weeding his flowerbeds, and he hadn't noticed any be-suited young men pushing prams.

Making my way back to the funeral home, I told myself they were sure to have shown up there by now – but once again, the receptionist confirmed there'd been no sign of them.

After several attempts to key in the number correctly, I managed to phone the office. My intention was to reach Annabel, and ask if Greg had phoned in, or if she knew his mobile number. But she was out at a meeting, and the secretary who took the call didn't seem at all clear as to who Greg was, let alone what his mobile number might be.

At that point, the rational, 'they can't have gone far' mindset deserted me completely. I heard myself whimper, suddenly no more than a child myself. I was back inside a recurring dream of my childhood: reaching up for a parental hand that wasn't there, finding myself lost, falling down through layers of terrifying worlds. I'd always awoken before reaching the bottom, but here it was now, after all these years: a world without Sophie. The street swirled around me and I was reduced to nothing more than the wanting of her; a hollow, screaming space at the heart of me. I bent double and vomited in the gutter.

Somehow I made it to the main road and flagged down a taxi to take me back to McKeith's. Ten minutes later I burst into the reception area in what could only be described as a hysterical state.

The receptionist was with a group of clients, showing them where to sign their names in the visitors' book and handing out visitor passes in plastic holders.

'Have you seen him?' I demanded, pushing to the front of the desk. 'Have you seen Greg, the work experience student?'

She raised an eyebrow and inclined her head to a seating area just off the main reception. Hardly daring to hope, I swung round.

Greg was there, stretched out on one of the chairs reading *The Economist*, nudging Sophie's pram back and forward with his foot.

'You bloody bastard! You fucking idiot!' I flew over and scooped Sophie out of the pram. I cradled her against me, and the world turned the right way up again.

'Oh, there you are,' said Greg. 'I told you I had to be back here for three. I told you I had to walk Radcliffe's dog.'

'You disappeared with my baby because you had to walk a *fucking dog*!'

'Yee-eees . . . speaking of which . . .'

He nodded towards Murray Radcliffe, who had materialised beside me. Shaking my head, I turned my back on them and buried my face in Sophie's neck, inhaling the powdery, milky scent of her. I didn't care at all, at that point, about the vomit splattered on my sleeve, the mascara trails down my face, or the cluster of plastic-badged businessmen looking on with amused interest.

★

An hour later, I was standing on the street outside the office, staring into the middle distance and jiggling the pram back and forth. I was waiting to flag down a taxi and trying to process what had just happened.

After my altercation with Greg, Murray Radcliffe had taken me aside, ushering me into a meeting room with an outstretched arm, casting a reassuring smile over his shoulder to the clients at reception.

'Cassie.' His voice was ominously calm. 'Do you know who Greg Robertson is?'

'Well . . . apart from being our work experience student . . . I'm not sure.'

'His father is CEO of Robertson Cathcart Group.'

Oh. It was one of the firm's biggest clients.

'The legal work is up for tender again next month. I've got five million pounds of business riding on this.'

So this seventeen-year-old twat was not someone to be messed with. But with my newly-found Sophie in my arms, I still found it difficult to care.

'You may also be interested to know that Bobby Spencer, employee of Braid Hills Funeral Home, has been on the phone for the last half hour. Making a complaint about you.'

70

'About me? Why?'

'He's claiming you pushed Elliot McCabe down the route of dismissal because of your own personal prejudices. He's threatening to raise tribunal proceedings against the funeral home, and to make a complaint about you to the Law Society.'

'But that's ridiculous. I'm not even acting for—'

'He says he overheard you telling Elliot that he was "taking the piss", and that your dismissal of the spirit world amounts to discrimination against him on the grounds of religious belief.'

'What? That's just—'

'He also said most of your attention during the meeting was taken up with a man standing outside the window with a pram.'

I sighed. 'I'm sorry. I know it wasn't ideal, asking Greg to help out. It's just that I didn't want to cancel my first meeting with Elliot. The nursery said I had to pick up Sophie immediately because she had terrible diarrhoea.'

As though on cue, there was a rumbling, squelching sound from Sophie's bottom, and the next second I felt something wet seeping through the fabric of her leggings onto my hand.

'Oh, poor love . . .'

Radcliffe's eyes narrowed just a fraction, but it was enough to convey his disgust, his utter contempt. 'I'll be making a note in your file. Now go.'

Standing on the street now, with Sophie cleaned up and my own face scrubbed free of mascara stains using scratchy paper towels, I faced the fact that my days at McKeith's were numbered. If they didn't pick me out with a conduct or competency dismissal, they'd nudge me into the redundancy firing line. Being a working mother was bad enough; being the subject of a Law Society complaint was worse; but swearing

71

in front of clients and calling the son of our biggest client a fucking idiot would surely finish me off.

I imagined a scenario where I had to go home and tell Jonathan that I'd lost my job. What would his face look like, I wondered. Would his jaw drop in shock or would it tighten with suppressed rage? Would he be angry with Murray Radcliffe, or disappointed in me?

Then I heard someone saying my name, and something made me pause for a second before I turned round.

Because it was Malkie. I knew it beyond a shadow of a doubt.

I'd been half expecting it for years, even more so since those mysterious missed calls after the birth, and the oh-so-close sighting in John Lewis. So really, I told myself as I slowly turned to face him, it was no big deal.

But nothing could have prepared me for the current that leapt through my body, singing through every nerve. The intervening years seemed to vaporise in a single sharp twist of longing. And there I was, standing in front of him, twenty-two years old again.

'Cassie.' His voice was still improbably deep; it resonated in places that didn't feel like they'd been touched since he'd gone.

'Malkie. Hello.' I was careful to keep an even tone.

'How are you? Long time no see. And this is your baby? Nice one! How old is he . . . she . . . now?'

'Five months,' I said, staring at his too-close-together eyes. The laughter lines and the slight thickening around the jawline suited him, taking the edge off his looks, while making him inexplicably more attractive. I fervently hoped he wouldn't notice I was covered in vomit.

'And a wee stunner, I see.' He peered into the pram.

'Yes. Yes, she is.'

'No smile for Uncle Malkie, though?'

'Er . . . probably not, no. She's had a stressful day.'

'And how's *married life?*'

I didn't miss the teasing tone, the hint of swagger.

'Oh, good, you know . . .'

I was reaching for the right responses, the responses of a contented wife and joyful new mother, but they seemed to have been stripped away.

'So what about you?' I asked. 'What are you up to these days?'

'I've just moved back to Edinburgh actually,' he said, tilting his head slightly on 'Edinburgh', and raising his eyebrows, as if testing my reaction.

'Oh right—' I began.

'Aaaaand . . .' he interrupted, his voice sliding upwards 'I'm working at McKeith's.' He pressed his lips together to suppress a smile.

I have to admit that I was surprised. I'd always imagined that Malkie would have ended up working at a hard-bitten criminal law practice in the Grassmarket, with wire grilles over the windows.

'McKeith's. But that's where I . . .'

Again, he interrupted me. 'I know,' he said, and he grimaced. But he did it like a little boy caught doing something a bit naughty, showing his white, even teeth and screwing up his eyes. Something inside me seemed to quietly slip free from its moorings. I thought I'd remembered everything about Malkie, but I had forgotten this. Oh God, I had forgotten this.

'I tried to phone you a couple of times actually, after I got your email, you know, about the baby.'

'Oh? Sorry, I must have missed your calls. You should have left a message.'

'Yeah, well, you know . . . I wasn't sure what to say. After all this time, and all that.'

The way his voice deepened on those last few words . . .

'I was trying to get in touch because I'd noticed that one of the addresses on the email list was this guy I used to work for in London who is now at McKeith's. Mike O'Farrell. And I'd been thinking of moving back up for a while and was going to ask you about McKeith's, how you found them to work for and so on. But in the end I just went ahead and got in touch with Mike, asked him if he was looking for any litigation lawyers, and here I am. It's my third day!'

'That's fantastic,' I said, vaguely registering that it was odd for McKeith's to be hiring in the middle of a redundancy exercise. It seemed to support my theory that it was all just an excuse to get rid of dead wood: troublemakers and foul-mouthed part-timers.

'Right, well. Better get back to it,' said Malkie. 'I've got a preliminary hearing tomorrow and there's a shitload of cases I need to read before then.' He winced, and rolled his eyes.

'Yeah, I need to get Sophie home, too. She's not too well today.'

'Okay, see you around then.'

'Bye.'

I lifted my hand in an awkward salute to his retreating back as he crossed the road. I suddenly felt exhausted, weakened by the force of my reaction to him. I bent down to kiss Sophie, breathing her in again and letting her centre me. When I looked up again he'd gone; had disappeared so quickly that I was left wondering if I'd really seen him at all, or whether it was all, somehow, just one more weary trick of the light.

8

'No, Mum, we definitely can't come!' I could feel my voice getting tighter. My mobile phone was struggling for reception as the car wound its way deeper into the valley.

'Look, sorry but you're cutting out. I'll have to go. Bye.' I pressed the red button and flung the phone into the footwell.

'What does she want now?' asked Jonathan.

'Keep your eyes on the road, would you? She wants us to go to Sweden.'

Mum lived with my paternal grandmother, Granny Britt, on a little island in the Swedish archipelago. Mum had raised me here in her native Edinburgh after my father's death, but she'd been drawn back to that blue-green island existence in recent years, returning to take care of her mother-in-law, who was no longer capable of living on her own.

They lived together in an old wooden house – dark and cool in summer, fire-lit and cosy in winter. The garden, with its four gnarled apple trees, was overgrown with wildflowers, and the scent of warm pine drifted across from the woods on sunny days. The beach was only a five-minute walk away – you could see the sea from the attic windows.

Going to visit them was out of the question. I hoped Jonathan would see that.

'Well, why don't we go then?' he suggested.

'Well, Jonathan, first of all there is the sheer logistics of three-hourly feeds whilst airborne. And the disruption of her sleep routine. She'd probably never sleep properly again.'

'I'm sure we could work something out,' said Jonathan.

It was this 'can do' attitude that annoyed me more than anything else. It was all very well to be blasé about somebody else's routines when you weren't the one who had to get up twelve times in the night when it all went to pot.

'Well, what if she had a cold, and her little ears were blocked up? It could be agonising for her. What if she had diarrhoea and we had to continually change her nappy in the plane toilet? What if we were delayed for eight hours at Stockholm, like the last time we went? There'd be no fresh milk for her, no sterilising facilities . . .'

And the last leg of the journey involved a tiny, shaky propeller plane.

'It's the propeller plane, isn't it?' crowed Jonathan. 'You're scared of the propeller plane!'

'I am NOT scared of the propeller plane. Don't be ridiculous.'

He chuckled.

'I'm not,' I repeated. 'It's just a logistical nightmare. If Mum wants to see Sophie she'll have to come over here – end of story.'

In fact, Mum had booked flights to come and stay with us, had been intending to come and help out during my first couple of weeks back at work. But two days before she was due to fly, Granny Britt tripped over in the kitchen, bruising herself badly. So Mum phoned to say she wouldn't be able to come after all.

I felt unreasonably hurt. I told myself that I shouldn't mind – that Granny Britt needed her more than I did. But a dark part of me turned the situation around and wondered what I would do in the same scenario, if Sophie was grown up and struggling with a new baby. Would I abandon Mum, badly bruised, in her rickety wooden house and come to help Sophie? Yes, I thought angrily, I certainly would.

We were on our way to a Babycraft weekend, to celebrate our babies' six-month half-birthdays. Jody, her husband (oh, what was his *name*?) and baby Vichard had recently moved to a big house in the country near Stirling, and they had invited the whole group to stay for a couple of nights.

'Just remind me,' said Jonathan, as the car struggled up a steep hillside road, 'why we are going away with the Babycraft people when you hate them?'

'I don't *hate* them, Jonathan. They are our support network, remember.'

'God help us.'

'If you had your way, we wouldn't have any friends at all!'

It was true – he didn't seem to need them. He played the occasional game of golf with work buddies, but apart from that, it was only ever Stephen . . . Stephen, who now lived with his wife, Moira, and their twin boys in a leafy suburb of Washington DC, but who telephoned every Sunday at eleven p.m. without fail for a brotherly catch-up. Jonathan had woken Sophie up last time, his voice booming through the house as he'd discussed the finer points of weaning with Stephen, debating whether puréed pear was easier to digest than apple.

'Anyway,' I pointed out, 'it'll be good for us to have a change of scenery. We can have invigorating walks and things.'

'And then we can get drunk in the evening and swap birthing stories. Molly can regale us with the tale of how they wanted to save the stump of Cameron's umbilical cord to make soup.'

'That is a complete fabrication, Jonathan.'

He snorted.

'It is,' I insisted. 'They wanted to save it to make a *necklace*.'

The truth was that this weekend was less about Babycraft and more about Jonathan and me. A change of scenery, some quality time together in luxurious surroundings, maybe some time to talk – this was just what I needed to forget my worries, bond with Jonathan again and put that silly encounter with Malkie out of my mind.

The house stood high on a hill overlooking fields and dark swathes of woodland; a landscape of soft greys and greens under a smirr of misty rain.

'Anyway, have you remembered their names yet?' demanded Jonathan as we hurried up the steps, him carrying Sophie in her car seat.

'She's called Jody, and the baby is Vichard.'

'Jody with the chubby cheeks who can't say "r". I know. But what's *his* name?'

'They've never mentioned his name. She just calls him sweetie. And as you well know, there comes a point when it is just too late to ask.'

He raised an eyebrow and rang the doorbell.

'Let's call him Tom,' I whispered. 'It might be Tom. I think it is Tom.'

The door opened and there was the man himself. 'Welcome to our humble abode!' he said, gesturing us inside with a flourish. 'Jody's been held up unfortunately – she's at her mum's with Richard, but she'll be back in time for dinner.'

We entered a large, square hallway, our boots clattering on the bare floorboards.

'I'm afraid we're only halfway through the renovations,' said Tom. 'The best bedrooms are in the dormitory wing.'

'Dormitory wing?' I echoed.

'Yes – this place used to be a boarding house for an old

school at the other side of the woods. But that's been turned into a swish hotel now.

'Anyway, this way!' he said, gesturing towards the staircase. 'I had a call from Shona earlier – she's been caught up with some court case in London for the last couple of days. She's representing some doctor who's about to be deported or something. She was meeting with the Home Secretary this afternoon so she won't be able to get up here tonight. Paul and baby Elgin are with her – they went down with her because she's still breastfeeding at night, so none of them can make it. Such a shame.'

He bounded up the stairs ahead of us. 'Mind the holes!' On the landing, some of the floorboards had been taken up, exposing dark spaces underneath. We stepped over and followed Tom along a dull soupy-green corridor.

'Careful – the lights don't work in this corridor yet, I'm afraid. We've had a few problems with the electrics.' After a few twists and turns, and a couple of heavily-hinged fire doors, we came to our room. Stepping inside, I saw it was furnished with two sets of old iron-framed bunk beds, and a grey threadbare carpet.

'There are sleeping bags there, and spare pillows if you need them,' said Tom. 'Sorry it's a bit basic just now.'

The windows rattled and a draught snaked up my legs. I thought longingly of the country house hotel up the road.

'I'll leave you to settle in. I'm making dinner in the kitchen, so I'd better get back to it!'

It took Jonathan three trips to the car and back to fetch all of our stuff, including the travel cot and highchair. Meanwhile, Sophie and I had found the bathroom – a large freezing room with a green painted concrete floor, set up with six baths around the outside and a row of sinks down the middle. Both windows had cracked panes. Hearing a low buzz, I looked up at the ceiling. The fluorescent lights, with their plastic covers, displayed the shadowy corpses of dozens of dead flies.

'What are we going to do?' I hissed at Jonathan, who was rubbing his hair dry with a greyish-white, fraying towel he'd found in the cupboard. 'We can't stay here!'

'We'll have to, Cassie-Lassie,' he said.

After negotiating the dark corridor and the holey floorboards once more, we found Tom downstairs in the kitchen. It was a large, country house-style kitchen, warmed by a dark green Aga. We knew that he'd made all the kitchen units himself from some rare and wonderful wood, and we made the appropriate appreciative noises.

He was stirring something pungent on the stove.

'I'm making a shellfish stew. I should have checked, actually – are you okay with shellfish?'

'Lovely.' Even the thought of shellfish made me shudder. Luckily I'd brought some of Sophie's jars with me, so she would be okay. Maybe I could sneak a few mouthfuls of her dinner, under the guise of encouraging her to eat.

'Actually, do you mind if I heat up Sophie's dinner now?' I asked. 'We really should try and get her off to bed before dinner.'

'Yes, go for it! And I need to get you both a glass of wine!' said Tom, leaping over to a cupboard and pulling out wine glasses.

Just then, the telephone rang in the hall, and Tom went out to answer it. We heard him saying, 'Oh no!' a few times and then he came back in, hands dragging at his cheeks.

'That was one of my clients. Their fitted oak bookcase has just collapsed! It's brought some of the plaster off the wall – and it's a Grade 2 listed building.'

'Oh dear,' I said. 'That doesn't sound good.'

'I'm so sorry,' he went on, grabbing his coat from the back of one of the kitchen chairs. 'I'm going to have to go up there and sort it out.'

I nodded sympathetically. He seemed in a real state.

'My reputation is at stake, you see, because this is a top-drawer client – very well connected. My God, this is a nightmare. I'm so sorry. Do you mind terribly . . .'

'No, of course not. You go on,' said Jonathan, giving him a pat on the back.

'Jody will be home very soon, I promise you. She'll look after you. Just help yourself to anything else you need . . .'

'Where are you going?' I called after him as he swept out of the room.

'Aberdeen,' he called back over his shoulder.

We heard the front door slam and stared at one another.

'Aberdeen?' Jonathan whispered, frowning. 'That's, what, a two-hour drive from here, at least.'

'I don't think he'll be back tonight, will he?' I said. 'I wonder what we should do with this shellfish stew.' I went over to the Aga and gingerly lifted the wooden spoon, so that the stew slowly slid off it and slopped back into the pan.

'You stir the stew, and I'll heat up Sophie's food,' said Jonathan.

'No, you stir the stew,' I said, raising the spoon again, as if poised to flick the residue over him.

He came up and grabbed me in a rugby tackle, lifting me off my feet. I squealed as Sophie looked on, her eyes wide and curious, her rosebud mouth slightly open.

The phone started ringing again, but by this point I was flat on my back with Jonathan sitting on top of me, trying to prise the spoon out of my hand.

'Get off me! Maybe we should answer that. Get off me!'

'No. I'm not getting off you until you've tasted this stew. It may need more seasoning,' he said with a wicked grin, trying to force the spoon towards my mouth.

The phone went on to answer phone, and we heard Jody's voice. 'Sweetie? Are you there? Can you pick up? I'm so sorry but I'm going to have to stay at Mum's. Vichard's been sick and he's got a bit of a temperature so I'd better keep him away from the other babies. Can you look after everyone? I'm really sorry. Give me a call when you get a chance. Bye . . . bye.' She hung up.

'Oh no,' Jonathan said. 'Vichard's not vell.'

'This is no joking matter, Jonathan! We need at least one host. Phone her back!'

He took the phone, and tried 1471, but it was a withheld number. I checked my phone but couldn't find a mobile number for Jody.

'So we are now stuck in this hellhole by ourselves!' Sophie, hearing the tension in my voice, began to howl.

'Well,' said Jonathan between wails, 'remember – the hypno-birthers will be here soon.'

Ah yes, the silver lining. A weekend alone with Molly and Dave.

'You say that as though it's a good thing. You do realise he was threatening to bring his lute?'

While we waited for their arrival, I heated up Sophie's dinner and fed it to her, spoonful by slow spoonful. Then, daunted by the prospect of the dormitory bathroom, we gave her a slippery, giggly bath in the kitchen sink.

'Shall we just pop her into her car seat and go home?' suggested Jonathan once we'd got her into a fresh nappy and pink-bunnied sleepsuit.

'We can hardly just abandon the house with Molly and Dave about to arrive. We're going to have to stay.'

So we set up the travel cot in a warm corner of the kitchen, and Sophie went off to sleep easily for once, tired after the car journey and her novelty bath.

'What are we going to do about dinner?' I was getting hungry by now.

Jonathan went and looked in the fridge, and came back carrying eggs, and milk, and cheese.

'Omelette?' he suggested. 'I can always rustle up something for the hypno-birthers later. But I think we need to eat.'

I nodded, and he began whisking up eggs. I found a grater in the cupboard and started grating the cheese.

We sat opposite each other at the enormous wooden kitchen table to eat, while Sophie slept in her travel cot in the corner.

I suddenly felt quite close to Jonathan – in this strange house, in this unlooked-for moment of solitude. Closer than I had done in a long time. He had been endearingly enthusiastic about making the omelettes, taking control of his environment with boyish delight, as if we were on a Famous Five camping adventure.

In this bright halo of country kitchen cosiness I seemed to see things more clearly. Jonathan and I had been acting more like co-workers than husband and wife since having Sophie. And – even worse – we were effectively working in shifts. Because she didn't sleep all that well, Jonathan would often send me off to bed at around nine o'clock, which was sometimes not long after he'd got in from work. He went to bed at around midnight, handing over responsibility for Sophie's night-time shenanigans to me. Weekends were no better – often one of us would do the chores whilst the other entertained Sophie. No, it was hardly surprising that we'd drifted apart a little, that we felt like strangers moving around each other in the house. And it was hardly surprising that we were both stressed

– me caught up in loops of horrifying worries, him with his inexplicable nightmares. But all this could be fixed, I was sure.

'So how are you feeling about things?' I began.

'Fine. What do you mean?'

'Well, since having Sophie. I was just wondering how you were feeling about things.'

'Fine. What do you mean?' he said again.

'We haven't really talked much, have we?'

'It's been pretty busy. What did you want to talk about?'

'I don't know. It's just nice to have some time to talk, isn't it?' I said it with a satisfied sigh, as though an evening alone in a semi-renovated boarding school was the answer to everything.

He shot me a questioning look.

'How do you think it feels, being a dad?' I continued.

'Fine,' said Jonathan. 'Great.'

'It's a lot of hard work, isn't it? More than I expected. I didn't think the broken nights would be so hard, for one thing.'

He frowned at me across the table.

'What? What's the matter?'

'Nothing,' he said with an irritated sigh.

'But it's so precious, isn't it – every scrap of time with her. When I was at Braid Hills Funeral Home the other day, I met this woman who was planning her own funeral. She'd actually taken her little daughter in with her. She'd obviously had chemo, her hair was all . . .'

'Jesus CHRIST, Cassie!' His fork clattered down on to his plate. 'I'm trying to eat my dinner!'

I put down my knife and fork, too, and stared at him. I felt as though the air had been knocked out of me. He pulled his face into a ghastly fake smile and tried to take it back.

'Sorry, darling. Go on.'

But then the phone rang. It was Molly, calling to say they'd

84

got lost and had been circling around Cumbernauld for the last hour trying to find their way back on to the M9. When I explained that both our hosts had disappeared and that Shona, Paul and Elgin were stuck in London because of their meeting with the Home Secretary, she decided they'd cut their losses and head back to Edinburgh.

Relieved of the prospect of having to play host to Molly and her family, we fetched our sleeping bags and pillows from the dormitory and settled down on the floor by the Aga. It seemed to conjure up a teenagey, sleepover sort of feel. How many years had it been since I'd lain awake with a friend next to me, talking for hours into the darkness? Probably not since Helen and I had shared a flat at University. I envied, in my younger self, that capacity for passionate, urgent exchanges. Suddenly it seemed imperative to feel that way again. I decided to ignore the fork-clattering warning signs and press on with my attempts to discuss dead parents.

'You know your dad?' I ventured.

'Yeees.'

'How did your mum cope when he died, having to bring you and Stephen up by herself? Did you have to help her a lot, being the oldest?'

'Well, school kept us busy – rugby and all that. And during the school holidays Stephen and I used to go and stay with Oma and Opa.'

I had heard this many times . . . about his fat jolly Dutch maternal grandparents, and his uncle and aunt with their six children. I had heard about uproarious games of hide and seek in their big house in the country, swimming in the lake every morning in summer, cycling through the flower fields in spring. And about the plays the children had written and performed on the verandah on warm evenings.

As he launched into describing it again, I thought I could see, in his face, a flicker of the child he'd once been. The nine-year-old, the six-year-old, perhaps ... an indefinable something to do with the curve of his lower lip, the stubborn set of his jaw. A child who'd had to grow up very quickly. I wanted to love all those of his former selves.

'Oma and Opa sound nice ... was your mum never tempted to move back to Holland to be nearer them?'

'No – she just got on with it,' said Jonathan, suddenly brisk again. 'We all did. There was no choice.'

What was he hiding, underneath this no-nonsense attitude? Images came into my mind: Jonathan sitting with his dad as he lay unconscious, wired up to monitors and machines; the day they'd spent in that timeless, twilight space between living and dying. My love, walking out of the hospital at dawn, blinking in disbelief at a world that was irretrievably changed.

'It must have been awful, not being able to say goodbye in the hospital, with him being unconscious and everything. What was the last conversation you had with him, before it happened? Did you get any sense that he ... knew, at all? That he was going to go, I mean.'

'I can't remember, Cass,' he said pleadingly. At this point I should probably have registered that he sounded tired, and not at all like a teenage girl.

'You must remember. Come on, I want to know. What was the last thing you ever said to him?' My voice came out like a whiny, demanding child. I was pushing him too far, desperate to tap into something deeper within him before the moment slipped away.

But then something went hard in Jonathan's eyes; hard and final like a book slamming shut.

'I think it was something along the lines of "I hate you, you fat, balding, freckly old arsehole." Now, *for the love of God*, can we talk about something else?'

★

Tom came back at around six in the morning, and was horrified to find us curled up in our sleeping bags near the Aga. We had to make up some story about Sophie falling asleep in the kitchen (glossing over the question of how the travel cot had materialised there) and us not wanting to leave her. We didn't want him to think we were ungrateful for the dormitory accommodation that had been offered, or the fly-graveyard bathroom.

Unfortunately we'd forgotten the pan of congealed shellfish stew, which Jonathan had abandoned last thing at night outside the back door. We had to pretend that we'd eaten some, but had only taken very small portions, being anxious that Molly and Dave might be hungry when they arrived, or that Tom or Jody might return home unexpectedly, needing food.

The atmosphere was a little cool, and we left later that morning since it was obvious that Tom wanted to get back up to Aberdeen to rebuild the collapsed bookcase. Jody had phoned to say that Vichard had been sick seven times in the night so it definitely wouldn't be sensible to meet up.

In the car, on the way home, I had an idea.

'Jonathan,'

'Yeeees.'

'You know your mum?'

He slumped dramatically in his seat. 'Oh, for fuck's sake, Cassie . . .'

'No, no . . . I was just wondering. You know how she went to stay with Stephen and Moira after they had the twins? Well, maybe she might like to come and stay with us for a while?'

'With us? For how long?'

'A few weeks, or maybe longer, depending on how it went?'

'Well, yes. That's a good idea.' His voice went deeper, the tightness rounded out into approval. 'You two have always got on so well. She could take the pressure off when you're working, what with Sophie's nursery pick-ups, and so on. And it would be company for you when you're not working. It must be lonely in the house with just you and Sophie. Maybe she could even get up in the night for Sophie sometimes, and give you a proper night's sleep. I know how tired you are.'

This came as something of a surprise – I'd thought he hadn't been listening.

'Shall we just ask her to come for a few weeks, and see how it goes?' I suggested. The idea of having easy company during those long days at home with Sophie felt like a weight slipping off my shoulders. But it was more than that. I sensed that Dita might provide an indirect way to bond with Jonathan. If he wouldn't talk to me, perhaps I could get to know him from the outside in, by trying to understand the things that were important to him.

Jonathan nodded, looking pleased. It was the sort of thing that pleased him; a domestic issue addressed, a mutually beneficial course of action agreed upon. We were safely back in our partner-parent roles.

'I think your mother and I will have lots to talk about.' It was a risky line, given the conversation of the previous night, but I said it in a teasing voice, with a sideways glance.

'Yes, you can discuss my many failings. I must be out of my mind . . . three females in the house to gang up on me.'

He shot me a strange little smile, and there was a flicker of connection between us as we turned on to the motorway slip road and headed for home.

9

If I had to pinpoint when things started going downhill, it would be one rainy Friday a few weeks later. Running on three hours' sleep, I'd dropped Sophie at nursery, struggled into the office, and made it through the morning on a heady mix of adrenalin and coffee. Bobby Spencer, the Braid Hills employee, had sent a second formal letter of complaint to Radcliffe and I'd been ordered to draft a reply, responding to each of the points Bobby had made. But I'd hardly been able to read the words on the computer screen – they'd seemed to swim in front of my eyes. By lunchtime I was barely able to keep awake. Our team had a 'learning lunch' training session so there was no time to go out and buy a sandwich, but I went into the kitchenette area to make another strong cup of coffee to take with me.

The tiredness was overtaking my life, and there didn't seem to be any end in sight, even though Dita had come to stay with us, as Jonathan and I had discussed. It wasn't that she was unwilling to help – before she'd even put down her suitcase and taken her coat off, she'd offered to be on duty for Sophie that night. She'd waved away my half-hearted objections, claiming that she would enjoy that quiet time with Sophie in the middle of the night.

The problem was, she proved to be such a heavy sleeper that she didn't hear Sophie crying, either that night or any night subsequently. So I was still getting up continually – blindly offering milk, cuddles or reassurance, though sometimes none of those seemed to work.

Dita, meanwhile, was happily convinced that Sophie had staged a miraculous turnaround, sleep-wise, since she'd arrived. She aired the theory that Sophie felt more settled now that she, Dita, was on hand to help out. Relaxed mum, relaxed baby, she'd said with a knowing smile. It seemed rude to shatter her illusions. Or to mention my own theory that the baby cries were masked, for Dita, by the sound of her own snores.

'Wakey wakey, sleepyhead!'

I jerked awake – I'd actually fallen asleep leaning against the kitchenette worktop, waiting for the kettle to boil.

It was Malkie. *God.* Of all the times to run into him. I hadn't seen him since that encounter in the street outside the office – the litigation department was far away on the second floor. There was no point in pretending I hadn't been asleep, but I hoped he wouldn't notice the dark circles under my eyes, or my flat wispy hair, which had still been wet when I'd rushed out of the house that morning.

'Hey, you,' I said. 'What brings you to our basement realm?'

'The upstairs microwave is broken,' he said. 'I need to heat this up.' He was holding a yellow polystyrene container that looked as though it was from the takeaway around the corner. 'Chicken piri piri baked potato,' he said with a grin, opening the lid to release a hit of garlicky fumes.

I pulled a face. 'Oh God, Malkie. How can you eat such stuff?'

He put it into the microwave and pressed the buttons. Then he leaned back against the counter, crossing his arms.

'So how's the world of employment law?'

'Oh, fine . . . great!' I didn't want to go into the whole Bobby Spencer fiasco. Malkie knew me from a time when I'd been the highest scoring law student in the year, with creamy skin and glossy, swinging hair. Now, there was no hiding the dark circles and flat hair, but at least I could feign some professional competence.

'You okay? You look a bit spaced out.'

'Just . . . er, a little dizzy. Too much coffee, probably. I'm fine.'

I wasn't at all sure that this was true. But I wasn't about to reveal that to Malkie – I didn't want him to know I'd become a neurotic wreck, the sort who'd spent the last three evenings Googling brain tumours.

With him standing in front of me, it all seemed so ridiculous, as though I could just step out of that skin, and go back to being who I was supposed to be. But who was that, exactly? The different versions of myself seemed to shimmer in front of me.

'Are you sure you're fine?'

Why was everything happening in slow motion? I looked up at Malkie's face, then at my own hands, stretching the fingers experimentally. I shook my head hoping that might sort it, but it was a mistake because something in my brain seemed to go into free fall. My vision lurched; I stepped towards the counter to steady myself but the floor seemed to slide from under my feet. I fell into him; I actually fell into him and he caught me, bringing me to rest on my knees on the floor.

'Woooahh, steady! Are you okay?' He was still holding on to me, his hands gripping my upper arms.

Sandra, one of the bossiest secretaries, came rushing over. 'Cassie? What happened? Shall I fetch the first aider?' She seemed to be speaking from somewhere very far away.

'Cassie?' repeated Malkie.

'No, honestly,' I said, rubbing my forehead with the back of my hand, hiding my eyes. 'It was just a dizzy spell. I just slipped, it's fine honestly.'

'Here, sit down,' said Sandra, wheeling a chair over. Her

voice wobbled, barely able to contain her excitement. I managed to stand up and lower myself into the chair but my legs shook and could hardly hold me. Malkie jerked forward, reaching for my arm to steady me.

'It's okay, Malkie, I've got her. Can you go and get Julie, the first aider? She's on the second floor. Now Cassie, just sit here and take some deep breaths.'

*

Malkie came down to see me a little while later.

'Feeling better now?'

'Yes, thanks. Much better.'

But my concern was mirrored in Malkie's face.

'I'm fine, honestly.'

'You should get it checked out. You don't look too well.'

'Don't worry,' I said in a whisper. 'Bloody Sandra has organised a GP appointment for me. Apparently they had a cancellation. I expect they bumped a poor sick old lady off her appointment – anything to get Sandra off the phone.'

'I'll drive you. I've got a stack of witness statements to work through and I was going to do it from home anyway, to get some peace.'

'No, it's fine.'

'I won't have you going on your own. No arguments, or I'll tell Sandra you've just fainted again and she'll phone an ambulance.'

*

Malkie brought his car round from the car park so I didn't have to walk. As I got in and pulled the door shut I felt the years fall away again, like pages sliding free from an old book. Many of our difficult scenes had been played out in his car, parked up at some desolate spot. It felt as though threads of old conversations were still hanging there, waiting to be continued.

I glanced over at him; he was frowning in concentration as he negotiated a right turn into the traffic on Queen Street. The dizziness had receded into a not entirely unpleasant wooziness, and combined with the adrenalin fizz of his close proximity it felt like being slightly drunk. Perhaps it would be okay just to surrender to it for a while, just to sit back and watch him.

With Malkie it had always been about chemistry. It had even started with an experiment in a grey concrete University tower block one rainy evening in June, the day after I'd finished my English Lit finals.

Helen and I had had to walk five floors up the stairwell to find the psychology lab, white and stark under fluorescent lights. Helen's friend Jo – who had appeared at our flat the night before, begging us to take part – was there to meet us, and she checked us off on her clipboard.

'Help yourselves to some refreshments,' she said, pointing to a table with white plastic cups set out in rows.

'Orange squash and custard creams!' remarked Helen. 'I feel like I've been transported back to Primary Three.'

'I know. I keep expecting Mrs Murray to walk in.'

We stood sipping our juice, glancing at the other participants – all young women around our age. It felt surreal to be a lab rat, under scrutiny in such clinical surroundings – my head was still full of T.S. Eliot, and the Brontës.

One by one, we were summoned to a table where we had to place a plastic mask over our nose and mouth. Jo screwed a series of jars – which seemed to contain crumpled t-shirts – on to a hose that was attached to the mask, and we were instructed to take several deep breaths.

The first four were variations on B.O., ranging from cheesy to acrid. But the last one was altogether different. It was an outdoorsy, rainy smell, like forgotten washing brought in from the line last thing at night.

After we had rated each smell Jo threw open a set of doors into an adjoining lab, where there were six tables set up, with a young male student seated at each one. Jo motioned to the first table. 'Cassie – you pair up with Malkie, please.'

Helen later told me that you could feel the chemistry, spitting and crackling in the air, as soon as I turned to face him. For me it felt like a state of heightened awareness, every sense tuned into him. While Jo gave us our instructions – which I registered only as an annoying background buzz – he sat back in his chair and put his hands behind his head, pulling back his elbows in a stretch. I glimpsed two dark circles of sweat, before he straightened up and smiled. 'Shall we get started then?'

He had to describe the house he'd grown up in, and I had to draw it on a fresh, white sheet of A3. However, I couldn't really concentrate on what he was saying. The sound of his voice was stirring me up, melting me, like a warm spoon in honey.

'Just take it a bit more to the left . . . that's it. Yes, that's it, right there . . .'

Whenever I drew something the wrong way he'd laugh in a knowing, masculine, spatially aware sort of way. Whenever I got something right he'd nod and grunt excitedly.

'Hmm,' he said afterwards, craning his head round. 'Doesn't look much like a council house in East Kilbride, but hey.'

I blushed. It looked like a crooked *Hansel and Gretel* house. Something a four-year-old might have drawn.

'Okay,' he said, picking up a pen. 'Your house next.'

I began telling him what to draw.

'Bloody hell,' he said, halfway through. 'That's the twenty-sixth window. Did you live in a stately home or something?'

'No,' I muttered. 'I grew up in a sheltered housing complex for the elderly.'

'What?' He screwed up his face like a wee boy.

'My mum was the warden. She was a nurse by training, but she took that job to fit around looking after me. We had a little flat on the ground floor.' I pointed over to one of the windows he'd drawn. 'There.'

'Cool,' he said quietly. He bent close over the paper and drew a tiny smiley face and a stick hand, waving.

Afterwards, I walked back to the flat in a daze, Helen laughing and pushing my back to propel me faster along the pavement.

Suddenly I swung round. 'What if he's not there next week?'

'He'll be there,' said Helen.

'Well it's obviously about pheromones or something, isn't it? What if this week was *attractive* men, and next week is . . .' My voice trailed off in horror at the thought.

'It doesn't matter. He's going into his final year of law, you said? You can always track him down in the law library.'

But I didn't need to worry. When we got there the following Thursday, Malkie was already there with his friend Kev, loitering beside the refreshments table.

'This week,' said Jo, 'We have a different task for you. Helen – you pair up with Kevin again, please. Cassie, you go with Malkie.'

I wanted to throw my arms around her, as though she was some kind of wild-haired, bespectacled fairy godmother.

This time we each had to describe our 'family', and the other person had to draw a picture of it.

'Well, there's my mum,' I began. 'She's big. Size twenty or so. But she's pretty . . . she's got nice skin and rosy cheeks and she always has expensive clothes. Usually she wears pearls.'

Malkie's pen hovered over the page, as though he wasn't sure how large he should actually make her – in the end he made her a tactful size sixteen or so.

'And you could draw me, I guess.'

He nodded, and with a flick of his eyebrows he put pen to paper again.

'I don't have a dad,' I said in a rush.

'Nah,' he said. 'Me neither.'

'I mean – he's dead. I don't remember him. Do you think you should put him in anyway?'

'I'll draw a father-shaped space,' he said.

How did he know? How could he have known that this was how I'd always thought of him? That I'd never been able to imagine him with a face, despite the slim Kodak envelope in the bottom drawer of Mum's desk, with its six faded holiday snaps and strips of slippery, baffling negatives.

In the next exercise, I was given a blindfold and Malkie had to direct me through an obstacle course, steering me round a series of cones, along a bench, and up and down a small set of steps. There wasn't supposed to be any physical contact, but he was so close that I could feel his breath against my cheek. At one point, I lost my balance and his hand shot out to steady me. A thought slammed into my mind, on the back of a thousand volts.

He is meant for me.

I stopped, and drew a deep breath, and it felt like the first time I'd ever breathed oxygen.

He lifted the blindfold from around my eyes, sliding it over my hair with two gentle hands. 'My turn now.'

'My goodness,' I said, after I'd walked him across the low wooden bench, the kind we'd used in school for gym. 'We're much better than everybody else.' Students were tumbling over cones everywhere and one girl was lying sprawled on the floor giggling. She pulled her partner over on top of her as he tried to help her up.

'Ha!' he said. 'That's because you didn't have any of the orange squash.'

He drew a hip flask out of the pocket of his jacket. 'Vodka,' he said. 'Kev and I thought it would make for a more interesting experiment. Want some?'

But when we turned up for the follow-up session the next week, we got to the lab to find a notice on the door, and a small cluster of experimentees standing around chatting. The notice said that the experiment had been cancelled – Jo had been forced to abandon her Masters, due to 'unforeseen circumstances'. A wave of disappointment hit me. However, a moment later Malkie came up behind us, hands thrust deep in the pockets of his shabby navy jacket. 'Anyone coming to the pub?' he asked casually.

I got really quite drunk and I don't remember much of the evening, or the walk back to Malkie's flat later. I registered that it was in a row of tenements somewhere near Arthur's Seat, four flights up an echoing stairwell, and that it had a distinctive smell – musty, sandy, damp, the smell of old stone.

As he shared his one-bedroom flat with another guy, he had turned the living room into his bedroom. It looked odd – a swirly carpet and an ugly fake stone fireplace, and a bed made up with navy and grey striped bedding. My head was spinning, so I lay down on it and shut my eyes.

Then it all came out – how I was supposed to be going to Massachussets to do a Masters in American Literature, how I desperately wanted to go but was so scared at the prospect of leaving everything and everybody behind. 'And I'm worried about what I'm going to do later. I mean, Emily Dickinson is incredible . . . and Henry James, and Hart Crane . . . and, oh God, all of them . . . but they're not going to get me a job, are they?'

Malkie, propped up on one elbow beside me on the bed, gave me a quizzical look, as though he wasn't sure who I was referring to. Ineffectual careers advisers, perhaps.

'Maybe I should do a law conversion course instead.'

'Maybe you should,' he said in a low, deep voice. 'We could play footsie in the law library.'

'Yes, but Malkie. It's because . . because . . .' Because of what? My head was spinning. 'Oh yes. Financial Security.'

'Yep,' he said, without missing a beat. 'That's something all those twats with rich parents will never understand.'

'Exactly!' I twisted myself up to look at him. 'They will never understand. All those people with two parents.'

He shook his head. 'They won't have a fucking clue.'

I fell back on the bed with a dramatic sigh. 'Have you got a traineeship yet, then?'

'Nah. I've had a few stage-one interviews with human resources, but I've never gotten through to stage two. They're only interested in one thing,' he said bitterly.

'What's that?' I breathed, horrified. Were the HR women after him for his body?

'What school you went to,' he said. 'They think I'm a scaff.'

'I think you're amazing.'

Then everything went quiet; the noise of the traffic and the passers-by outside seemed to fade away. And there in the room, on that bed, there was a pause; a sense of something being weighed in the balance. Silently it resolved itself, as he lifted his hand to stroke my hair. I could smell cigarettes off him, and something else; the essence of him, that far-away rainy night scent.

He lowered his face and closed his mouth over mine. Silver lightning coursed down the backs of my legs. I pulled his narrow body on top of mine, and he paused to look at me, and murmured three words. They were the same words looping through my mind. 'We fit together.'

At around midday, I woke up to Malkie groaning, 'Jings . . .' in a voice even more gravelly than normal. I felt the bedsprings bounce as he sat up next to me. Thrilled to be in bed with someone who said things like 'Jings', I opened my eyes and gazed at him admiringly as he stumbled through to the kitchen to get two pint glasses of cold water and some paracetamol.

We took a bus into town and went to Princes Street Gardens. We picked our way down the grassy slope, past office workers with their shoes kicked off, sunburnt students, and young families with buggies and picnics and sensible hats. We found a spot under a tree, and lay on our backs, staring up at the leaves as they shifted gently in the breeze. Green against the deep, deep blue.

Malkie eventually broke the silence. 'I'll wait for you, you know.'

I sat up and turned to look at him, awkward in his old navy jacket, jeans and grey trainers. His face was even paler than usual, almost white, with a sheen of hangover sweat.

'I know that you're going away. But I'm kind of in trouble here. I think I've fallen for you.'

So why did he look almost ill at the thought of it? His eyes were heavy, full of discomfort.

He walked me to the bus stop, where he grabbed me into a brief, fierce hug, then turned and walked away without a word. I ached for him. Oh God, I ached for him. But already, it felt more like a death than a beginning.

★

It was about half past four by the time I left the doctor's surgery – the appointments had been running behind. Malkie was still waiting for me in his car. I shimmied into the passenger seat and pulled the door shut with a clunk.

'What did they say?' he asked, handing me a cold bottle of juice and a packet of paracetamol. He must have gone to the corner shop while he was waiting for me.

'How did you know I had a headache?'

He shrugged. 'You just had that kind of hazy look.'

It was strange. We'd hardly spoken for nearly a decade. But this little bit of drama had cut through the awkwardness, and the old dynamic had clicked back into place. It was undeniably still there, this connection that was grounded in physical chemistry but was not limited to that. He'd always 'got' me, effortlessly, instinctively, without the need for stumbling explanations.

'Oh, she just said there were millions of different things that can cause dizziness. Most of them not serious. She said I should make a note of when I feel dizzy to see if I can see a pattern or connect it with anything I'm doing. Maybe if I've not eaten for a long time or something. Or if I'm particularly tired – but that's all the time, really. I did say that, but I don't know if she was actually listening.'

I released a shuddering breath.

'You sound *stressed*,' he said. 'What's the matter?'

'I don't know. I feel a bit wound up.'

'Wound up how?'

'Like something terrible is going to happen. Or sometimes . . . I feel a bit spooked. Like somebody might be following me or something.'

'Jesus, Cassie. Somebody's been following you?'

'No. At least I don't think so. I think you're right, I am a bit stressed.'

'Being tired won't help. It must be hard with kids around.'

'Yeah. Only one kid. She's only little.'

He put his left hand on the gearstick and wiggled it. But rather than starting the ignition, he turned to me and spoke again, his voice soft and improbably low. 'Cassie, I don't want to say the wrong thing, but something seems up with you. What is it we're talking about here? Is it stress, or is it something else? Post-natal depression?'

It was like an arrow through me. He was ruthless in his directness, the way he shone it into all those places I wanted to hide. I wanted so much to just give in and say that I didn't know, that I didn't understand any of it. But I had a feeling that if I said that, he might reach for my hand, or lift my chin with his finger, the way he always used to, and then where would I be? I could accept that he might hanker after the past, after the young, glossy me he'd given up so long ago. But the idea that he might love what I'd become . . . well, it would simply unravel me.

'She didn't say anything like that.'

He gave me a look. 'The doctor? I wasn't asking what *she* thought. What do you think?'

I gazed through the windscreen at the sweep of the Georgian terrace: cold, hard, beautiful stone.

'I feel like I'm disappearing.'

He was quiet for a minute or two. I realised, by the tension in my hands, in my jaw, that I'd been braced for the change of subject, or the humorous twist that I'd come to expect from Jonathan.

But Malkie just turned towards me, and looked me straight in the eye. 'That doesn't sound good.'

And suddenly it seemed a little easier to breathe.

★

Sophie grizzled all the way home, kicking her little feet against the inside of the cosytoe, and arching against the buggy straps. I had thought she might be pleased to be collected earlier than usual, but she seemed upset by the change in routine.

What had just happened there, with Malkie? The question drummed itself into my mind again and again, as relentless as my headache as I pushed the buggy up the hill in the rain.

Nothing – nothing had happened. He'd asked how I was feeling after my doctor's appointment, and I'd told him. He'd asked if there was anything he could do, and I'd asked him to drive me to the nursery. That was it – one colleague helping another out, giving her a lift on his way home.

Colleagues? Would I have had that conversation with Annabel Masters, or Sandra the secretary?

Friends, then. Maybe enough time had passed now. Maybe it would actually be fine to have *more* of those conversations with him. We could walk to the sandwich shop together at lunchtimes, and I would feel him next to me like the sun on my skin, but it would all be okay. Made safe by the label of 'friends'.

But then Helen's voice cut through my thoughts. *Friends? Come on, Cassie. He broke your heart, time and time again.*

Yes he did. But he *had* my heart. He had my heart, in the first place, to be able to break it.

Whatever I'd felt, lying next to Malkie in his uncomfortable bed in his dingy flat, it had never been *hollow*.

It was a truth that my imaginary Helen didn't seem to have any answer to.

As we turned on to Ravelston Dykes, Sophie stopped grizzling . . . and started bawling. I picked her up and carried her wedged on my hip, pushing the buggy with one hand. It didn't make any difference, only that the wailing was closer to my ear.

'Oh Sophie, Sophie. What's Mummy going to do?'

Rather eerily, she stopped crying the moment that I opened the front door. I knew the house had been empty all day because Dita was visiting friends. But there was the sense that someone had been there. A feeling that the air in the house had just settled. I hesitated on the threshold and called out.

'Hello? Dita? Are you there?' No answer. I noticed one of Jonathan's slippers lying in the middle of the otherwise tidy hall. I didn't think it had been there when we'd left the house this morning. Then again, we had been in a rush.

'Jonathan?' I didn't expect an answer – there was no way he'd be home at this time.

I stepped inside and it was then that I noticed a small slip of paper lying beside the mail. I leant down rather unsteadily, Sophie still balanced on my hip, and picked it up.

I'm watching you

I gasped, and spun around to look out onto the street, pulling Sophie against my chest. Nobody was there. I scanned

103

the parked cars, but the few that were there all looked empty. A taxi drove past. Then a lady on a bicycle.

I went back into the house and locked the door.

I carried Sophie upstairs and looked round all the rooms, checking they were empty, checking nothing had been moved. I drew the blinds and curtains, thinking it might make me feel safe. It didn't work though – it just gave the house a dim, closed-in feel.

I went back down the stairs slowly, looking straight ahead – trying to get out of my head the idea that we weren't alone in the house. I went into the kitchen and rummaged around under the sink with one arm, crushing a protesting, backwardly horizontal Sophie against my chest with the other.

'Hold on, hold on . . . here we are, Soph.' I sat back on my heels and showed Sophie what I had found. 'Nice wasp spray.'

Weapon in hand, I went back up to the bedroom and phoned Jonathan.

'There's some madman watching the house!' I explained about the note, struggling to find enough breath to complete my sentences.

There was a long silence. At first I thought he was shocked, but then I heard a couple of faint clicking noises.

'Jonathan. Are you typing?'

'Hmm?' Another long pause. 'Nope.'

'Listen, this could be serious. It could be a stalker.'

'Don't be silly, Cassie. It's probably just a promotional thing. Maybe for that new pizza place that's opened in Roseburn?'

'Why would they send a slip of paper saying "I'm watching you"?'

'We'll probably get another one tomorrow with a twenty per cent off voucher.' Jonathan was completely unflappable.

As I rang off a thought came to me. Bobby Spencer from

the funeral home. It had to be him, getting back at me for his dismissal. Goodness knows how he'd got hold of my address.

A key turned in the front door. I rushed out to the landing and looked over the banisters just in time to see Dita coming in, laden down with shopping bags. By the time we'd got downstairs, she'd gone into the kitchen and was standing there looking bewildered. She was surveying the chaos all over the floor by the sink: bottles of bleach and laundry liquid, a carton of fabric softener lying on its side in a puddle of pearly fluid, an avalanche of freezer bags escaped from their box, a scattering of clothes pegs . . .

It was the sight of this – this crime scene of panic – that finally made my legs go weak, and my head go dizzy, forcing me to sit down on the nearest chair.

★

'Bobby Spencer?' said Jonathan later that evening while we were doing the dishes. 'I thought you said he was a five-foot midget?'

'So?'

'Hmm. Doesn't sound like the stalker type to me.' Jonathan was still very sanguine about the whole thing, even after he had looked at the note and conceded that it was 'a bit odd'.

'That's very illogical. A stalker could be any shape or size. The main thing is, we know that he hates me.'

'Sweetheart, why would anyone hate you?' His rubber-gloved hands were covered in soapy bubbles, but he twisted towards me and kissed my hair. 'He might have issues with how you handled the business about his dismissal, but he doesn't *hate* you.'

'The way I *handled* it? You almost sound like you agree with him!'

'Of course I don't agree with him. Oh Cassie, let's try and forget about it for tonight. Let's talk about something else.'

He put a clean saucepan on the drainer and I picked it up, drying it slowly.

'Well there is something else I need to tell you, actually. I had a bit of a strange turn at work today. I sort of went dizzy and fell over.'

'Did you? Are you okay?' He turned to face me.

'I went to the doctor's – they had a cancellation.'

'And what did they say?'

'Oh, nothing really.'

'Oh, right. Maybe you're just tired. I'll cover Sophie's wake-ups tonight.'

He went back to rinsing the soap bubbles out of one of Sophie's bottles. There was no concern in his voice, but I thought I'd better pass on the doctor's reassurances anyway.

'She didn't seem to think it was a brain tumour or anything.'

'Cassieeeeee!' his voice slid up, rich with affectionate mockery. 'Have you been watching *Holby City* again?'

'Jonathan, I don't know why I even BOTHER talking to you.' I shoved the tea towel into his chest and walked off.

10

Late one evening, not long afterwards, I initiated a heart-to-heart with Dita. Jonathan had been away on business for a few nights, and Dita and I had fallen into the pattern of having extended toast and tea sessions at bedtime. It was a delaying tactic, on my part – I didn't want to go to bed. Since the arrival of the note, I'd started a complicated process of checking the doors and windows, sometimes twice or three times. After the completion of this exercise, I would go to bed and lie awake in the dark worrying – about my dizziness and other suspicious symptoms, about Jonathan and his nightmares, about Bobby Spencer and his complaint, about who could have left the note and what they might do next. A week had passed without further incident, prompting a self-satisfied, 'See?' from Jonathan. But I couldn't shake the ominous feeling that settled over me whenever I was by myself in the house.

The late-night chats with Dita were a good way to keep all this at bay, however. Buttering our third round of toast, we got onto the subject of Dita's family in Holland (Oma and Opa and all that) and it seemed natural, somehow, to say that I had asked Jonathan about his father. I wondered if she would flinch and stiffen, like Jonathan, at the mention of the subject, but she simply nodded and raised an enquiring eyebrow.

'Did Jonathan have a falling out with his dad before he died?' I asked. 'I hope you don't mind me asking ... it was just something he mentioned which made me wonder.'

Dita looked surprised for a moment, then shrugged and gave a half smile. 'Oh, it was just one of those silly things,' she said. 'I kept telling him, afterwards, that it didn't matter – that his dad would've been laughing about it. But I don't know if Jonathan ever came to see it that way. You see, he'd asked his dad if he could go on a weekend to Newcastle with some of his rugby friends. He was only fifteen, the youngest of them, and Frank thought they were planning to be drinking most of the weekend, so he said no. I felt for Jonathan, in a way – he was always the one who came up against the boundaries, being the eldest, and so much more outgoing than Stephen. Frank used to come down harder on him.'

For a brief moment, he flashed into something real, this blank face on Sophie's family tree. He was a parent trying to feel his way, just like Jonathan and I were now.

'Jonathan was really angry about it, and just as Frank was leaving the house to go to work, he shouted something out – that he hated him, or something like that. Frank didn't look round, he just got in his car and drove away.'

I wondered whether Dita remembered Jonathan's actual words, whether it hurt her to remember them too.

'It was later that day he collapsed. Someone phoned me from his office. It took us ages to get to the hospital, because it was raining heavily and the traffic was dreadful. Jonathan spent the day and half of that night by his dad's bed, gripping his hand and saying, 'I love you, I love you,' over and over again. Frank couldn't hear him – he was unconscious. When he finally passed away, Jonathan stopped speaking. He didn't speak for three days afterwards.'

'But any dad would have known . . .' I began.

'I know,' agreed Dita. 'It was just one of those things. Jonathan and his dad were so alike in some ways. I expect

Frank would have been trying to hide a smile, even as he drove away that morning.'

'Was Frank a good father?' I asked.

'Yes, he was a wonderful dad. He worked so hard, such long days, trying to give us all security. But he took every opportunity to spend time with the boys, too. When they were little he would come in from work and sit down on the floor, still wearing his suit, so he could build Lego with them. He took them camping, and taught them to light fires and tie knots and all that kind of thing. He'd sit and listen to Stephen's violin practice every night, and drive him back and forward to orchestra rehearsals. And when Jonathan got into rugby, he drove him around to sports fixtures all over the country – every weekend without fail. He would stand on the sidelines and watch, whatever the weather. He wouldn't shout out or anything, not like some of the other dads – he was a bit shy like that – but he knew he was there just the same.'

'And was he a good husband, too?' I spoke hesitantly, wondering if I was overstepping some invisible boundary. But I was keen to hear the answer; the question of what constituted a 'good husband' – or a 'good wife' for that matter – was very much on my mind.

Dita smiled, and patted my hand. 'Yes, he was. I loved him very much. But I had my regrets too, when he died. I had an affair, you see.' She glanced up, scanning my face for a reaction. 'About a year before he died.'

I nodded, and she went on.

'Frank and I were a good match on many levels. We had fun, and we were very fond of each other. We were a good team, good parents together. But I used to feel there was a whole other dimension to me that he just didn't ... get. The man who was my lover – well, he was very passionate, into poetry and music and all that kind of thing. He used to talk to me – really listen – as if I was a really fascinating person.' She gave an ironic laugh. 'I got addicted to it. But although I felt at the time that he knew me better than anybody had ever done before, when I look back I don't recognise that woman. I don't relate to her much.'

'What happened?'

'Well, this man – Tony, his name was – was one of Frank's old schoolfriends. So we all knew him quite well. He used to come round for dinner sometimes . . . but then we ended up on a museum committee together. We went out for a drink once, after a meeting, and got talking.' She shrugged her shoulders and sighed heavily.

'So you were thrown together by circumstance.' *Just like Malkie and me, both working at McKeith's.* The thought seemed to come from nowhere. I dismissed it. 'Sorry, go on.'

'I ended it as soon as I came to my senses. But I always wondered whether Frank knew, or suspected at least. I think perhaps the boys did too.'

'But nothing was ever said?'

'Nothing was ever said. And . . .'

'No, don't worry, I won't say anything.'

We were quiet for a minute. She sat biting her lip, gazing down at her feet.

'So why do you think Frank knew?' I asked.

'That last year, he seemed to withdraw from me somehow. Nothing you could put your finger on, but still . . . something. I didn't say anything because I wasn't certain whether he knew or not, didn't want to make things worse. But secrets, things left unspoken . . . they can . . . I don't know. I think I might have broken his heart, Cassie. I think I might have.'

I was shocked to see a tear trickle down her face.

110

'After he died, of course, I fell in love with him again.' She tutted and rolled her eyes. 'Of course I did. So predictable.'

'Why?'

Her voice when she spoke was low, measured. 'All that love had become twisted into the fabric of everyday life. I couldn't see it for what it was. When everyday life was finished, the love sprang up again, everywhere. Everywhere, uncontrollable, like a hillside on fire.'

I sat for a moment, trying to absorb what she'd said, wanting to think about it a little more. But Sophie's baby monitor, which I'd placed on the table beside me, burst into life. Her cries were high-pitched, terrified, as though she'd woken from a bad dream.

'I'll go,' said Dita, springing to her feet. I felt a pull towards Sophie – she'd need me if she was frightened. I wanted to go to her, but Dita was already halfway out of the room.

'You just relax,' she called over her shoulder. 'Let me do this. Nana Dita is on the case.'

11

The Babycraft crew was coming round to our house for a 'get-together', arranged in the wake of the country house weekend fiasco. This had seemed like a good idea at the time, but on the big day, having clocked up three half-hour blocks of sleep the previous night, I found it almost inconceivable that I could have agreed to this. Sophie had woken only twice, but Jonathan had woken at around four with one of his nightmares and I'd lain awake for the rest of the night.

Dita had a headache that morning and Jonathan was out playing golf with clients, so I took Sophie with me to Marks and Spencer to buy food for the guests. My usual indecisiveness about food shopping ballooned into total paralysis. I had been intending to make wholesome curried chickpea soup and home-made bread but I emerged, an hour later, with ten packets of sausage rolls and three Victoria sponges. It might have had something to do with Sophie having an explosive nappy incident whilst we were perusing the vegetables, and a long interlude when I had to change her nappy and clothes crouching on the floor of the customer toilet.

By the time I got home I was so exhausted I could barely stumble through to the kitchen to switch on the oven to heat up. I shook my head, wondering at my audacity in thinking I might have the time or energy to make curried chickpea soup . . . and home-made bread?

First to arrive were Molly and Dave – the hypno-birthers – and their baby son Cam.

'Oh look,' said Jonathan as we watched them park the car from the sitting room bay window. 'It's Camomile.'

'Don't!' I said, whacking him on the arm with an empty sausage roll packet, scattering flakes of puff pastry over the carpet. 'One of these days I'm going to actually call him that by mistake. It's Cameron, as you well know.'

'Oh, yes, sorry, Cameron,' said Jonathan absently. Then, as we watched them approach the front door, he frowned deeply. 'My God. How unfortunate. Is it normal for a seven-month-old to have such an enormous head!'

'It's boys,' I explained. 'They make the baby girls look all dinky.'

Before we'd even taken the hypno-birthers' coats, Jody arrived with Tom (possibly – we still didn't know the man's name) and the baby. Shona was next, with her husband Paul following behind carrying little Elgin. She was looking radiant. Before she'd even got her coat off, she enthused about how fantastic it was to be back at work.

'I'm defending a groundbreaking medical negligence case,' she announced, as she swept into the living room. 'God, I can't tell you how good it is to get my teeth back into something.'

Paul, following in her wake, weighed down by Elgin and his changing bag, raised his eyebrows at me in a comical, long-suffering sort of way. He'd begun married life as an accountant, and had then left to become an out-of-work actor, so had pretty much been forced to assume the role of stay-at-home dad to Elgin when Shona went back to work.

After a while I left them all to it, and went into the kitchen to help Dita prepare all the sausage rolls. Jonathan followed me and begged to be allowed to join in. 'It's enough to put me into a coma,' he complained. I just threw a bag of rice cakes at him and told him to start doling them out to the babies.

113

'I must say,' said Dita, after Jonathan had left the room. 'I feel rather embarrassed after the last time. You know – when I mentioned vaginas. I think I will just stay out of the way, if that is all right with you.'

'No!' I said, shocked. 'You can't stay here in the kitchen like a servant. Come through and say hello, at least.'

So we went through. Surveying the living room, I did feel a little weak at the knees. Cameron was crumbling up the rice cakes and grinding them into the carpet with his little fists. Vichard was dangling his beaker upside down, dribbling (surely sugar-free?) cranberry and acai berry juice over the cream couch. A strong smell of poo pervaded the air. Sophie was bawling, stranded in the corner, whilst Jonathan tried to hand out cups of tea, although all our visitors appeared to be oblivious to this. I went over and rescued her. I picked her up and pointedly held her up, pretending to sniff her nappy area. 'Oh dear,' I said in a loud voice. 'Has somebody got a dirty nappy?' Nobody took the hint, however, so I sat down next to Shona, and bounced Sophie on my knee.

'So what's your case about?' I asked her. As a fellow lawyer, I felt it was appropriate for me to feign interest.

'Oh, well,' she began, lightly clapping her hands. 'I'm defending the GP of this woman.'

'Oh?'

'Yes. This woman had been to her GP dozens of times in the previous twelve months with various imaginary complaints.'

I hooted with slightly overdone laughter at this. 'Ha ha! A total nut-job, then!'

Shona looked at me, surprised. I quickly realised that this was not the basis of the litigation, and put on a serious, inquiring expression.

'Anyway, eventually she became convinced there was an

alien growing inside her. She went to the GP eight times, insisting he had to do something because the alien wanted to take over. The GP tried to refer her for psychiatric assessment, but she wasn't having any of it.'

I giggled again. 'So why was she suing the doctor?'

'Oh, it was her family that was suing. Not her – she was dead by then. Because she was right, in a way, about the alien. She had a tumour growing in her liver. It was too late by the time they found it.'

I felt sick with panic. I excused myself, saying I had to check on the sausage rolls. When I got back, after taking several deep breaths in the kitchen, I went to the opposite side of the room and planted myself firmly next to Dita, judging her to be the person in the room least likely to be having conversations about fatal tumours and inattentive GPs. As if on cue, a wave of dizziness came over me. I tried to ignore it and concentrate on what Dita was saying to Shona's husband Paul.

'So Paul,' Dita was saying. 'Cassie was telling me that you are an actor. How interesting!'

Paul nodded, his expression grim.

'Is that something you might be able to continue doing part time once Elgin is perhaps in nursery?'

'Ooooh, yes,' chipped in Jody, overhearing. 'Maybe you could apply to be a presenter on CBeebies. There are quite a few male ones. Some of them are quite dishy. I'll freely admit I have a bit of a crush on Little Cook Small from *Big Cook, Little Cook.*'

'Really?' I queried. 'I would have thought Big Cook Ben was more appealing. At least he is a normal height, and doesn't have to ride on a wooden spoon to go and collect the ingredients.'

Suddenly Paul stood up.

'You know what?' he said, his voice shaking. Everybody

stopped talking and looked at him. 'This is all complete and utter crap. You're all sitting here eating your sausage rolls and drinking your tea, pretending life has never been better. Why doesn't somebody just come out and admit it? Our lives are basically over. I love Elgin, but I can't DO anything any more. From the minute he wakes up until the minute he goes to bed, I can't do anything. I can't have a cup of coffee or read a bloody newspaper. I don't even have time to take a piss. And do you know what? I hate puréeing vegetables. I hate sterilising breastpumps. I hate CBeebies. I hate being covered in baby sick. I hate parent and baby groups and Babycraft get-togethers. I hate that we can't go out for meals. I hate that we can't go anywhere decent on holiday. I hate that I'm so fucking tired I can't even sleep.'

My pulse was racing. It was a strange feeling, listening to Paul. As though a door was opening just a crack, letting a slice of light fall across the floor of a darkened room.

Jody whispered across to me, her hands clamped firmly around Vichard's ears. 'He's finding it tough. You know, he was on the verge of landing a part in *River City* when Shona got pregnant and he had to turn it down. After years of working up the ladder, you know, he had to give it all up just when he was reaching his peak.'

'But do you know what the worst thing is?' Paul went on, tears catching at his voice now. 'There is no fucking escape. There's no end in sight. There'll be nothing left of me, for as long as I love him. And I'll love him for as long as there's anything of me left.'

Perfect sense. It made perfect sense to me. I wanted to go up to Paul and wrap my arms around him. But nobody moved. Nobody said a word. Finally, Molly's husband Dave broke the silence.

'Listen, mate,' he said gently. 'Have you tried Bach Flower Remedies?'

The tea party went downhill after that. Shona ushered a tearful Paul, and a (by that time) tearful Elgin, out of the house with courtroom-style briskness. She blamed a recent attack of flu, saying Paul wasn't quite himself, but that he'd be fine after a good night's sleep. But when would he be likely to get that?

The others made their excuses too, and left. Within ten minutes, the house was empty of guests. I closed the front door and leaned my hot forehead against the wood for a moment or two before going into the living room to find Jonathan.

'Poor Paul,' I began. 'I really felt for—'

He shook his head, his expression a mask of withering contempt. 'Appalling,' he said. 'Just appalling. A terrible, incontinent outburst. He needs to stop wallowing in self-pity and face up to his responsibilities. The human race would grind to a halt if everyone succumbed to that kind of self-indulgent attitude. We all just need to knuckle down and get on with it.'

He swept out of the room bearing plates of sausage rolls and rice cakes. I sank onto the sofa and put my head in my hands.

Dita came in and sat down beside me with a sigh. She patted my knee. 'I think if it's all right with you, Cassie dear, I will steer well clear of these gatherings in the future.'

*

The next morning, daily activities felt arduous, effortful. Getting Sophie dressed, trying to pull clothes onto her thrashing arms and legs, took an age. By the time I'd cleared the breakfast dishes and put on a load of washing it was nearly

117

lunchtime. I felt a sudden, surprising flash of anger towards Dita, who'd gone away to Linlithgow that morning to stay with friends overnight.

But this feeling, this heaviness, wasn't Sophie's fault – or Dita's. Something had been creeping into the edges of my mind for months, and now it was time to face it, just for a moment. I gave myself just a tiny space to think about whether Jonathan and I would make the distance.

Since Sophie's arrival, I'd soothed my worries by telling myself that we just needed to learn how to communicate better, that if he seemed like a stranger sometimes, then I'd just have to make the effort to get to know him. But nothing I said seemed to get through to him – every conversational opening was brushed aside with a jokey comment or a change of subject, or stopped in its tracks with a heavy, irritated sigh.

He had no idea how closely I'd identified with Paul's frustration and his loneliness, or how relieved I'd been to hear that he, too, had found himself imprisoned in a cage of stifling, relentless, terrifying love.

And he had no conception of how worried I'd been by the anonymous note – how my pulse raced when I glanced out of a window or went for the post. He didn't see that I'd only just grown comfortable with the house again, after it had shifted in some indefinable way with Sophie's arrival. He couldn't see that it was now changing into something else again. I hated how it felt when I came home to find it empty, with its pockets of silence and still, dead air.

'Well, Mum's here most of the time, isn't she?' he'd said when I tried to explain. His tone of voice seemed to add the question – *What more do you want me to do?*

Perhaps worst of all, he was still having the same nightmares, still calling out for his father in the night, but denying in the morning that there was any problem. He wouldn't let me get inside his world, and he didn't seem to have any interest in getting inside mine.

I took Sophie to John Lewis – wanting to be around people – but the trip wasn't a success. She hadn't had her nap, and was very grumpy. She didn't want to sit in her buggy, yet didn't want to be carried. She kept throwing her beaker on the floor in the café and screamed when I took her to get her nappy changed.

As I cleaned her up in the baby change room and disposed of her nappy in the foul-smelling bin, I acknowledged that even my connection with Sophie could get buried, a little, when I felt exhausted. And I knew beyond a shadow of a doubt that I loved *her*. So maybe simple tiredness could explain away this grey, flat feeling towards Jonathan, maybe it was nothing to worry about.

But that didn't change the fact that I craved something more meaningful than a puzzled frown, or an uncomprehending grunt whenever I tried to express my feelings. I wanted him to leap on any observations I made, I wanted his eyes to flare with recognition, I wanted him to finish my sentences, the way Helen used to do.

The thought made me long to talk to her. Once again, the time difference precluded a phone call, but I sat down to type an email when Sophie finally went down for her nap, back in the cool quiet of the house.

Hi Helen,

How are you? I wish I could chat with you properly and hear all your news. I miss talking to you. Things are a bit ropey here, to be honest. It's not Sophie – she's getting on really well. She's trying to crawl, bless her – rocking backwards and forwards on all fours, as though she's going to launch herself off like a rocket. But she can't manage it yet – she just kind of flumps on her tummy and looks cross!

No, she's wonderful.

It's just that everything else seems to be going wrong. Maybe it's the tiredness, I don't know. But Jonathan and I are hardly communicating at all, and

I imagined Helen's look of surprise. As far as she knew, Jonathan and I were as solid as a rock. It seemed too much, too late to be telling her all this, in one big ugly lump. A low-voiced conversation over a glass of wine would have been one thing, but to see it down there, in black and white . . .

Malkie's turned up again, and I'm wondering if I've married the wrong person.

I hovered the mouse over the 'delete draft' tab – this wouldn't do at all. But suddenly a wild scream tore out of the baby monitor, which was resting on the table by my elbow, and I accidentally pressed 'send' instead.

'Bugger!' I hurried up the stairs to Sophie – I'd have to email Helen later and explain.

But Sophie cried for nearly an hour, by which time it was time to start making her tea, then feed her, then mop the kitchen floor (splattered liberally with puréed butternut squash), then watch *In the Night Garden*, and then get her in the bath and off to bed. By the time I sat down to email Helen again, she'd already replied – she must have checked her emails before her early morning beach run.

Cassie – WHAT??? Malkie? Are you serious? We are talking about the commitment-phobic, chain-smoking, vodka-swilling git who dumped you FOUR TIMES?!!

I'm worried about you. Can you try talking to Jonathan? How about getting some help in the house, or a nanny to help out with Sophie? How about a night nurse, so you can get some more sleep?

Is there anything *I* can do?

Yes. Move back to Edinburgh. Get pregnant and have a baby, even though you've never wanted one. Come over for coffee so Sophie and I don't have to be alone in this house. Walk round the Botanics with us and feed the ducks. Make me laugh at Murray Radcliffe and Annabel Masters so I can stand up to them. Keep telling me that I'm not doing everything wrong, and that the Babycraft lot talk out of their arses most of the time. Keep telling me I don't really love Malkie. Just come back.

★

It was nearly eight o'clock by the time I'd emailed Helen back with reassurances ('I'm fine - really! I was just tired . . .'), and Jonathan still wasn't home. I tried his mobile. He was clearly in a bar somewhere. I could hear music and talking in the background, and the signal was patchy.

'Didn't you get my message?' he shouted over the music. 'I'll be home around ten—'

The line went dead. Where was he? What was he doing? Why was he in the pub when I was sitting at home alone?

I did a third circuit of the house, checking the doors and windows were locked, then sat down on the sofa with the landline phone and my mobile beside me, along with the baby monitor and keys for the back and front doors. I switched on the television and flicked through the channels for something reassuring and familiar, something to disperse the silence. I settled on *Midsomer Murders* – I'd never managed to stay awake through a whole episode. But I was still sitting upright, hugging my knees, when Jonathan's key turned in the lock at quarter past eleven.

'Hi, Cassie-girl,' he called out from the hall, on his way into the kitchen.

The atmosphere in the house corrected itself instantly – like the lights going up at the end of a film. The tension ebbed out of me and I had to make an effort to gird myself up for the confrontation I was determined to have with Jonathan. After ten minutes or so, he came into the room carrying a plate of cheese-on-toast. He had pulled his tie loose and the top few buttons on his shirt were undone. He looked good, and I felt a stab of possessiveness.

'I made some for you,' he said, coming over to sit next to me. 'I'm sorry I'm late home, kiddo.'

'Are you going to tell me what you've been doing?'

'I took Paul out for a drink.'

'*River City* Paul?' I was so surprised that I forgot to maintain my icy tone. 'Why?'

He shrugged. 'Someone had to.'

'After yesterday's appalling, self-indulgent outburst?'

'Look, Cassie, that's not exactly fair. The guy's obviously under a lot of pressure. I just thought maybe he might need someone to talk to, okay?'

'So you were nice to him? You didn't tell him he was incontinent and wallowing in self-pity and all that?'

'Cassie, what are you talking about?'

I looked at him in astonishment. 'That's what you said!'

'Well . . . I can't remember. Maybe I did. I was just a bit wound up that he'd spoiled your party when you'd put so much work into it all.'

'Ten packets of sausage rolls? Hardly.'

'Yes, but I know how tired you've been, with Sophie not sleeping. I know it's been tough on you.'

'So what did you say to Paul?'

'He's finding it hard, that's all. He was really into this acting thing. He's had to put it all on hold – indefinitely. And it's not easy for him. Being a stay-at-home dad, there aren't the same support networks. Not like you have with all the other mums.'

I thought dubiously about the Babycraft girls, my support network. More like a web, entangling me in sticky despair about my non-breastfeeding and other failures.

'He told me something awful,' went on Jonathan, after a pause.

'What?' I said, wide-eyed. Did Shona beat him or something?

'He takes Elgin to Oceanic Experience every day. You know, that big aquarium.'

'What do you mean, every day?'

'He says there's nothing else to do,' said Jonathan, shaking his head. 'And Elgin seems to quite like looking at the fish.'

I paused in horror to contemplate this. Oceanic Experience, every day. 'That simply cannot be,' I said finally.

'It's true. Shona takes the car to work and it's the only thing within walking distance. He says he can do the walk in around forty-five minutes on a good day, when Elgin stays in the buggy. But it can be quite windy crossing the Forth Road Bridge.'

Jonathan spread himself out on the couch and slung his arm round me. Then he began flicking through the channels.

I snuggled against him, filled with affection at the thought

123

of his attempt to reach out to Paul. But, from this more comfortable place, I still wondered about the strength of his negative reaction to Paul's outburst yesterday.

Then I remembered the poor woman whose family was suing her GP, and my reaction on hearing about her hypochondriac tendencies. I had rushed in with my laughter, falling over myself to place some distance between her and me.

'Do you ever feel like Paul? You know, the way he talked yesterday?'

He considered this for a moment. 'No,' he said. 'My job is to look after you and Sophie. Falling apart simply isn't on the list of options.'

A wave of tenderness swept over me. Poor Jonathan. Working so hard. Denying himself even the right to his own feelings.

'We'll get there,' I whispered, my voice suddenly thick with tears. I untucked his shirt, and slipped my hands underneath, to feel the warmth of his skin against my cold fingers.

12

I was finding it hard to concentrate. The faint whine of bagpipes had been drifting in through the office window all afternoon, but that was an occupational hazard in this part of town. Sometimes I even appreciated the holiday feel of it, and the implicit message that I should really be somewhere else enjoying myself – buying shortbread in Jenners or visiting Edinburgh Castle – and certainly not reviewing share purchase agreements or worrying about brain tumours.

What was more distracting, though, was the coach-load of tourists that had been milling around on the pavement outside for the past forty-five minutes. They kept peering down at us through the railings in a curious but vaguely disappointed way, as though we might be the first point of interest in a not very interesting guided tour.

As usual, I jumped when the phone rang.

'Elliot McCabe here. More paranormal problems, I'm afraid.' He gave a gusty sigh.

'Really?' I reached for a pen.

'I've got an employee who's been signed off on long-term sick leave, giving work-related stress as the reason. I eventually got round to requesting a doctor's report. It arrived this morning and it says . . . let's see, yes . . . "*Re David McLaren . . . The patient came to see me in May this year complaining of severe headaches and insomnia. Reassurance was given, and advice on dealing with symptoms. However, the symptoms did not settle over time, and on the fifth visit the patient broke down. He complained that he had experienced unusual events at work, which had led him to believe that his place of work was haunted by a poltergeist. In particular, he was distressed by an incident when a coffin fell off a workbench, seemingly propelled by an invisible force. His work involves night shifts and he has become so anxious that he feels unable to attend work. A mild antidepressant was prescribed, and David has been referred for cognitive behavioural therapy in the hope that this may alleviate his symptoms."'*

'I see. Not very helpful, is it? What you really need to do is make the doctor say when this David character is likely to . . .' – *get his arse back into work* – '. . . um, be fit enough to return to the workplace.'

'It's not just that. I'm concerned he might sue the company for causing some kind of mental illness.'

'Hmm. Unlikely. He would need to prove that the company took no action over whatever was causing the stress. Our argument would be that action was impossible, because the problem was all in the employee's mind.'

'What if he says we should have got rid of the ghost?'

'We would need to stick to the line that the . . . er, manifestations were a subjective phenomenon.'

'But should we not do *something* . . . even by way of a gesture . . .'

'I suppose you could make some very mild attempt . . . like putting garlic cloves in each of the affected rooms or something.'

'No. Garlic is for vampires—'

'Well then celery sticks or something. Just make it up, Elliot – play him at his own game.'

He sighed heavily. 'My other concern is a claim under Health and Safety legislation.'

'Health and Safety legislation?' I envisaged Elliot rushing

up to the poltergeist as it was about to chuck the coffin across the room, telling it to bend from the knees and not from the back.

'Yes. There's a health and safety angle to everything in the funeral business. Believe me, I've had my fingers burnt before—'

'Elliot—' I cut in. 'Have you heard from Bobby Spencer at all?'

'Not since he phoned me threatening to raise a tribunal claim. Why?'

I had a sudden image of Bobby, looming over the funeral home like it was a dolls' house, orchestrating this whole debacle like a manically grinning, ginger-haired puppeteer.

'Could you let me know if he surfaces again? And tell him to deal with McKeith's in future rather than talking to you direct.'

'Will do. Look, I have to go now – I have a meeting. But could you please prepare a note for me with a clear recommendation as to how we should proceed. If you could get it to me by the end of the day, please.' And he rang off.

Time to get creative, then. I stared up at the Japanese tourists again, hoping for inspiration, until I looked at the clock and realised I had to leave for the nursery in less than an hour.

Bullet points were the way to go. I recommended that Elliot should arrange for an up-to-date risk assessment, preferably to be undertaken by an independent risk assessment consultancy. I suggested that David McClaren should prepare a statement for the assessor so that he could check for any non-subjective explanations, e.g. electrical faults, infestation by rats or mice, evidence of the presence of drugs or other hallucinatory substances. I asked Elliot to get back in touch after the risk assessment had been completed, so I could provide further advice as to how to proceed at that time.

For one mad moment, as I shut my laptop, I dared to hope that I'd never hear from Elliot McCabe again.

13

From time to time I receive student newsletters from Oakenwell College, Massachusetts. My former landlady still forwards them assiduously from the Morningside flat. I keep thinking I should tell them to take me off their mailing list but part of me likes receiving these missives. They're like communications from a parallel world, snapshots from a life I chose not to live.

I was in the living room one morning in late September when one of them popped through the letterbox. Sophie was planted on the floor, playing with a toy giraffe, bashing it on the carpet in the V-shaped space between her short chubby legs. The outline of her head, dipped in concentration, and the delicate little stem of her neck, formed the shape of a perfect question mark. It seemed to emphasise her newness – the infinite possibilities of her.

In between extended moments contemplating my daughter, I was checking the contents of her changing bag: sterilised empty bottle in an insulated holder, carton of baby milk, flask of hot water to heat bottle, Infacol wind drops, antibacterial hand gel, nappies, wipes, changing mat, nappy sacks, spare change of clothes, two bibs, two muslin cloths. I was planning to take her for a walk in the Botanic Gardens.

'Scissors, scissors, scissors,' I muttered as I went to retrieve the mail. I was determined not to forget this final item – necessary to open the milk carton quickly at the crucial moment.

The newsletter, when I saw it, struck a chord. I'd been

thinking about Malkie – and that era of my life – all morning. Not that this was exactly unusual, since our little heart-to-heart in the car outside the doctor's. But when I took it into the living room and flicked through it, I found another little piece of my past waiting for me on the last page. It was a photograph of a painting by one of the students – a seascape under moonlight. Underneath, I recognised the lines of an Emily Dickinson poem I had once written about whilst at University. I remembered an autumn afternoon spent curled up in a sunny window seat at the library, inhaling the smell of warm wood and old books.

> *Each that we lose takes part of us;*
> *A crescent still abides,*
> *Which like the moon, some turbid night,*
> *Is summoned by the tides.*

I sank back on the sofa, suddenly caught up in a fierce, inexplicable longing. But Sophie started wailing – her giraffe had toppled out of her reach – so I dismissed the feeling, gathered myself up and got us both ready to go.

It was a cold, dull day, and it wasn't until around half past two, when we were walking back through Inverleith Park, that the sun broke out from behind a pearly bank of cloud to the south.

'Ah look, Sophie! Sunshine.'

She gurgled in her buggy. I stopped and bent down to kiss her nose, hoping for one of her ravishing smiles, but she wasn't looking at me. She had tipped her head back and was surveying the canopy of one particular tree with a thoughtful, wide-eyed stare. A few trees in the park had already turned a satisfying Halloween orange, but the leaves of Sophie's tree were caught at a point of luminous, washed-through green, about to tip into yellow. I wheeled her across the grass to a bench that overlooked Inverleith Pond, eased her out of the buggy and held her against my chest so she could look over my shoulder at her tree. Her breath was damp against my neck, and I could hear the little catches as she swallowed. Within a minute or two, though, she laid her cheek on my shoulder with a big sigh, and fell asleep.

The skyline was spectacular from here: Arthur's Seat in the distance, Edinburgh castle on its bulk of rock, the panorama of domes and church spires, enticing green glimpses of parks and private gardens. I could trace with my eye the neat patterns of elegant New Town crescents and terraces, places where I had walked a hundred times but which were unfamiliar from this vantage point. I thought of all the lives being lived there, all the dramas being played out in my city and all the streets that fell under the sweep of my gaze.

And what about the lives I could have lived? All those paths seemed to spiral back to one central, incontrovertible point. Malkie – again – and me, teetering on the brink of adulthood all those years ago.

*

Because you see, I never went to Massachusetts.

Malkie and I had one summer together – a glorious, shimmering summer in my memory, although in fact we only saw each after dark. He was stacking supermarket shelves from ten a.m. until six p.m., and I was working in a bar near the Museum of Scotland, in long busy evening shifts that ended at midnight. Each night I crawled back to his flat, reeking of smoke and beer, showered, and joined him in bed, my bare skin sweet with the smell of Johnson's Baby Soap. In the mornings, we'd sleep late – he'd set his alarm for 9.25 a.m. – just enough time for him to shower, shave and pitch up at Tesco.

One afternoon in August, I went to the University library and emailed Oakenwell College to tell them I wouldn't be coming, and then dropped by the Law faculty to see about getting myself onto a law conversion course.

For a while, I tortured myself by gazing at the Oakenwell brochure: the chapel nestling between soft green lawns, vistas of maple and elm trees, leaves aflame with breathtaking fall colours. And I would scan through the various course reading lists, my heart beating fast as though I was in touching distance of Emily Dickinson herself, in her Amherst attic, or Willa Cather, on the wide-open Nebraska plains.

But I couldn't leave Edinburgh – being with Malkie made me feel as if I'd just woken up after twenty years of sleepwalking through my life.

When term started again, there was a shift in our relationship, as subtle and inexorable as the inching of summer into autumn. It wasn't a physical change – my body still responded, deep inside, every time I saw him. The sound of his voice, full of Glasgow grit, provoked the same reaction. And he seemed as caught up in me as he'd ever been. But some kind of new awareness, a question mark, seemed to hang over the relationship.

During the week we studied together at the law library after lectures, and then I'd spend Saturday at his flat. We would watch the football, if it was on, and then we'd make dinner; clumsy meals of pasta and supermarket garlic bread, or chicken kiev with oven chips. On special occasions it would be 'Secret Recipe Bolognese', the only meal Malkie knew how to make from scratch – knowledge passed down from mother to son when he'd left home to go to University.

If I was in a relaxed mood, chirpy and light, all would be well and the time would flow easily between us; but increasingly, I found myself trying to think of the right thing to say, and it would be a relief when he finally took me to bed, where we didn't have to talk, but just let our bodies fit together. We would always have music on; for months we had the same CD on repeat, which started with an Aerosmith rock ballad, 'I Don't Want To Miss a Thing'. He would murmur the words, buzzily, into my skin as he kissed my throat. And then afterwards we would fall asleep face to face with the bedside light still on, the navy blue duvet thrown back off our too-warm bodies.

Somehow, though, that connection between us seemed unstable, like a rare element forged in an intensity of heat and light. I would leave his flat on a Sunday morning after staying over, and everything would feel perfect, light, sparkling, between us. But as soon as I had left I would start fretting about why he hadn't asked me to spend the day with him too, and the next night. A knot would form in my stomach, tightening harder and harder until he phoned.

He finished with me the day after my birthday, saying he wasn't ready to commit. Every time I asked 'Why?' or 'What have I done wrong?' his eyes grew a little more distant, as though it was the questions themselves that were breaking us apart. So I stopped asking them, and within the week he was knocking at my door, saying he'd made a mistake. Twice more, over the next eighteen months or so, he finished it, then changed his mind. And each time he came back to me, the moments became even more precious, knowing as I did by then that there was very little chance he would ever really be mine.

By the time we entered the dying days of the relationship,

we'd given up on those ordinary everyday things that we couldn't quite seem to get right – watching television together, eating meals, going to the pub. We just used to lie in bed together, wrapped in each other's arms, listening to music. There was an unspoken agreement that the Aerosmith was now out of bounds, but there were plenty of other mournful tracks to listen to, which all somehow expressed the paradox I was living through – that misery could be transformed into something beautiful. And I would try to get my head around the enormity of what was coming, would ache with the loss of him even as I was lying there beside him.

Late one evening, he turned up at my flat unexpectedly. I knew why he'd come, in the way I could always read his emotions. Wordlessly, he drew me into a hug, and stood, rocking me gently. Then, hand in hand, we walked to his car.

We drove up around the road that circles Arthur's Seat, and then climbed up on foot as far as we could go. We sat on a concrete bench in the darkness, staring the end of our relationship in the face. Suddenly, he threw his head back and cried in a broken voice, 'I can't bear this. I can't do this any more.'

I gathered all my courage and said what I knew to be true now. 'You're never going to love me, are you.'

He shook his head. 'We have to stop.'

I sat quietly, feeling only compassion. I knew this was nobody's fault, not any more. We'd both tried. I knew the feelings he had for me, understood their limitations. I knew that he'd tried to turn them into something that could bear the weight of a future together. And I had tried to step back from him, tried to be strong enough to function within the uncertainty. But every time, we found ourselves playing out the same pattern, and every time, we fell apart along the same fault line. There was nothing more to be done.

I looked out across the city below us, the lights twinkling from a thousand different streets. And I realised that, however hard and long I looked, even if I knocked on the door of every house in every street in the world, even if I walked through every crowd, tapped the shoulder of every stranger with dark hair and a shabby navy jacket, I would never find another Malkie. It hit me then, the loss of him. It resonated through me, like a perfect note in a heartbreaking song. And then it settled in my bones so that it ached to move, to take a single step.

★

I felt shaky, as I got up off the bench and tucked Sophie back into her pushchair to begin the walk home. That poem, finding its way to me, had been almost like a warning. For the part of me that loved Malkie was still there, under the surface. Always, since the day of Jo's psychology experiment. It was true – of course it was – that just when you thought it had dissolved away, pain and longing could reappear, terrifying and undiminished. In certain seasons, when the tides are strong, when the wind is blowing in from a certain direction. And autumn had always been a bad time of year for missing Malkie.

Where did that leave me, I wondered, as I pushed the buggy along past Waitrose and meandered along Orchard Road towards home. God, the very air seemed to smell of Malkie that afternoon . . . the tail end of summer, a crispness in the breeze, the autumn flame catching at the leaves. With a searing twinge of sadness for Jonathan, I acknowledged my feelings. It seemed there would be no getting over this. No getting over it at all.

14

'You know, I've been thinking about Braid Hills Funeral Home,' I announced to Jonathan. He groaned and sagged in the driver's seat – we were on our way home from B&Q, having spent a scintillating afternoon looking at mixer taps. We'd been planning a trip to the park but soft drizzle had been falling all afternoon, the October colours muted under a low grey sky. As we crawled through traffic the wipers swished back and forth in a reassuring sort of way, lulling me into a conversational mood.

'I'm just wondering whether, somehow, Bobby Spencer could be behind all this trouble they're having. What if he's . . . I don't know . . . faking the ghosts or something? Could he do that, do you think?'

'Bobby Spencer, the five-foot-nothing ginger evil genius?' Jonathan still found it amusing that I had suspected Bobby of planting the anonymous note.

'It just seems strange,' I persisted. 'Or maybe he's putting the other employees up to it, somehow. Maybe he's still in contact with them. What do you think? Do you think I should look into it, or suggest that Elliot gets in touch with him?'

'I think you should stay out of it. He hasn't pursued the Law Society complaint, right? Or lodged a tribunal claim? Well, don't give him a reason to change his mind.'

'I suppose.' I turned round to look at Sophie.

'She's asleep,' I murmured. 'A wee ten minutes won't hurt, I suppose, though it is kind of late in the day.'

'My mother . . . had an affair once, you know,' announced Jonathan out of nowhere. An unpleasant smell drifted into the car – we were driving past the sewage treatment works on Seafield Road.

'Oh?' I said faintly. He had paused, mid-sentence, to negotiate a lane change, which made it unclear whether his emphasis had been on 'mother' or 'affair'. For a moment I had a terrible feeling that he was about to accuse *me* of having an affair, and had offered up the example of his mother's infidelity by way of comparison. I had to remind myself that nothing illicit had actually happened with Malkie – other than in my mind.

'Yes. With this appalling man, Mr Caravaggio,' he went on, pulling the corners of his mouth down.

'Mr Caravaggio?'

'Yes. He was an old schoolfriend of Dad's. He was called *Tony* but he made us call him Mr Caravaggio.'

I couldn't help laughing at the withering contempt in his voice.

'But he had an ice cream van, which he used to bring round to the house, so we put up with him.'

'He had an ice cream van?'

'Yes, it used to play that tune – 'Just One Cornetto'. He ran a couple of Italian restaurants too. But then he sold up and bought a taxi, as far as I can remember.'

I wondered why Jonathan had chosen this moment to bring up the affair. He and his mother seemed to have had a bit of a falling out in B&Q. I wasn't sure what it was about, exactly, as I had been carrying a fascinated, dribbling Sophie around the mocked-up kitchens and bathroom suites. But Jonathan had been huffing impatiently when I'd caught up with them again, and Dita had just raised her eyebrows at me, and shrugged behind his back. He'd then decreed it was time to go home, but she'd stayed behind, saying she'd do a bit more shopping and get the bus back later on.

Whatever the argument had been about, surely it was not grounds to expose Dita with regards to her affair. But I was afraid I'd be drawn into difficult territory if the conversation continued, so I changed the subject.

'So, Braid Hills. If you were me – if you were the lawyer – what would you do?'

It was a question Jonathan loved to be asked – a way of engaging him on almost any topic. He smiled and settled himself into his seat more comfortably.

'Outline the facts of the case again,' he said. 'Let's knock this one on the head.'

As we drove on I stifled a smile at the way Jonathan had taken the bait. He had always been so invested in the idea of me as a lawyer, so eager to get involved. At the time we'd first met, I had been in the process of applying for coveted legal traineeships, and he soon developed a habit of offering unwanted career advice. In retrospect, the most useful advice anybody could have given me at that time would have been 'people who look like Bambi should not go into law', but his advice veered more to dealing with office politics, how to impress the partners without being annoying, long-term career planning – that type of thing. He seemed to adopt my burgeoning legal career as his own personal project.

Given the nature of our first date, I should have seen it coming. When Jonathan had phoned, the day after he'd extracted my phone number outside The Underground, he'd sounded quite mysterious. He wanted me to meet him at one o'clock the next day, at the Caledonian Hotel on Princes Street.

I decided to dress casually in my ancient Armani jeans and

my favourite black velvet hoodie. But when Jonathan swept up to meet me by the old-fashioned revolving doors, he was wearing a pinstripe suit and carrying a briefcase.

'Hi, Cass,' he said breezily, ushering me in with an out-stretched arm. I thought it was a bit cocky of him to shorten my name when I had only known him five minutes.

However, all this was forgotten when we went into the lobby and he gestured to a large sign which read: Torquil Forsythe & Chalmers – Annual Corporate Round-Up.

'What's this?'

'I thought you'd be interested in this, since you're applying for legal traineeships.' He led the way through double doors into a conference room, and located two empty chairs in the front row. 'Torquil Forsythe is one of Edinburgh's biggest law firms – you know that, right? And I'm a client of theirs, or at least Wraithe's is, so I was invited to this corporate round-up. It's just a few seminars giving an overview of corporate law developments over the last twelve months.'

'What? But I'm wearing a hoodie!'

'Don't worry.' Jonathan settled into his seat and began leafing through the spiral-bound booklet of PowerPoint slides that had been handed to him on the way in.

Before I had a chance to say anything else, a dark-suited man walked up to the lectern.

'Ladies and gentlemen – welcome. It's great to see so many of you here today for our whistle-stop tour of what has been a fascinating twelve months in the world of corporate law . . .'

There were five seminars, beginning with: 'When is a share sale not a share sale?' after which point I nearly lost the will to live. The final talk was presented by three newly qualified assistants, who had been given permission by a client to give

139

a blow-by-blow account of a recent transaction. The highlight of this was apparently when they were down in London for meetings, and suddenly learned that the deal was closing at another law firm on the other side of the city. They realised they would have to draft the final clauses of the share sale and purchase agreement in a taxi on the way to the completion meeting.

The talk finished to thunderous applause. I stared at Jonathan in bewilderment.

'You see, Cassie,' he said, 'THAT is what it's going to be like being a corporate lawyer.' He banged his hand down on his knee and I jumped, spilling my glass of still mineral water down my top.

'You'll need to think on your feet, and draft contracts in the back of taxis,' he went on. 'But once they see how smart you are, you'll be straight on the track to partnership, and you'll be on half a mil a year before you know it.'

I smiled sweetly, making a mental note never to return this man's calls ever again. We were married eighteen months later.

*

Of course, none of Jonathan's advice about Braid Hills (which centred around paying each of the 'loony' employees to resign) helped when Elliot McCabe phoned again the next day, late in the afternoon. I nearly didn't answer the phone – I had shut down my computer and was rushing off to collect Sophie. Dita, who usually did this on a Monday, had phoned to say she'd been persuaded to stay for tea at the house of an ancient friend.

'All hell's broken loose. I've had four employees raise official grievances about the haunting.'

'Four?' I didn't like the sound of this at all. I put my laptop bag on my desk and sat down again.

'That's not even counting David McLaren, who's still off sick. One of them is threatening to resign and claim constructive dismissal. But the thing is, they've approached me as a group, asking me for permission to take part in a television programme.'

'Oh – about employment grievances?'

'Not exactly, no. The name of the programme is *Workplace Phantoms*.'

Silence. This was worse than I thought.

'They've backed me into a corner. If I don't agree to it, that will prove that I'm not taking it seriously. And David McLaren has emailed me to say that his therapist thinks it's a good idea.'

'So what does the programme entail?'

'Well, they're bringing in a team of experts. Three professional ghosthunters from Florida, a priest experienced in carrying out exorcisms, a psychic to give her view as to what is causing the manifestation, and a sceptic, a psychology professor from Glasgow. They plan to conduct interviews with all of the employees who've supposedly had paranormal experiences, and carry out an all-night vigil.'

'So what does this have to do with employment law?' I asked, bewildered.

'Well, the thing is, Murray Radcliffe was on the phone earlier – it was just a courtesy call to ask how things were going. But when I told him about the filming and my concerns about it, he was kind enough to offer your services. Suggested that you could be on hand for the vigil. Er . . . at no additional charge. Just backup for me, really – make sure nobody oversteps the mark at any point during the night. I think the employees are playing silly buggers and if I tell them the company's lawyers are going to be there that might make them rein it in a bit.'

'Well it would be very unusual for . . .'

'I appreciate that. I wouldn't have thought of it if Murray hadn't suggested it. But now I come to think of it, I really would feel happier with you on board.'

So Radcliffe had landed me in it again – fantasising, no doubt, about Elliot's wife with her position on the board of Turley Sturrock.

'And Cassie, I've decided I want to settle the Bobby Spencer case. Can we bung a couple of grand at him and get him to go away? I just don't want to have a tribunal claim hanging over me on top of all this.'

'Fine. I'll draw up a compromise agreement. Are you sure?' I wondered if I should try and talk him out of it – tell him to stick to his guns and we'd fight the tribunal case. I should at least try and appear confident about the prospects of winning, given that I'd backed Elliot's decision to dismiss. But the truth was, the case could go either way, and it would cost Elliot a great deal just to have me defending at the hearing, even if we won. And if Bobby was prepared to go away for a couple of grand, that sounded like a good deal. Christ, I'd even pay it myself.

'Yes. Offer anything up to three thousand.'

'Really? I'll start at five hundred and see where we get to.'

I bumped into Murray Radcliffe in the lobby, as I was making a dash for the front door.

'Ah, Cassie – did you speak to Elliot McCabe?' he asked.

'I did. I'm not sure how much use I'll be at the vigil, but . . .' I stopped. Jonathan was always telling me off for saying that sort of thing.

But Murray regarded me with a slight wince, as though

thinking I might have a point. 'Hmm. That new associate – Malkie Hamilton. He's got media law experience. He led a big case involving a television company at his last firm. Have a word with him about going to this vigil. Pull out all the stops for this one, Cassie.'

'Yes. Yes, Murray. Consider them . . . pulled.'

So I was under orders to spend the night with Malkie. Was someone trying to tell me something, I wondered, as Murray swept past me and up the stairs.

★

When I got home, I popped Sophie into the Baby Bjorn and we went round the house tidying up, turning on lamps and closing the curtains. She was adept at crawling now, and I could no longer leave her in the baby chair, or in a nest of cushions with her toys. And I liked to feel the warm weight of her against my chest, especially when we were alone in the house.

In the bedroom I laid out pyjama bottoms and a t-shirt on the bed, and unstrapped Sophie so that I could put her down while I got changed. Moving over to the window to draw the curtains, my eye was drawn to something on the back lawn. Stones from the rockery had been placed on the grass and arranged to form letters a foot wide.

YOU

A shock of adrenalin ripped through me. I drew the curtains so hard that the stitching gave way at the curtain hooks on one side, and the fabric flopped down, leaving a grey triangle of exposed sky. I grabbed the bedside phone and called Jonathan.

'Shit,' he said, and paused for a moment. 'It's probably just some local kids.'

But what local kids? And why?

'I think I should come home, though. And just to be on the safe side, you should get out of the house. Take Sophie and get her into the car. Drive to Sainsbury's. I'll meet you there.'

My breathing slowed down a little as I pushed Sophie's buggy through the automatic doors and headed towards the café. I ordered a cup of tea, and a piece of toast and a yoghurt for her. That would have to do for her dinner, poor thing. The cashier, seeing how much my hands were shaking as I pulled coins out of my purse, carried the tray over to a table.

Sophie's mouth pulled downwards into a cartoon pout when I slotted her into a high chair and presented her with the toast. Her current favourite meal was butternut squash and chicken purée and anything else was liable to be met with extreme disapproval.

'Come on, Soph, have some nice toast.'

Her mouth opened, red and wide, and she began to howl.

'Shush, shush, Sophie . . .' I picked her out of the high chair and pulled her into my chest, but her shoe knocked over the cup of tea, soaking my leg with scalding water.

Gasping with pain, I tried to blot my skirt with napkins, while Sophie's screams rose in pitch and intensity.

'Could I give you a hand, dear?' I turned to see an elderly lady with white curly hair and large spectacles. She looked vaguely familiar.

'It's Cassie, isn't it? And this young lady will be Sophie, unless I'm very much mistaken?'

With mumbled thanks, I handed Sophie to her and started mopping up the tea on the table and the floor. Sophie stopped crying, staring with great curiosity into the old lady's plump, lined face.

A café assistant appeared at my side with a mop.

'Why don't you sit with us, dear?' said the old lady, gesturing to a table opposite, where a man was seated in a wheelchair. 'I'll hold the little one while you have some tea. There's plenty left in our pot.'

I sat down in the chair she indicated. 'I'm sorry, but I can't quite recall . . .'

'I'm Jean. Jean Forrester. And this is my husband Gerry, though I don't think you've met him. I don't think he was around that day you came in for the waxing.'

I looked at her blankly, thinking of car washes.

'I'm the receptionist at *Brand New You*.'

'Oh, that's right!' Brand New You Image Consultancy – basically a beauticians with a fancy name. I'd gone there, using up Christmas vouchers from my mother, when my eight-month pregnancy bump had made the usual leg-shaving routine impossible. 'We chatted while I was waiting for my appointment. We talked about baby names. And you suggested the name Sophie, because that's your granddaughter's name.'

'And then you sent me such a lovely email, to say that the wee darling had been born!'

'Oh . . . that was my husband actually, he sent—'

'Such a kind thought, dear. It made my day! Now, Gerry, love, pour Cassie a cup of tea.'

My hands were still trembling as I took the cup, and the tea sloshed into the saucer.

Jean tutted softly. 'Now, now, dear. Whatever's the matter? What has got you into such a state?'

The floodgates burst. I put my face into my hands and sobbed, quite unable to speak. Jean jiggled Sophie on her knee, and Gerry solemnly handed me tissues from Jean's handbag.

What was it that had got me into such a state? What was it,

really? Was it the fact that I had nearly poured boiling water over Sophie's foot, proof of the fact I didn't deserve to be a mother? Was it the barrage of intrusive thoughts telling me that either Sophie or I was about to die? Or was it my suspicion that I didn't love my husband any more?

'Somebody's been watching the house.'

Jean gasped. 'Oh, my! No wonder you're upset.'

I explained about the note and the 'YOU' spelled out in the garden.

'Youths,' decreed Gerry in a low, rumbly voice. It was the first time he'd spoken. 'It'll be one o' them gangs. I've seen them hangin' about.'

'It could *be*,' agreed Jean, eyes wide behind her plastic spectacles.

'Possibly. But I'm worried it might be someone like . . . this undertaker's assistant . . .'

Jean looked sceptical.

'I was helping his boss with preparing a case to dismiss him. I'm an employment lawyer.'

Jean raised her eyebrows and nodded meaningfully at her husband. 'Oh yes – I remember now. You mentioned that in the baby email. Did you hear that, Gerry? This lass is an employment lawyer.'

'Are you having . . . employment problems?'

'Oh, my dear, we *are*! But I couldn't possibly trouble you with all that now.'

'It's okay. Tell me. I'm fine now.' Strangely, I was. Without doing or saying anything much at all, Jean and Gerry had sucked all the anxiety out of me, and I felt calm for the first time in weeks. I took Sophie back onto my knee. Jean poured some more tea for herself, carefully holding a wodge of napkins under the spout of the teapot to catch the leaks.

'They're trying to force me out,' she said. 'They're saying I can't bring Gerry to work with me any more—'

'Cassie!' It was Jonathan, sweeping over in his dark suit and overcoat, exotically professional among the orange tables and chairs. 'Are you all right?'

'Jonathan. It's okay. Jean and Gerry have been keeping me company.'

He gave them a peremptory smile and nod. 'Let's get you home, then, Cass. It's Sophie's bedtime.'

I handed Sophie to him, and was about to thank Jean and Gerry, and say goodbye, when I hesitated. I would normally run a mile from anything like this – becoming involved in someone's employment dispute. But somehow, these two . . .

'Do you need help, at all . . . with your employment dispute? I'm not really supposed to . . . but I hate to leave you in the lurch. I could give you some pointers, get you started at least, though I probably wouldn't be able to take it much further.'

'Oh no, dear. We don't want to get you into trouble. What was the name of your firm again?'

'It's called McKeith's, but . . .'

'Well maybe we'll get in touch through McKeith's. We'd want to go through the proper channels.'

I smiled, ashamed to mention my astronomical hourly charge-out rate. We rarely acted for individuals, and when we did they were invariably loaded. These two didn't look as though they'd fall into that category.

'Well, you have my email address, if you change your mind. If you just . . . you know . . . want to have a chat about it. Or a coffee . . .'

'Okay, Cass?' said Jonathan, his arm outstretched now to usher me away.

'Goodbye, then,' I said, still not moving.

'Goodbye, dear,' said Jean. 'And goodbye, little Sophie.'

I hesitated as we turned out of the café area, wishing for a moment that I could go back, sit down again, and let Jean pour me another cup of tea. For some reason I felt that these two elderly people belonged in my life; that I needed them in ways I couldn't yet understand.

★

'Should we phone the police?' I asked Jonathan later, as we sat at the kitchen table. Sophie was in bed and Dita, back from her visit, was heating up shepherd's pie for dinner.

Jonathan had been round knocking on all the neighbours' doors. Nobody had seen anything, no strange man nipping through the gate into the back garden, no mysterious cars parked up.

'What have we got to report, though, Cassie? A note through the door and a few stones moved around? I mean, it's hardly *Crimewatch* material, is it.'

Dita turned round to face us, shrugging with oven-gloved hands. 'You know, I had a similar problem many years ago . . . somebody bothering me with notes and phone calls. Oh, nothing that you'd have known about, Jonathan. You were only young. But the police said they couldn't do anything. We just ignored it, and eventually it stopped.'

'That was a while ago, though, Mum, it might be different now. I think I've heard that the police advise people to write everything down . . . build up a dossier of evidence. So I suppose we should get a notebook and record these two incidents, and the dates. And then . . .'

We can go to the police the next time something happens. Those

148

were the words that he didn't say. Because things would keep happening, I felt sure of that now. Why wouldn't they?

'We could also make a note of the neighbours we talked to,' I added. 'And we can clip in the original note, and a photograph of the stones.' I said it almost as a kindness to him, so that he'd have something to do – a plan of action with steps to be taken and crossed off.

He seized on the suggestion – and the idea that we could do anything to control this thing – and rushed off to the study to get his camera, even though it was now pitch dark outside.

'I wouldn't worry about it, you know,' said Dita after he'd gone. 'I don't think these people are out to harm us. Why don't you go through and watch some television – let's have a TV supper on trays!' She spoke as though I was about five years old. But the idea of being mothered, just then, was appealing. So I called Jonathan down, saying the dossier could wait till later, and we settled down in front of an episode of *Rebus*.

He seemed to sleep easily that night, snoring away as usual, star-fishing across the bed so that I was squeezed onto the edge. I stayed awake for hours, staring into the fuzzy grey of darkness and listening out for every creak in the old house as it settled for the night.

15

For the first time in ages, Jonathan and I were getting ready to go out for dinner. Dita was going to babysit, and was taking charge of Sophie's bedtime routine so we could have some time to get ready. I had put on new matching underwear (purchased in accordance with Helen's advice: 'Maybe try and pep things up a bit?') and I was trying on a new dress, which Jonathan had bought for me earlier that day. He'd actually presented it to me in a gift box with a big bow. I never usually wore red, on account of my hair being a sort of reddish brown, but I was pleased at this romantic gesture from Jonathan.

Or was it romantic, I wondered. Perhaps Jonathan and Helen were both trying to tell me something – that I normally looked a fright. I sighed, scrutinising myself in the mirror. Against the deep red of the dress, my arms looked white and flabby. I went to the wardrobe and started rummaging around for a black shrug I knew I had somewhere. This was to be a Babycraft dinner party, and rather perversely, this made me want to shed any trace of mumsiness.

Jonathan came out of the en suite, fastening one of his cufflinks.

'Cassie, sweetheart,' he began. 'Is there any particular reason why there's a can of wasp spray in my underwear drawer?'

'Hmmm? Oh here it is.' I pulled the shrug from where it was lying balled up at the bottom of the wardrobe. I straightened it out, only to find there was a small hole under the left arm.

'In addition to the can that I found in the hall bookcase yesterday, hidden behind my copy of *Animal Farm*?'

Jonathan's fiction collection was very discriminating, comprising only three titles – *Animal Farm*, *Moby Dick* and *The Moonstone*.

'Oh, don't start quoting *Animal Farm* again,' I said. 'Or *The Moonstone*.'

'But why the wasp spray? Do we have a wasp problem? In November?'

'Self-defence,' I said, applying lipstick to tightened lips.

'Why?' he asked, bemused. 'Do you suspect it was wasps that rearranged the rockery?'

I whirled round. 'Oh yes – it's *so* funny, isn't it. So funny that some nutter's been watching the house.'

'It was three weeks ago now, Cassie. Nothing else has happened. No sign of anyone watching us. I think we can relax a little bit now, don't you?'

'No.'

'I'm sorry. Of course we won't relax on our night off. What was I thinking? But ... hmm ... you look nice.' He grabbed me around the waist with a playful growl.

A taxi came to pick us up. We waved goodbye to Dita, who was standing at the front door holding a curious and distinctly unsleepy-looking Sophie wrapped in a fluffy white towel, her damp hair mussed up into wispy tufts.

It was nice to sit quietly in the taxi as it rumbled over the cobblestones into the heart of the New Town. I breathed in Jonathan's familiar woody aftershave, and I nudged up against his arm, trying to remember the last time we'd been out together as a couple. He wasn't exactly getting into the spirit though. He was highly suspicious of what our hosts, the hypno-birthers, might give us to eat, and kept muttering about going to McDonald's afterwards.

'Hello,' I whispered as Molly opened the door of their tiny little mews house. 'Did you manage to get Cameron off to sleep?'

'Oh no, don't worry. He never goes to sleep until we do. He's helping with the cooking.' She led us into the kitchen where Dave was preparing a salad in a bowl that was about two feet wide. Cameron hung suspended from his chest in a baby sling, a wooden salad fork flailing dangerously in his fat little fist.

'Actually,' went on Molly as she poured me a drink, 'we've got other friends here tonight – Sebastian and Poppet. They're having their kitchen done, so they're joining us for dinner. I know they're not Babycraft, but they are lawyers so I'm sure you and Shona will have lots in common with them. They're in the other room. I'll introduce you in a moment. Dave! Watch Cameron with that salad dressing . . .'

Clutching my glass, I went over to Paul, who was chatting with Jody and looking strained and pale, as though he might need to be rescued.

'How are you getting on?' I asked. 'Any luck with the acting at all? Or is it still all on hold just now?'

'Yeah, it's pretty hopeless just now,' he admitted. 'We thought of putting Elgin into nursery for a couple of mornings. That was Shona's suggestion, anyway. But obviously, that's not going to free me up for acting work. Even when he's at school, it wouldn't work unless we got a nanny or something . . . and I don't think we can justify that.'

'Oh, don't worry,' said Jody with a cheerful smile. 'Before you know it he'll be at university and out of your hair.'

Paul's face fell even further.

'I'm sure you could do something before then,' I said, although I didn't really believe it.

'Well anyway,' said Paul, 'I've started a blog about being a stay-at-home dad. It's called *Dads Aloud*. It's a bit of an outlet. As well as trying to keep the old creative brain ticking over. It's actually building up quite a following. I've been asked to guest blog on some other sites, too.'

'That's great!' I said.

'Blogs. Ughhh,' said Jody, and went over to get herself another drink.

At the dinner table, Molly had seated me next to Sebastian, the male half of the lawyer couple we didn't know. He spent most of the first course (cauliflower and mung bean soup) with his back turned to me, talking to Shona, who was on the other side of him. I drank two glasses of wine quite quickly and amused myself by making faces at Cameron, who was strapped into his bouncy chair on the floor, looking rather perplexed at the toy ladybirds velcroed around his wrists and ankles.

But when Shona got up to help clear the plates, Sebastian turned to me.

'So, Cassie, you're a full-time mum then?'

'Ha! Is there any other kind?'

He gave a slow blink.

Crikey. 'But I also work part time at McKeith's.'

'Ah! And what do you do there?'

He looked marginally more interested in me, but it was obvious he was trying to find out if I was a secretary or a lawyer.

'I'm an employment lawyer . . .'

'Ah right! Poppet's an employment lawyer! Hey, Poppet!'

He motioned proudly across to his girlfriend, a few places along on the other side of the table, and she turned to face us. She was a perfectly presented woman – sleek, poised and pointy like a Siamese cat. But distinctly ruthless-looking, not at all poppet-like.

'Have you come across each other at all?' wondered Sebastian.

I shook my head sadly.

'Last month, Poppet was featured in *Law Today*. They described her as Scotland's go-to lawyer for third-generation cross-border TUPE transfers.'

I raised my eyebrows and smiled appreciatively.

'She's hoping to be made up to partner within the next year. What about you, Cassie, what's your special field, within employment law?'

The table had fallen silent, and all eyes were upon me.

'I specialise in ghost law.'

Everyone looked at me, confused for a moment.

'There's no such thing,' scoffed Sebastian.

'There's no such thing!' echoed Jody, her voice dripping with condescension. 'Can you imagine, at university: "I'm just off to my tutorial in ghost law." ' She dissolved into laughter at her own joke.

'I'm Scotland's go-to lawyer for ghost-related employment dispute resolution.'

'Ghosts?' echoed Poppet. She raised her eyebrows and put her hand over her mouth, as if trying to hide her amusement.

I nodded, chewing a piece of bread carefully before replying. Paul caught my eye from the other end of the table and the corner of his mouth twitched in a conspiratorial smile.

'Or subjective employee experiences, as we prefer to call them at McKeith's,' I said, keeping a straight face. 'Since my first case, a few months ago, I've had forty-six new instructions relating to paranormal employment issues. It seems that employers were just too embarrassed to seek professional advice before, and thought there were no lawyers in the marketplace to cater for them. But now the word has got round and the floodgates have opened.'

'Forty-six new instructions!' breathed Poppet, not laughing any more, thoughts no doubt turning to new revenue streams which might bolster her bid for partnership. 'What sort of scenarios are you dealing with, then?'

The wine was undoubtedly going to my head now. I nodded gravely, in the manner of one professional to another, and began.

'Well, without breaking client confidentiality, most of them are about alleged hauntings in the workplace. Employees going off sick with stress, that sort of thing. Last week I had a construction company where there had been three serious accidents on one particular site, where they were trying to build a house. One of the builders had actually been thrown backwards off some scaffolding. None of the workmen were prepared to go near it after that. But it meant that the construction company was five weeks behind schedule with that particular plot, and were going to be in breach of contract with regards to the completion date.'

The scenario was loosely based on an episode of *Scooby Doo* that we'd tuned into by accident when Sophie had been playing with the remote control the day before.

'Oh, gosh,' said Jody, wide eyed. 'And what did you advise?'

'I asked them what they would do if they had encountered another problem with a site, you know, for example if they had discovered archeological remains or something. And I told them to treat it in exactly the same way – get in an expert.'

'What kind of expert?' asked Shona with a sceptical frown. She was coming back from the kitchen carrying the enormous bowl of salad.

'A panel of experts,' I clarified. 'An independent risk-assessor, a priest, a sceptic and a fortune teller.'

I was slurring my words slightly by now. But I was enjoying the attention – everybody at the table was lapping up every word I had to say.

'And what happened, did they resolve it? Are they going to get the houses completed on time?'

'Yes,' I announced, beaming.

'That's good,' said Sebastian. 'We've got friends who have just reserved a house at that new Silvermains development, and they've just been told that completion will be delayed for three months! And can anybody guess what they're paying for it?'

The conversation went safely on to property prices. I sat back in my seat, took a long sip of wine and raised an eyebrow at Poppet, who was staring intently at me across the table.

16

Malkie had offered to drive us both to Braid Hills for the *Workplace Phantoms* vigil. He came to my office just as I was tidying up my desk.

'Ready to go?'

'Just about,' I said, leaning down to slot files into my filing cabinet. 'What are you going to wear, by the way?'

He shrugged and cast his eyes down over his narrow body, clad in a black suit with faint grey pinstripes.

'I thought we probably needed to wear suits,' I said, nodding. I had given this careful consideration. 'Since he wants us to be a sort of cautionary, sobering presence.'

Malkie looked me up and down and raised an eyebrow. I was wearing a navy suit with a neat cinched-in jacket and a skirt that clung to my hips but kicked out slightly at the knee. The ensemble was finished off with kitten heels and cherry pink lip gloss.

Not that I was trying to impress him – definitely not. Helen had phoned just yesterday to give me a stern pep talk about how the Malkie thing was all in my head – 'a post-natal hormonal delusion' – and she'd told me to take a magnesium supplement.

'Shall we get going then?' He touched my upper arm – the lightest of touches – and my insides melted. Magnesium, indeed.

We chatted briefly about our days as we walked to the car, but there was a slightly awkward silence as we drove off and waited in the queue of traffic on the main road. Our previous conversation in the car, outside the doctor's, seemed to weigh heavily in the air. Suddenly it seemed imperative that I should direct us away from that and back into the safety of small talk.

'How is Jo Cranston getting on these days? Are you still in touch?'

Jo Cranston, mastermind behind the body odour experiment, had been going out with Malkie's best friend at university.

'Kevin's bird? His ex? Nah. Haven't heard from her in ages. Last time I heard she was training as an accountant.'

'Really? Jo? I can't quite picture that somehow.'

'Me neither.' He gave a short laugh. 'But it's better than going around causing train wrecks in the name of psychological research.'

It felt exquisitely intimate, this reference to our failed relationship. What should I say? My lips hovered around something I had read in a magazine that lunchtime.

'It was a painful time for both of us,' I said softly. 'But I could never wish that it hadn't happened.'

'What?' said Malkie, looking confused. 'Oh no, sorry. I was talking about Jo's sleep deprivation experiment. She used Kevin as one of the subjects. He fell asleep while he was driving home and ploughed through a level crossing barrier. Had a very near miss.'

My insides curdled with embarrassment. 'So, this vigil. What are the parameters, legally speaking, do you think?'

'Parameters?'

'Well you're the media lawyer. What's fair game for the programme makers, and what's not?'

'Yeees . . . about that. I'm not sure where Radcliffe got the idea that I was a media lawyer.' He shot me a sideways glance.

158

'What, you mean you're not?'

'I once defended a case for a radio station.'

'Well, there you go. Defamation or something, was it?'

'Not exactly. The cleaner fell down the stairs.'

'Oh right,' I sighed. '*Bloody* Radcliffe.'

'He really seems to be wetting himself over the idea of pitching to Elliot's wife.'

'Do you want me to get the basics of defamation off Wikipedia?' I reached for my phone.

'Nah, I'm sure I can wing it. How hard can it be?'

'I'll just check anyway.'

'Go for it,' said Malkie. 'The traffic's dreadful; you've got at least ten minutes.' Though it was actually more like fifteen by the time we'd crawled through the busy city centre, through the Meadows, then up through the Grange towards the Braids.

Already parked in the courtyard at Braid Hills Funeral Home were two black vans, with the words *Workplace Phantoms* emblazoned on the side in edgy white lettering. A stubbly young man with a camera was busy taking shots of the house.

Elliot was standing around looking uncomfortable in a dark overcoat. He visibly relaxed when he saw us, and came up to us offering his hand.

'Thanks for coming, Cassie . . . and . . . Malcolm, isn't it? Well, as we discussed, I really just want you here to keep me right, as far as what's reasonable or not.'

'Pleased to meet you,' said Malkie. 'I think it's best if we just keep a low profile for now, and let them get on with it.'

It was the first time I'd heard him speak in a professional context, and I noticed that he smoothed out the Glasgow edge in his voice, carefully rounding off all his 't's. I wondered if this was something he did on purpose, had perfected over the years, or whether it was unconscious. I felt a twinge of tenderness for him, editing himself to play the successful lawyer.

Malkie and I watched at a distance as Elliot and the employees went into the house along with Madame Sinistra, the psychic, and Father Pritchard, the priest. For some reason, the sceptic, Brian, stayed in the van eating a packet of crisps. The format, we'd been told, was that the employees would point out the areas where they'd witnessed 'activity'. Then, for the vigil, the professionals would leave the employee in the room in question, with all the lights turned out, and retreat to the van whilst the night vision cameras recorded every breath, blink, tremor and flinch of the poor soul locked up in the dark room.

During all this, we stood outside in the freezing cold, with Elliot coming out every so often to report what was happening or to ask for our opinion on something. We'd made it a condition that, although the employees were allowed to say what they'd experienced in the house, they weren't allowed to comment on how it had caused them to experience stress-related problems or comment on any aspect of their employment with the company.

We knew from Elliot that much of the 'activity' in the house had been centred on a particular turn in the stairs. One employee called Donald had reported seeing a figure hanging from the light fitting, although it had disappeared by the time he'd run to fetch help. On another occasion he'd complained to Elliot that something had thrown him against the banister, and that he'd nearly lost his footing and fallen down the stairs.

Elliot was anxious about whether Donald should be allowed to mention this on film, given that a fall might be a health and safety issue. I deferred the question to Malkie, expert on stair accidents. He hazarded an opinion that a narrowly escaped fall could probably be mentioned without attracting too much liability.

'I'm a bit uneasy about it all,' said Elliot. 'They keep leaving him to sit on the stairs in the dark, with a night vision camera to film his reactions. But they've had to do it four times so far, because there's a problem with one of the night vision cameras. He's getting rather distressed.'

'But that's progress,' said a throaty Glaswegian voice behind us. It was Madame Sinistra, sweeping past us on her way to one of the vans. 'Malfunctioning equipment is a classic sign.'

'Look,' I said, trying to still my chattering teeth. 'Things don't seem to be moving very quickly. We might as well make ourselves useful while we're here. Do you want us to look over the notes of the grievance hearings? Or even any employment policies that might need updating?'

It was a desperate ploy to be allowed to go inside into the warm, and it worked. Elliot showed us the way to a cramped office, filled with filing cabinets, in the modern extension at the back of the house. It was out of the way of the filming and could be accessed through the garden by a back entrance. Malkie and I sat there for what must have been an hour or two, reading through the documentation as slowly as possible.

Eventually he scraped his chair back from the desk and stretched his arms. 'Well, this is just too much excitement for me. I'm going out for a fag. Will you be okay here on your OWN?' He did a comedy eyebrow waggle.

Twenty minutes later he hadn't returned. Where had he got to? Honestly, Malkie and his cigarettes. I remembered how, when he lived on the top floor of the tenement, he'd been too lazy to go up and down the stairs to buy cigarettes, and had set up an arrangement with the young lad from the corner shop below. He would phone him and wait five minutes before leaning out of the back window and lowering a small empty paint tin down on a long piece of string. Rashid would appear in the alleyway, remove the money from the tin, and replace it with the cigarettes and a neatly folded till receipt. One drunken night Malkie even attempted to buy a bottle of vodka this way, but it didn't survive the ascent, plinking onto the cobblestones below.

I decided to go and look for him and made my way out to the back garden. It was quiet out there, except for the wind sighing through the trees and the crunch of gravel under my feet. A prickle crept down my spine as I glanced towards the rooms at the back of the main house, dark behind Victorian sash windows.

It was then that I heard the noise – a very faint banging noise coming from the direction of the house. I stepped off the gravel path and began to approach the window nearest to me. My heels sank into the damp lawn but I kept walking. A strange feeling had come over me, a sense that somebody needed my help. I walked right into the flowerbed and put my face to the window, cupping my hands around my eyes.

A hand on my shoulder.

'Jesusssss! For fuck's s-ssake, Malkie.' My teeth were chattering uncontrollably now and I couldn't seem to catch my breath.

'What's up?'

'There's s-ssomething in there, banging.' But even as I spoke I realised that the banging had stopped. The silence was so complete it almost seemed to buzz.

Malkie stepped forward and peered into the window.

'Hmm. I can't hear anything now. It was probably one of the ghosthunting lot setting up a piece of equipment.'

'But Malkie,' I said. 'Can we check? Have you got a torch or something in the car?'

'Okay,' he said in a sing-song voice, 'I'll get a torch. But if this is a wind-up . . .'

He came back a minute later and handed the torch to me. I clicked it on and shone it into the room. I couldn't see much, but it appeared to be a meeting room. I could make out the edge of a table, the back of a chair, in the weak, wavering beam.

'I can't see anything,' I muttered. 'Here, you have a look.'

But as I pulled back the torch to hand it to Malkie, the pale disc of light dropped downwards and fell on something just on the other side of the window.

The gleam – the merest flicker – of a small, white face.

I dropped the torch.

'Did you see that, Malkie? Did you see that?'

'No – what?' Malkie was scrabbling around in the flowerbed for the torch.

'Fuck's sake, Malkie. *For fuck's sake*. It was a child.'

★

'Elliot, can I have a word?' I had peeped my head round the front door. He looked pleased to be called away and led me into a cramped office just off the reception area. The employee, Donald, was sitting on the stairs looking uncomfortable while a man with a camera hovered around him, and three investigators were crouching on the ground fiddling with a piece of equipment wired up to a laptop.

'Elliot – the meeting rooms at the back of the house?' My words were falling over each other, slippery with panic.

'Yes?'

'I think I just saw a child in one of them. I heard a noise, and looked through the window. Is there a child on the premises? Have any of the investigators brought a child?'

He frowned and shook his head. 'No, definitely not. You must have been mistaken.'

'I think she might have been trapped. I think she might have been trying to get out. Could you just go and check?'

'Okay, I'll check.'

'Don't say anything, will you. I mean, to the investigators?'

'Oh. No, all right.' He seemed distracted – or maybe just weary of matters paranormal.

Malkie was waiting by the car when I came out.

'There are no children,' I said. 'It was a ghost.'

It sounded so ridiculous, spoken solemnly in the dark. Malkie's mouth twitched and my fear buckled into laughter. I laughed so hard that I had to lean backwards against the car.

'I hope you didn't tell the investigators?' said Malkie. 'Tell me you didn't.'

'I didn't tell them,' I said, finally catching my breath. But when I looked up at him, somehow the laughter had turned to tears. I choked back a sob, and wiped my cheek with the back of my hand.

Malkie looked at me appraisingly. 'You okay?'

I smiled and nodded, causing one more tear to spill down my face.

'I think it's time to call it a night. Just wait here a second.'

He strode into the house, but came back a few minutes later shaking his head. 'Elliot wants us to stay till the bitter end.'

I glanced uneasily at the house. 'No children, I suppose? In any of the meeting rooms?'

'No children,' said Malkie lightly.

I sighed. 'You know, I thought it was Milly, for a second. The last time I came here I met a little girl. She was here with

164

her mother, who was dying. They were planning her funeral. Milly was acting it out, with a little white carriage, and horses with pink ribbons. It's silly, though. Why would she be here at this time of night?'

'Maybe she was just at the back of your mind, because you were back here again. That's pretty heavy stuff, planning your mother's funeral when you're only – what?'

'Six or seven, I'm guessing.'

'Jesus Christ.'

He closed his eyes for a second. I recalled Jonathan's reaction to the story, his face crumpling in disgust, his fork clattering onto his plate.

We stood there for a moment or two. Then Malkie opened the boot and pulled out a black cable-knit jumper.

'Put this on. You're shivering. I've got a blanket in the back there, too. Why don't you lie down and doze for a bit.'

'What will you do?'

'I was just going to sit here in the front and keep an eye on things from here.'

'Will you put some music on?' I asked.

He scrabbled in the footwell for a minute or two.

'*Best Hits of the '90s* okay for you?' He put it on and it must have been the neurological effects of all the excitement or something, but I fell asleep instantly.

When I woke up it was around half past three in the morning. Malkie was standing outside having a cigarette. I rubbed my eyes and got out of the car to join him.

'Did I miss anything?'

'Nah,' said Malkie. 'They're saying there hasn't been much to go on. Not much EMF activity, nothing on camera. Nobody saw anything.'

'Oh well,' I said softly. 'Just as well I didn't say anything. They would have insisted on interviewing me for the programme! Radcliffe would've been really pleased about that – a loony lawyer getting freaked out on *Workplace Phantoms*!'

'Two loony lawyers,' said Malkie with a smile. 'You had me pretty freaked out, too.'

On the car stereo, a new tune started playing – the first, hesitant, achingly sweet notes of the Verve's 'Drugs Don't Work'. The plaintive, sweeping melody that spoke of love, and loss – well, it just undid me.

I looked up at Malkie to find his gaze resting on me.

'I must look a mess,' I said, searching for something to say. 'Have I got mascara all over my face?'

'I've never seen you look more stunning.'

I stood still, barely daring to breathe. 'Do you remember this song?'

'Come here,' he said, pulling me towards him, as if to comfort me. He held me close to him and I laid my head against his shoulder, near to his heart. I could smell the cold night air on his clothes. Our bodies fitted together again as if they'd never been apart.

We swayed ever so slightly to the music, pressing our bodies closer at the hips.

'Don't worry,' he whispered. 'I won't let anything happen. I know you can't.'

But it had happened. It had happened already. It was as though all the cells in my body had loosened, shifted, and aligned themselves towards him like iron filings to a magnet. I don't know how I summoned the strength to finally push him away and say that we should be getting back. Malkie clutched my head against his chest, briefly, his fingers tangled through my hair. Then he released me, and drove me home.

17

When I got home, at around half past five, Sophie had just woken up for the day and Jonathan was crashing around the kitchen trying to heat up her bottle.

'Hello!' He came over to give me a stubbly kiss. 'How's my favourite wife this morning? How was the vigil?'

I'd decided in the car on the way home that I had to tell Jonathan about what had happened with Malkie, and immediately, before I lost my nerve. Once there was one lie nestling in the space between two people, there was always just enough room to tuck in another one, and then another.

I followed him into the living room and told him while he gave Sophie her bottle. The extreme tiredness helped. It made me feel distanced from myself, as though I was telling somebody else's story, as though that tangled mess of emotions didn't really belong to me.

Jonathan kept his eyes on Sophie throughout my account. His eyebrows went up and the left corner of his mouth went down. When I'd finished he paused, as though assessing the evidence.

'So.' He rubbed his nose with the back of his free hand. 'A litigation lawyer and an employment lawyer dancing to "Drugs Don't Work", one of the most depressing songs of the last century, in an undertaker's car park.'

He paused again, narrowed his eyes and shook his head. 'You know, I just can't get excited about that.'

A giggle bubbled up. 'It's not the most cheerful song in the world, is it?'

'A dirge, definitely.'

'I'm sorry, Jonathan. I wasn't myself. It was just a really odd night.'

But he was already getting up out of the chair, holding Sophie against his chest.

'Why don't you go to bed for an hour or two?' he said. 'Mum can look after Sophie. Do you definitely have to go into the office today? It's not one of your usual days.'

'Unfortunately, yes,' I said to his retreating back. 'I'm doing a lunchtime seminar which Radcliffe wouldn't let me out of. And I've got to finish a report too, because the client's going on holiday on Friday.'

I went back to bed, but I couldn't sleep. My confession hadn't damped down the adrenalin that was coursing through my body, jerking me awake every time I started to drop off.

Possibly because that confession hadn't been quite complete. Wrong-footed by Jonathan's low-key reaction to my story, I'd lost my nerve to tell him the last thing. When Malkie had pulled up at the house to drop me off, he'd grabbed my hand and asked me to meet him for a drink after work tomorrow. 'Just to talk everything through,' he'd said.

I told myself now that it was irrelevant, as far as Jonathan was concerned – Malkie just wanted to clear the air, to make sure things weren't awkward around the office.

But something about the look in his eyes, and the feel of his hand as he'd grabbed mine, rather tended to suggest otherwise.

★

'Hah!' exclaimed Annabel Masters, as though she were executing a particularly devastating karate move.

I jerked awake, realising with horror that I must have nodded off over the age discrimination case report I was reading. I had successfully delivered the client presentation over my lunch hour, but now I was flagging. My body ached as though I was coming down with flu.

Annabel, who'd been out at court all morning, tossed her coat onto the back of her chair and slammed her briefcase onto the desk.

'There you are,' she said. 'Has anybody told you yet?'

'Told me what?'

'I was at the Project Manhattan completion dinner last night.'

'Oh? And?'

'We're standing there having canapés, right – Radcliffe, and the clients, and a whole bunch of lawyers from other firms – and ... oh God, it's so funny. Poppet McCrae suddenly appears beside Radcliffe and me. She tells him that she's not being stretched enough at Prentice's, that she's looking for a new challenge, and that she'd be the perfect person to head up our Paranormal Services Team. He says, "What?" and she tells him how she's got ideas for growing this side of the business, tackling it as a multidisciplinary approach, with lawyers from construction, litigation, employment. He asks what on earth she's talking about and she says she's been speaking to someone from McKeith's – couldn't remember the name.'

Here, Annabel gave me a pointed look, but I merely shrugged.

'And apparently this McKeith's lawyer told Poppet she'd been involved in advising about a haunted construction site.

So then Poppet tells Radcliffe this story about somebody being thrown off scaffolding by a ghost, and McKeith's arranging a team of experts to sort things out. According to this mysterious source, McKeith's could hardly keep up with the instructions that were flooding in – and that's where she, Poppet, would come in.'

I wasn't in the least surprised that Poppet would try to steal my job.

'What did Radcliffe say?'

Annabel laughed. 'He said, "I don't know who has been making up ludicrous stories about the firm, but Paranormal Services is not one of our practice areas, nor likely to be. When I get to the bottom of this, heads are going to roll, believe me. I'd thank you not to besmirch the name of McKeith's by referring to this again." And then he walked off. You should have *seen* Poppet McCrae's face. Absolutely priceless!'

'Oh God.'

'I wonder *whose* head will roll,' said Annabel, with an arch smile.

When Radcliffe's secretary phoned down later, asking me to go up to his office, Annabel looked up and raised her eyebrows, her mouth twitching with amusement. With wobbly knees, I got up from my desk and embarked up the three flights of stairs that would take me to my doom.

I knocked on the door, feeling like a nervous schoolgirl called to the headmaster's office.

'Come!'

It was a beautiful room with wood panelling and tall Georgian windows. Set into two of the walls were full-height bookshelves. These held his volumes of the *Stair Memorial Encylopaedia*, and various sets of dusty old law reports, although rumour had it that if you looked hard enough you might come across the odd PG Wodehouse or John Grisham. On the far wall was a fireplace, and today a fire had actually been lit.

I realised, remembering the clink of glasses that I'd heard on the way up the stairs, that the fire had probably been lit because Radcliffe was hosting one of his 'evenings' tonight. This would be for his 'magic circle', the ten or so of his clients from whom was extracted the bulk of the firm's revenue.

As I walked into the room he didn't look up, but motioned to me to sit down on one of the chairs by his enormous mahogany desk. I sat there, breathing silently and deeply, seeing if I could relax the tension in my neck and shoulders. A strange feeling of stillness began to ebb through me. What will be, will be, I told myself, listening to the slow tick of the clock on the mantel, and the scribble of Radcliffe's pen. I stared out of the window at the darkening Edinburgh skyline, as the afternoon crept into evening.

After several minutes I did start to wonder whether he'd forgotten I was there, and was wondering whether it would be polite to give a slight cough, when I heard an unmistakeable snoring sound emanating from somewhere near my feet. I jumped back with a little squeal, whereupon a grey muzzle and a pair of black eyes poked out from beneath Radcliffe's desk and viewed me reproachfully.

I had forgotten Bailey, Radcliffe's ageing black Labrador, who could frequently be seen padding around the office. When I'd first joined the firm, my daily duties had included feeding, watering and walking him twice a day. This had surprised me at first. (I had imagined that I would be doing the whole Ally McBeal thing from day one, appearing in the Court of Session and attending tense but dramatic all-parties meetings, if not actually yet rising to the dizzy heights of drafting contracts in taxis.) However, I soon came to enjoy these little outings with Bailey, his claws scritching along the New Town pavements in eagerness to reach Queen Street Gardens where I'd let him off the lead and let him root around looking for interesting stones.

'Ahhhh . . . Cassie. Thanks for coming in to see me.' He stood up, and started pacing the room. Bailey jumped up and capered around him, wagging his tail, perhaps thinking it was time for a walk.

'Right then, so Roger White's been in touch about this Forrester case.'

'Sorry, what?'

'A new case for you. I thought you were aware of it already – a Mrs Forrester? Interesting little set of circumstances.'

My anxiety about the dinner party rumours receded a little, to make way for a fresh flood of anxiety about this new case. I was billed, in the firm's marketing literature, as a specialist in employment litigation, but in fact, I found this idea appalling. It had been a long time since I'd done any appearance work.

Roger White was a magic circle client, so I'd have to be sure not to screw this up, whatever it was. Radcliffe had no doubt summoned me because he wanted to be able to announce to him, in person, that the wheels of this new case were in motion.

Radcliffe stopped pacing for a moment and plonked himself in one of the comfy leather armchairs by the fire.

'Right,' I said. 'And have you got any details about the case?'

He gave me an odd look, vaguely surprised. 'Well, it sounds like a constructive dismissal case, or will be. She's alleging unreasonable treatment, but there's no legal precedent, as far as I can see. It's a tricky one. I'll bet it ends up in the tribunal.'

Oh great.

172

'And it's a *pro bono*, by the way.'

What? He was waiving the fees? This was getting all too confusing. Who was this needy, well-deserving Mrs Forrester?

'Sorry, but . . .' I cleared my throat and tried to speak more confidently. 'Is there a business connection between Roger White and Mrs Forrester?'

'I doubt it. He referred to her as his Auntie Jean. And *Auntie Jean* only wants to deal with you. Something about running into you in Sainsbury's? She says she's got a "connection" with you.' He winced with mild distaste at this last statement.

Of course. Lovely Jean, who'd calmed me down in the Sainsbury's café.

'I said you'd meet her tomorrow. Would you call her to arrange a time, please?'

Radcliffe stood up to hand me the file, and I turned to leave.

'One other thing, Cassie.'

I held my breath. Was this the part of the conversation where I got reprimanded over the Poppet debacle? I couldn't stand it any longer.

'I heard about the completion dinner,' I said. 'I heard about what Poppet McCrae said to you.'

'And?'

He was giving me a chance to confess.

'The thing is . . . I think I'd better explain the situation to you. I mean, how Poppet got this idea.'

Radcliffe, standing behind his desk, arms crossed, was frowning now.

'You see, I was at a dinner party last week. I made up a . . . well, a scenario . . . about a . . . sort of, paranormal problems, at a building site. It was just a bit of fun. It was one of those . . . awful dinner parties . . . where you can never think of anything to say, and I was a bit drunk. It didn't even occur to me . . .

173

that I might be besmirching the name of McKeith's. I'm so sorry. I was very . . . unprofessional. Please . . .'

I couldn't find enough breath to get the words out. My legs had gone numb. I managed to take a step back and leaned against the bookcase as a wave of dizziness swept over me. A volume of the All England case reports toppled down onto the floor next to my foot, but I suspected if I bent down to pick it up, I wouldn't be able to get up again.

Radcliffe sat down behind his desk and began rifling for something amongst his papers.

'*You* made it up? That surprises me. I thought it was quite funny, actually.'

'What? But you said . . . that heads would roll.'

'Oh, I just said that to shut that stupid Poppet woman up. She's irritating in the extreme.'

'Oh! Goodness, that's a relief—'

'But, Cassie. I have to say, this concerns me. More than anything else, I have to question your attitude. I mean, how do you react when a client piles on the pressure? This shaking and stuttering – what's that all about? Where's the confidence? I just don't see it, Cassie. It concerns me. A great deal.'

'No, of course I don't—'

'Well, I think a competency review is appropriate, in light of what I've seen today, and your conduct in general in the last few months. You'll be familiar with competency procedures, naturally. I want you to copy me in on all correspondence for this new case, write up file notes of all telephone conversations and meetings, and email me reports each week with an update of how things are progressing. At the end of it I'll interview the client myself to get a viewpoint as to you personally, how you've come across, how you've dealt with things and so on. Is that all clear?'

I could feel my face burning with shame. My job was to advise employers about how to implement such procedures. I'd never dreamed that I would be subject to one myself. As I left the room, part of my very identity seemed to fall away. What was I, anyway? A new mum? A mildly unfaithful wife? A failed lawyer? It all seemed so impossible.

18

Reeling from the meeting with Radcliffe, I decided to catch a bus home rather than embark on the half-hour walk in my shaky state. But the traffic was heavy and progress very slow. I stared out the window as we edged along in the dark, condensation creeping up the glass. We crossed over the Dean Bridge, and the precipitous gully of the Water of Leith a hundred feet below. We inched past elegant New Town crescents before advancing west along Queensferry Road.

I checked my phone – there was an email from Helen, asking how the vigil had gone. Picturing her face if I were to tell her about the 'Drugs Don't Work' moment, I slid my phone back into my bag. I'd build up to telling her later. And I'd also have to tell Jonathan about the competency review. I could just imagine his face, too . . . and my mum's, if I were ever to tell her – which I'd have to, if I lost my job.

I focused on the November gloom outside, trying to banish the procession of disappointed faces from my mind.

Although you never knew with Jonathan – on occasion he'd been incredibly supportive with work crises. Once, as a newly qualified assistant, I'd come home in tears, laden down with boxes of files and a hideously complicated section of a public sector outsourcing agreement to draft for a transaction that was completing the next day. A colleague had supposedly been dealing with it but had gone on holiday and dumped it on my desk with a post-it note.

Jonathan had made cheese-on-toast and large mugs of tea,

and had then gone onto the local government website and found and printed off copies of all the current regulations dealing with employment transfers from the public sector. Then, while I drafted, he flicked back and forth through the legislation double-checking that my cross-references made sense. By the time we'd finished, and crashed out on our bed, fully clothed, it was four a.m. and dawn was breaking.

I thought wistfully of that night now, as I tinged the bell to get off the bus. At that time, I'd still believed that I was at the start of a bright and promising career; that I could rise to the top and succeed with the best of them. And Jonathan had bolstered me up in this belief from the moment I'd met him, taking a close interest in me, and all the future possibilities of me. Which had now, it seemed, wound down to this: a part-time job doing the cases nobody else wanted to do, and an impending competency review.

I did screw up the courage to phone him – after first popping upstairs to see Sophie, who was in the bath. She was smacking the water with her hands and soaking poor Dita. I took off my suit jacket and knelt down to kiss her, leaning over the side of the bath so she could wrap her wet, pudgy arms around my neck.

'Oh Jonathan,' I said with tears in my voice, once I'd shut myself in the study with the phone. 'Radcliffe has put me on a competency review procedure.'

'Are you at home? I'll be right there.' The phone clicked as he hung up. If I'd announced an imminent nuclear attack, I don't think I could have elicited a prompter response.

'Right,' he said as he walked in the door, throwing his coat and briefcase down in the hall. 'Tell me everything.'

Jiggling Sophie – now clean and in her pyjamas – on my knee, I told him the shameful story.

'Where does he get off, treating you like that? Come on.' He led the way to the study and fired up the computer.

'Okay, so first off, he bothers you on maternity leave – in fact, you'd only just got home from hospital, hadn't you? – insisting that you had to head up a new case. And threatening you with redundancy.'

'Hmmm.'

'He has a go at you for taking the work experience student to Braid Hills, even though you were showing initiative and would otherwise have had to cancel the meeting.'

I nodded again, while Jonathan typed.

'Then he drops you in it with this *Workplace Phantoms* nonsense, something you clearly shouldn't have been involved in in the first place. Then, even though you've had to stay up all night doing that, he insists you go into the office the next day to deliver a presentation. And then, after you've had no sleep for – what, thirty-six hours? – he's surprised when you feel a bit shaky when he lays into you?'

'When you put it like that . . .'

'He's an *arse*. Right, don't worry, Cassie. I know you're upset, but just take the feelings out of it for a minute. Let's be pragmatic. All we need to do is make a note of all this. Then if he tries to get rid of you using this stupid competency review thing, you just show him this list and say you'll take him straight to a tribunal.'

Jonathan finished typing the document while Sophie wriggled and strained in my arms. He'd taken me aback with how supportive he was being over this. It made me want to go to him with all my other worries, place them all in his arms and let him take care of them for a while.

'There!' he announced once he'd finished typing. 'All sorted. Hey, Cassie-Lassie, what's wrong?'

178

'Oh, Jonathan . . . I just feel so bad.'

'I told you, none of this is your fault . . .'

'Not about the competency review. About – you know. What happened. Last night.'

Jonathan looked longingly at the computer screen, as though there might be a list he could draw up to get round the issue of my almost-infidelity.

'Well,' he said, swallowing. 'Nothing really happened, did it?'

'No, but . . .' I let the silence speak for me.

'It's what you wanted to happen,' he said in a low voice. 'That's what this is about, isn't it?'

'There was a part of me that went straight back to being twenty again,' I said. 'I felt so . . . I don't know . . . beautiful; a young, free thing.'

'You are beautiful,' said Jonathan, taking my hand and kissing it. 'I've not been paying you enough attention recently, I know. Why don't we—'

'It's not that.' Now I'd started, I couldn't stop there. 'I love you. But it made me . . .'

'Wobble?'

How many times had I wished that Jonathan would be the sort of husband that finished my sentences off for me? But not in these circumstances, not sentences laden with shame and dismay and truths that could barely be faced.

'Yes. I suppose that's right. It made me wobble.'

How could I find words to say what I really felt? That the way I felt in Malkie's arms had made me wonder whether I'd accidentally ended up on the wrong path in life. Whether that moment last night was like a door opening through parallel worlds, a way back into the life I was supposed to be leading.

'Have you ever wobbled?' I asked, suddenly suspicious about why he was taking things this well.

He thought for a minute, a deep frown creasing his forehead. 'Have I ever bumped into an ex-girlfriend and felt a thrill? Have I ever wondered what life would have been like if we'd stayed together? Sure. I think that happens to everyone.'

I felt a surge of love for Jonathan. He always knew just the right thing to say, to put things in perspective, to place them in the context of a reassuring, secure normality.

'But it hasn't struck you off balance, like this?'

'Not really.' He looked uncomfortable. 'But then, I don't know what your relationship with Malkie was like. Maybe it was pretty special. Any relationship with you would be pretty special.'

I was speechless at this last comment . . . couldn't think how to respond to this generosity. But then Jonathan snapped back into take-charge mode.

'Listen, you go and get Sophie off to bed. I'm going to make you a nice cup of tea, and some toast, because I don't think you've eaten anything today, have you?'

I shook my head.

'Ah-ghu,' said Sophie, grabbing a fistful of my hair. 'Ah-hoo.'

'Then I want you to watch *EastEnders*, then get tucked up in bed and get a good night's sleep. I'll even make you a hot water bottle, how does that sound? I'm going to go out on a limb here and say that I think the way you're feeling has at least something to do with lack of sleep, and low blood sugar, and the after effects of that stupid vigil thing. Then tomorrow, and the next day, and the next, we'll see what we can do to get you un-wobbled.'

'So you're okay about it, then. Sort of.'

'I'll level with you, Cass. I don't see this as a deal-breaker.

180

The fact that you came right back here and told me all about it – that's the most important thing. I think you'll feel back to normal soon.'

But what if Jonathan's un-wobbling plan, the hot water bottle and everything, didn't work? What if I still felt the same way tomorrow? Next week? Next month?

'We're meant to be together, Cassie. We'll get through this.'

I nodded. Sophie nudged my chin up with her head and buried her face into my neck. She was trying to tell me she was ready for bed.

'Anyway, that's what I have to think, isn't it? Because the alternative is pretty grim, Cass.' His voice was crisp and businesslike now, as he turned and left the room.

19

I shivered as I waited for Jean Forrester to buzz me into the tenement, and it wasn't just because of the cold, drizzly November afternoon. I'd been jittery all day at the thought of this case, with its looming threat of a tribunal hearing, and scrutiny by Radcliffe as part of the competency review. The buzzer echoed up the stone stairwell as I swung the door open and went in.

The flat was on ground level, and Jean was already standing at her door smiling a welcome at me, drying her hands on a yellow checked tea towel. As I approached she threw the tea towel across her shoulder and held out her hands, as though I were a favourite niece come to visit.

'Hi,' I said, smiling back, feeling like a nine-year-old and forgetting to be lawyerly.

'Come in!' She gestured towards the interior of the flat with a little flourish and a nod. Her white hair looked stiff, as if it had been recently set into curls – perhaps even in honour of this very occasion.

'And how's the little one doing? Is she sleeping?'

'Oh, she's really well, thanks. The sleeping's not great, but we'll get there.'

The living room hadn't been touched in thirty years, decoration-wise. The sofa, covered in a brown, bobbly material with flecks of orange, had armrests like enormous chocolate Swiss Rolls perched on either end. In a matching chair, drawn up close to the old-fashioned gas fire, sat Gerry, dressed in smart trousers and a neatly pressed blue shirt.

'Hi Gerry, how are you?' I shook his white, gnarled hand.

'Nae bad, nae bad,' he said. 'Sit down, sit down! You must be . . . er . . . welcome!'

Jean left momentarily then bustled back in with a tea trolley, steering its squeaky wheels to a halt at my knees. On the trolley stood a teapot, cups and saucers, a plate of sandwiches and three different sorts of cake. I took the plate she brandished at me, and accepted a slice of cream cake.

Jean poured me a cup of tea, and placed it on a little side table before sitting down beside me on the sofa.

She leaned forward with an urgent, confiding expression. I wondered whether she was about to launch into the details of her employment dispute. I balanced my plate of cake on my knee and reached for my briefcase to get out a pen and notepad.

'These cakes,' she began. 'I order them from the bakers in Morningside Road to pick up every Monday. You need to order, because the popular ones are all taken by nine o'clock.'

'Well, this is superb,' I said.

'There's a fruit layer that I sometimes get if the raspberry sponge isn't available to order.'

'Mmmm,' I said, munching.

'There's a problem with the jam supplier, so I'm told,' she continued in a confidential tone. 'Unreliable. So they don't have the raspberry every week. And definitely not if you don't pre-order.'

'Right. Well, that's very organised of you. And this is very kind of you, you really didn't need to . . .'

'Nonsense,' Jean scoffed. 'It's no bother. I go for the cakes every Monday anyway. They're—'

'No more trouble from that gang, I trust?' cut in Gerry.

'Oh! No – nothing else. Thanks for asking. We're hoping it was just a one-off.'

We sat in companionable silence for a moment or two, the fire hissing in the background. I felt transported back to a simpler time, as if I was sitting in my granny's front room, no pressing issues other than to decide if I wanted to spend the afternoon dressing up, going to the swings, or jumping around her living room like a flea, allowing myself to step only on the furniture.

'So, do you want to tell me about your work situation?' I asked, when I thought I couldn't put it off any longer.

'Well,' said Jean. 'As you know, I'm a receptionist at Brand New You. An image consultancy, they call it. It used to be just a hypnotherapist, Mr Weeks, and his wife Mary, who's a chiropodist. Mr Weeks had built up quite a practice, you know, even in the days before the alternative therapies became popular. You may have heard of him if you move in golfing circles – he's a specialist in golf hypnotherapy. At one point – gosh, well, it would be back in the Eighties I suppose – there was a rush of middle-aged executive types needing help with golf issues – mental blocks, that sort of thing. It's surprisingly common, by all accounts, just when you're about to take a swing. To be troubled by a mental block.'

I raised my eyebrows. 'Really? How interesting. Golf is not a subject I know much about.'

'Of course,' she went on, 'there were always other issues behind it. Mid-life crises, stress, childhood problems, that sort of thing. But by advertising himself as a golf coach Mr Weeks made it easy for them to come to him. He'd bring out all the issues, while seeming to tackle the golf, and then send them on to Mary to sort out their feet. So by the end of it they were ready to go back home to their wives.'

'Hmmm ... how interesting.' Jonathan played golf; he was surely a prime candidate for all this, what with his nightmares and refusal to discuss his dad.

'No need for fast cars, mistresses or any of that song and dance,' she went on, pursing her lips and shaking her head. Gerry shook his head too.

'And the added bonus of the feet,' I said reverently.

'That's right, dear. Anyway, the business grew very successful. Hypnotherapy and the like became more popular. A counsellor, Dickie James, joined the practice. Certainly, the appointment books were always full.

'There's a staff room behind the reception area, overlooking a sunny little garden courtyard. And when Gerry had his hernia operation a couple of years ago, Mr Weeks and Mary said I could bring him in to sit in the back room while I worked, so I could keep an eye on him.'

Gerry nodded solemnly from his woolly brown armchair.

'And that just sort of became the arrangement. Gerry got used to it, even after he recovered from the operation. He's seventy-eight now! I know you'll find that hard to believe.'

I raised my eyebrows and nodded at the ancient-looking Gerry, trying to look impressed.

'Gerry would drive in with me in the mornings, and sit in the back room, maybe reading or listening to the radio, or writing his poetry. He's a gardener by trade, you know, but he did an English Literature course through the Open University – oh, when would that be? – about ten years ago.'

'I studied English Literature, too,' I said, with a shy smile towards Gerry.

Jean gave a brief nod of approval and then continued. 'He looked after the courtyard garden, planted it out with lavender and suchlike. Made a lovely trellis with honeysuckle and clematis around the back door. We got a little bench and put it out there. Made it into a nice peaceful area where the clients could sit while they waited for their appointments, if it was a nice day. Then they decided to use it for Tai Chi classes and outdoor yoga in the summer.

'That sounds really nice. Very relaxing.' I was almost falling asleep, just thinking about it.

'It was. And then, since Gerry's legs got bad, it's become more of a necessity, taking him into work, because he can't manage very well at home by himself. It was fine at first, because Mr Weeks saw both of us as more part of the family, really. He was grateful to Gerry for the work he'd done in the garden, and Gerry would chat to the clients and show them the garden while they were waiting for their appointments. Put them at their ease, sort of thing.

'But last year Mr Weeks retired, and his son Wilf took over the business. He's one of these new lifestyle coaches. No training to speak of. He's rented out the rooms in the clinic to other new types. A beauty therapist, which is fine. But then there's Dr Bourne, who does that botox, non-surgical facelifts, and all sorts. And they've rented new rooms upstairs for a clothes therapist, and a hair consultant. Hence renaming the business *Brand New You*.'

I looked across at Jean, with her cream jumper, tweedy skirt and opaque, flesh-coloured tights, and understood the root of the problem.

'Mary's still there. Wilf can hardly get her out, being his own mum. But the likes of these new clients, they're not really interested in feet as much. Her appointment book has been looking quite empty of late. It's the clothes therapy and suchlike that they're all into now. But the thing is, now Wilf has announced that they want to convert the staff room into another consulting room, since they want to hire a . . . well, a sex therapist, dear. A relationship coach, they call it. But the thing is – they say that Gerry won't be able to come to work with me any more. But I can't leave him at home on his own. So I'm going to have to resign. But I really don't want to. We need the money, you see. And the thing is, dear, I just wanted to ask you: is there anything I can do?'

I'd never heard of a case so rich in employment issues. It was almost like an exam question – the sort I'd always been rather good at.

'Well. If they're making it impossible to do your job, that could be constructive dismissal.'

'And can I do something about that?'

'Yes. You've been taking Gerry into work for so long that it's arguably become your contractual right. Then there's sex discrimination . . .'

'How could it be sex discrimination?' Jean leaned forward, fascinated.

'Because you're a woman, and women are more likely to have caring responsibilities. Not allowing you to bring ageing relatives into work is a restriction that is more likely to impact on a woman than a man . . . so you can argue it's discriminatory.'

'No!' whispered Jean.

Gerry frowned a little at 'ageing relatives'.

'It's the same with age discrimination. Not allowing you to bring . . . incapacitated family members . . . into work is a restriction that is more likely to affect older workers. They'd argue against it, but it's worth a shot. Then there's the whole issue of disability discrimination by association. And the argument that Gerry himself might be an employee. If he's been doing the gardening and keeping clients entertained, that could be a possibility. It would mean that all the employment protection laws would attach to him in his own right.'

Goodness, this was actually fun. I could barely stop talking. Jean was starting to look bewildered.

'I'm not saying that any of these arguments would win a tribunal case. They're all a bit of a long shot, actually. But the point is, you could still lodge a claim, throwing all sorts of employment legislation into the pot. Just the thought of the lawyer's fees might be enough to stop them in their tracks.'

Jean looked shocked and excited, and held a hand up to her mouth.

'First of all, what you need to do is lodge a grievance. Do you know who's in charge of human resources?'

'Yes! It's Wilf's girlfriend, Chantal-Marie. She just started last month, and already she's laying down the law. Ideas above her station.'

'Okay, well that's fine, I suggest you lodge a written grievance with Chantal-Marie and see what happens. I'll help you write it. Then there'll be a meeting.'

'Oh dear, I don't know what I would say if I had to go to a meeting like that. And I'd need to bring Gerry too, you know. I can't leave him.'

'We'll all go,' I said.

'Do you want some more cake, dear? It'll only go to waste.'

I detected that the discussions of the grievance hearing had made Jean anxious, so let the conversation drift on to other subjects. I heard about Norma, organiser of the church sale of work, who was apt to underprice the baked goods (she'd let officialdom go to her head) and the old man in the upstairs flat who played his keyboard late at night, keeping everybody awake. The other neighbours were going to convene a meeting to discuss what should be done.

By the time I got up to leave, the nausea and shakiness had gone. I felt calm, clear headed, and *well*. I'd forgotten about the competency hearing, other than to vaguely register that I'd have to type up my written notes of the meeting before putting them on the file, since the paper version was smudged with cream.

Jean showed me out, closing the sitting room door behind us as we went into the hall.

'Dear, I think I might need to have another wee meeting with you – on our own. There was . . .well, an incident at work, involving Gerry. I don't like to bring it up in front of him, but . . . I think you should be aware.'

'That's fine – yes, we'll meet up again. We need to go over the grievance letter anyway. How about . . . a week on Thursday? Three-ish?'

'All right then – shall we meet at the Copper Kettle on Stevenson Street? They do a good scone there. Lovely jam and proper fresh whipped cream.'

She eyed me beadily, as though daring me to suggest that aerosol cream would be a perfectly adequate substitute.

I gave a deep nod, and promised to see her there.

20

Bar Twenty-Nine was just around the corner from the office. Without needing to confer, Malkie and I headed to a small dark booth tucked away at the back. There were no other customers, apart from a group of people who seemed to be in the awkward early stages of an office night out, their small talk echoing too loudly across the empty room. Malkie sat playing with a coaster, looking down at his hands, while I summoned over the waiter.

'So what's up?' I asked, once we'd ordered coffees.

'Cassie.' He raised his eyes to mine. 'The way we were at Braid Hills. Let's just say, I haven't felt that way with a girl since we were last together. And I just wanted to tell you – I think I made a mistake.'

'A mistake? Then, or now?'

He rubbed his forehead with the heel of his hand, eyes squeezed shut, as if he was in pain. When he spoke it was barely audible. 'Then.'

Vindication for all those years of longing swept over me in waves. It trickled down my back, making me want to gasp. As Malkie continued, I felt like a different person within my body. My cheekbones felt sharper, my eyes darker and deeper. A scent seemed to rise like heat off my skin.

'I was too young,' he said. 'I didn't realise what we had.'

'I did.'

'I know you did. And I just don't know what I was holding out for. I thought that since I was still so young, there must be more to come . . . you know. But there wasn't, after you. There just wasn't.'

'Why didn't you get in touch with me then? I spent months, Malkie. I spent years, with you on my mind, every day.'

'I guess I just got carried away with other things. I did go out with a few people. I even lived with a girl for a couple of years. Gaby. She was everything I thought I was looking for. Sassy, confident, sporty. She could be one of the lads when she felt like it, she could give as good as she got.'

'Not like me, then.'

'Just different. I was the one begging her for commitment, if you can imagine that.'

'Not really.'

'It didn't work out. She was what I thought I should want, but she wasn't right for me. When I finished with her, I thought I'd just need to keep looking for the right person. But when I saw you that day on the street outside McKeith's, I knew it was your face that I'd been looking for. I don't know what it is about you. But it was like you reached into me and flicked the "on" switch. It was always like that with you.'

Why had it taken him nearly a decade to realise it?

'So anyway.' He brought down his palms on the table in a gesture of finality. 'I just wanted you to know. I know you're married, I know you've got a little girl, and a life you can't leave behind . . . that you probably wouldn't want to leave behind. But I felt like I had to set the record straight. It felt wrong to just never tell you.'

'What?'

'That you were The One.'

Silence; and a twisting sensation where my heart should have been. Words were circling in my head but they were all impossible.

191

'*Malkie*,' I whispered finally. It wasn't a rebuke, neither was it a capitulation. I was pleading with him; pleading for him to have said those words all those years ago.

'I was so stupid.' His voice tightened and he shook his head. 'I didn't know it was love. It was right in front of me and I couldn't see it. And now, I—'

'You don't *know* me. I'm not the same person as before.'

'I do know you. I can see that this motherhood thing has knocked you for six. I can see that you're full of anxiety – you're practically buzzing with it. You think you don't know who you are any more, but I can tell you, Cassie, you're still the same. I could feel it, when I held you that night. My body knows you. My . . . my *heart* knows you, for God's sake. We fit together.'

Of all the things he could have said. Maybe if I stayed very still I would manage not to break into all the different pieces of me.

The wife and mother in me knew that I had to leave. But there was part of me that was unfolding like a flower in the light and warmth of this attention, and it wanted me to linger at that table with him, raking over the coals, playing a little with the fire before it had to die.

Then there was the part of me that had been searching for Malkie's face in every stranger in every street, since the night he'd left me; it was crying like a desperate child, clinging on to my arm, pulling me down, begging me to stay.

What if Malkie was talking to the real me? What if he'd found her and pinned her down with his straight talking and the look in his eye? If I got up and walked away, maybe I'd be leaving her behind forever.

I'd love to be able to say that I came to a decision there and then, that I knew, deep down, what to do. But when I stood up to leave, it was because I had to go and collect Sophie from nursery – there was no one else to do it.

'I have to go,' I said. 'I'm sorry, but there's nowhere we can go with this . . .'

He nodded. He didn't make any attempt to hold me back, but his face was white, clammy, almost panicky.

I left the bar and took the back route down a street of mews houses, their windows bright in the wintry gloom. Clattering over the cobbles, I knew I'd reach the nursery if I just put one foot in front of the other. I focused on Sophie – how her face would light up when she saw me, how her pudgy hands would wave upwards, opening like little stars, to be lifted.

★

It was about ten o'clock that night when I heard Jonathan's key in the door. I came downstairs and found him in the kitchen.

When I saw him standing there, his tie pulled loose and his hair sticking up at the front, he looked so reassuring and familiar that I just wanted to go up to him and hold him, and be held. But I hung back – just said a quiet hello and sat down at the table.

'Sorry I'm late, Cassie-Lassie. That drinks thing went on.'

'It's fine.'

He was surveying the contents of the fridge, rubbing his thumb and two forefingers against the thick stubble on his cheeks. A kick of desire came out of nowhere. Perhaps I was seeing Jonathan through the eyes of that sleek, alluring version of myself with the sharper cheekbones.

'Jonathan. I need to tell you something.' My tone of voice was all wrong. It sounded as though I was about to tell him

193

that the phone bill was higher than usual this quarter, or that I'd arranged for the plumber to come and look at the cistern.

'I went for a drink with Malkie after work.'

Jonathan, piercing the film lid on his microwave risotto, didn't look round. But there was a fraction of a pause between piercings.

'He told me that I was The One, but I told him that nothing could happen between us. I'm just telling you.'

'How bloody juvenile,' he muttered under his breath, sliding the container into the microwave and throwing the fork into the sink with a clang.

'Sorry?'

'Jesus Christ, Cassie. It's just one drama after another with you, isn't it. It's like *Sweet Valley High* around here. *High School* Bloody *Musical.* This is a very simple scenario – he just wants to get his leg over. Now just grow up, would you? Get over it. I'm not discussing this again.' He set the microwave, jabbing the buttons with a vicious finger, then sat down at the table and snapped Dita's *Evening News* open in front of him.

I'd been prepared for accusations, maybe even shouting or tears. But this impatient dismissal was worse. I stood up, my legs shaking, suddenly unable to be in the same room as Jonathan. I'd go upstairs, I thought, and phone Helen. I'd tell her about the vigil, and this whole awful mess, and listen, unflinchingly, to her no-nonsense advice on how to climb out of it.

But as I walked up the stairs I felt for a moment a terrifying reversal that made my pulse race. I didn't have to confess my sins to Helen, or grovel to Jonathan. I could just walk away from all this. I could call Malkie right now, and tell him I'd made a mistake. I could be round at his flat in half an hour. I imagined his smile as he opened the door; how I would drop my bag on the floor and walk into his arms. I imagined

194

the weight of him on top of me; how I would pull my knees around his hips; how it would feel when he pushed inside me.

My phone sat tauntingly on the bedside table. It would be so easy.

★

Something woke me. For several moments I lay, disorientated, not understanding where I was. I was at Malkie's flat, wasn't I? Lying with him in his bed, our bodies flung out across crumpled sheets. My pulse thudded with the finality of what I'd done. But slowly, grainy dark shapes resolved themselves into the surroundings of my own bedroom. I hadn't made the call. Relief flowed through me, cold and sharp.

But there was a noise in the house. Something. I got to my feet and went out into the hall. There it was again – deep gasps of breath. I thought at first that it was laughing. But no . . . when it came again, it was a high, keening sound, deepening to a throaty wail at the end of each cry. It wasn't Sophie, I knew that much. It sounded barely human.

But it seemed to be coming from her room.

The stalker had got in.

Before I'd had time to think, my legs had covered the few yards to the nursery. It was dark in there, with just a faint greyness creeping in at the edges of the blackout blind.

A figure was standing over her cot. Bending over her. Crying.

I stood for a second, torn between running back to our room to wake Jonathan and rushing at this shape, getting it away from my daughter's cot, tearing it apart with my bare hands if necessary. Until it leaned right into the cot and spoke to her, and then I knew.

'I loved you. I loved you.'

It *was* Jonathan.

And he was talking in the past tense.

I snapped on the light. The second it took me to get to her cot stretched and unwound, long enough to contain the possibilities of a thousand wretched outcomes.

She was rolled up in a little ball, face down in the cot.

'Sophie!' I put my hands around her ribcage and lifted her off the mattress. Her arms and legs flailed.

I pulled her close and she wrapped herself around me, soft pink gingham warm against my skin. I swung round to face Jonathan.

'What the *hell*—'

But he was just standing there, standing over the cot with staring, glassy eyes, his face wet with tears.

'Jonathan . . . are you . . . *asleep*?'

I put my hand on his shoulder, gave it a little shake. He didn't respond.

Perhaps Dita would know what to do. I went to wake her.

'Ach . . . we'll soon sort him out. Don't worry.' She swung her legs out of bed and shrugged on her dressing gown.

'But Dita, I thought . . . I though he'd . . .'

She went up to Jonathan, put her arm around his shoulders and led him firmly out of the nursery and back to our bedroom, where she got him into bed. She stroked his hair back from his forehead, then turned to me, motioning me to go out into the hall.

'Cassie, relax. He's sleepwalking – I've seen it before. It'll pass. He went through a phase of it in his teens.'

She seemed completely unfazed, as though we were talking about an outbreak of athlete's foot or pimples.

'But Dita, I thought . . . he was talking like Sophie was . . . dead, or something.'

196

'It can look frightening, I know. But he won't remember anything about it in the morning.'

'He's been having nightmares about his father. Do you think this is connected with those in some way?'

She shrugged. 'Grief is a funny thing. It resurfaces when you're not expecting it. That's just the way it works. This sort of thing is bound to come up from time to time . . . nightmares and so on. It was a shock when he went. None of us were prepared.'

'Is there something about his father that . . .' – *that neither of you are telling me* – ' . . . that might be bothering him, in particular? Is there anything that I should know? If this is affecting his relationship with Sophie, then . . .'

'Cassie, please. It might look alarming but there is really nothing to worry about. I've seen him sleepwalk many times before, and he's never come to any harm, or hurt anyone else. We both know he's not an aggressive person when he's awake, so why would he be when he's asleep? No. He was just a little bit sad, that's all. I'll stay up for a while and listen out, make sure he's settled down. Go and put Sophie back to bed, and get some sleep yourself. We'll talk about it again in the morning. But I'm sure there's no need to worry.'

I put Sophie back in her cot, but I didn't go back to bed. I grabbed a blanket from her wardrobe, and curled up on the floor beside the cot.

21

The Copper Kettle was a reassuringly traditional coffee shop, with a brown painted exterior and steamed-up windows. I arrived a few minutes early and sat at a wobbly wooden table watching shoppers milling past on the pavement outside, pink-cheeked and well wrapped up against the cold.

They didn't seem deterred by the man who was standing on the street corner wearing a Santa hat and beard over a skull mask, and a large 'Santa is Satan' placard. I'd seen him a few days ago on Princes Street, too. I noticed that the few locks of hair escaping from beneath the furry white band of the hat were ginger, and it made me think of Bobby Spencer. Could it be him, watching me from behind the skull mask? Positioning himself on street corners around Edinburgh so he could spy on me undetected?

I forced the image out of my mind. I had more pressing things to worry about. Jonathan and I had both had doctor's appointments that morning. He'd agreed to see the doctor after the sleepwalking episode as one of a range of measures – including giving up cheese-on-toast before bed, turning his BlackBerry off at night, and a sturdy stair-gate across the doorway of our room. However he'd emerged looking smug.

'Sleepwalking is *not* a sign of mental disorder, Cassie,' he'd said reproachfully as we left the building. 'The doctor said these episodes mostly just pass of their own accord. She suggested I try putting lavender oil on my pillow. Can you pick some up for me?'

I didn't tell him that I already had cupboards full of the stuff at home, or that the doctor had frequently made the same suggestion to me, in her desperate attempts to get me out of her office. Today's visit had been my third this month. This time it was dizziness again and she'd taken a blood test 'to exclude one or two things.'

What things? I'd been too afraid to ask, but the possibilities were racing now, as I stared out into the street at the Satan-Santa.

'Cassie!' It was Jean. 'Are you all right, my dear?'

It was a relief to surface from my imaginings. 'Hello! Yes, I'm fine! How are you? Is everything okay now?'

'Oh yes, dear. Sorry I'm a few minutes late. Gerry had a bit of a funny turn this morning and I wanted to make sure he was all right before I left. He's fine now. He's watching the football with a Tunnock's Caramel Wafer. That'll keep him quiet for a bit.'

We ordered coffee and scones, and Jean started talking about her case. I listened intently, enjoying the feeling as the analytical, practical side of my brain whirred into life.

'So,' she began. 'As I mentioned, the other day, my employers are alleging that there was a . . . well . . . an incident involving Gerry at the clinic.'

She stirred her coffee, and tapped the teaspoon delicately against the china rim of her teacup before placing it back down on the saucer. At the next table, a dark-haired mother appeared with her toddler son. As she was folding up their coats and scarves and stowing them on the buggy, the boy stood up on his chair, reached across the table and emptied a pot of sugar sachets onto the floor.

'Oops,' I said, and bent down to help the mother pick them up.

When I returned my attention to Jean she nodded and went on. 'There was this one client. She was called Nina Deneuve. She'd been to the clinic a few times for the odd facial or massage, but had then phoned up asking to book in for "The Works". They had set this up as a marketing gimmick. It was supposed to be like on those television programmes. The client would first of all see Wilf, the lifestyle coach, to sort out their personal issues and so on. Quite often, they would be talked into booking a series of six or ten "confidence building" sessions. He took them to bars and the like, and made them approach strange men. What nonsense. In my day, it was the men who did the running.'

I nodded vigorously. At the next table, the little boy was pulling at his mother's arm. 'Miwksake, Mama. Stawbelly.'

'Then, the client would see Dr Bourne, the cosmetic surgeon, who would make recommendations for whatever they needed – a chemical peel or what have you. Then they would have their hair done, and see the beauty therapist. A lot of it's in the eyebrows, you know. They don't tell you that. But get the eyebrows right, and they frame your face, take ten years off you. Then there's the clothes therapist.'

'What does a clothes therapist actually do?' I asked. 'Is it just a question of choosing some new clothes?'

'Oh no, dear. They delve into all your personal issues; for example you might point-blank refuse to wear yellow, because of an experience as a child. Perhaps you wore it to a children's birthday party and were teased about it, or something of that sort. The clothes therapist would then have to desensitise you so that you could wear yellow again. Maybe making you walk around the town centre in a yellow coat and hat. And the idea is that this would liberate you, and allow you to make more healthy clothes choices.'

'Oh dear. And what if you just don't like yellow?'

'Oh no, dear. If you say you "don't like" any item of clothing, that just reflects an inner conflict. And then you would have to go through the desensitisation process. It's actually best to say you like everything – that's what I tell the girls when they check in for their appointments. On the quiet, of course.

'But it's an expensive business. You have to put £700 on deposit just to pay for the clothes that the therapist chooses for you.'

'Gosh. Just for the clothes? And the therapist purposely chooses things you don't like?'

'Yes. But the idea is that you will like them by the end. Anyway, back to Nina Deneuve. "The Works" was being advertised in all the Sunday newspapers, and there had been a fair few clients coming forward for it. It was a big money spinner. And the girls really did look a lot better, more confident, once they'd completed the course of treatments.'

'That's great,' I said. I wondered whether my involvement in Jean's case would preclude me from booking in for 'The Works'. God knows, I thought, I could do with it. I thought I could probably get round the clothes therapist by pretending to dislike navy and black.

'But the thing is, dear . . .' Now Jean leaned forward, as if to drop a bombshell, and paused dramatically. 'They don't push the chiropody! That's not even advertised as part of the package!'

She sat back, triumphantly, and placed her teacup back in its saucer with a loud clack.

'Maybe it's not seen as so . . . glamorous . . . as the other things?'

'That's as may be, but to my mind it's because they want to get Mary out! I think Wilf's been planning that for some time, ever since he took over the business.'

'But, you were saying about Nina Deneuve?' I had to steer Jean away from her conspiracy theories.

'Yes. So, this Nina Deneuve had booked herself in for "The Works", and she was in the waiting room, waiting to see Wilf for her first assessment. Gerry was in his wheelchair that day. He can walk, you know, but some days when his legs are bad it's easier for him just to use the wheelchair.

'Anyway, Gerry wheeled himself up to this Nina, and struck up a conversation. I think he was just trying to be friendly as she did look a bit nervous, if truth be told. I wasn't really paying attention, since I was on the phone booking in some more clients. But ten minutes later, Nina got up, swept over to the desk and announced that she wanted to cancel her entire treatment regime! Well, I was flabbergasted. Didn't know what to say. I had to enforce the cancellation charge, but that was just half the cost of the first session, only about £50. It meant thousands of pounds in lost income, if you took into account the full treatment regime.'

She shook her head and carefully poured another cup of tea. At the next table, the little boy pointed out of the window suddenly, knocking over his milkshake. 'Mama! Scaywy Santa, ook!' He burst into tears and buried his head in his mother's lap.

I went over with a handful of napkins and tried to help clean up the mess until a waitress appeared with a cloth. The mother smiled a thank-you at me, continuing to stroke her son's curly head as he sobbed.

Jean, looking out of the window, shook her head and tutted. 'Excuse me, dear. I must just pop out for a second.'

She exited the coffee shop and marched up to the scary Santa. She stood there for a minute or two, talking animatedly and wagging a finger. The skull mask dipped dejectedly towards the ground as it received its dressing-down.

I was overcome with admiration. Never in a million years would I have mounted such a challenge. I would have remained rooted to my chair, thinking about the potential consequences. Would I be interfering with the Santa's freedom of expression? Possibly even discriminating against him on the grounds of religion, contrary to the European Convention on Human Rights as incorporated into UK law? And what if he had a knife hidden under his red velour costume?

But that was no way to live. Maybe I needed to be more like Jean. If something wasn't right, you should do something about it. You should step up and take control.

Finishing her tirade, Jean pointed firmly down the street. The Santa took off the placard, tucked it under his arm, and walked off.

Jean came back into the coffee shop. She patted the toddler's shoulder. 'Now don't worry, you wee soul. That wasn't the real Santa. He was a naughty man just pretending, but he's gone now.'

The child looked up from his mother's lap, his face trailed with tears and snot. He hiccupped, and stuck his thumb in his mouth.

'Thank you,' said the mother.

Jean waved her away with a smile and shuffled back into her chair.

'Now, where was I, dear? Oh yes. Nina Deneuve cancelling her treatment. Well, anyway, when Wilf realised what had happened, he asked to speak to me and Gerry in private. He asked Gerry what on earth he'd said to Nina, as it had obviously made her change her mind. Gerry was grumpy about it. He said, "I can't remember. I think we had a good chat about different brands of incontinence pants." And he wheeled himself out in a huff.'

I realised that some reaction was expected of me. I raised my eyebrows and gave a thoughtful nod.

'It was just a week or so later that Wilf took on this Chantal-Marie woman as his *PA and HR manager*. Stuff and nonsense, I say.'

And who could begin to argue with that? When you were with Jean you couldn't help feeling that the world was being set to rights, and that the process would be completed before very much longer if she had anything to do with it. I shook my head gravely and began to butter another scone.

22

Sophie took her first steps on Christmas Eve. She waited, bright-eyed, until she had a full audience. Mum had just flown in from Stockholm – Granny Britt's niece had taken over her caring duties for a few weeks – and was seated in the best chair in the living room having a cup of tea. Dita was hovering over the coffee table, cutting a chocolate Yule log she'd made in honour of Mum's arrival, debating with Jonathan how big the slices should be.

Sophie stood up in the middle of the room, her sturdy pink feet planted wide apart (I had ignored my mother's loud protestations about bare feet in December). She clapped together the two plastic frogs she was holding, and said a very loud 'Gaaaa'. Then she transferred all her weight to her left foot, and dragged her right towards it. She teetered onto the right one, wobbled there for a moment, and flumped on to the carpet.

'That was a step!' Jonathan leapt to his feet. 'That was definitely a step.'

'Try again, Sophie!' shouted Dita.

'My baby,' I whispered. 'My little baby.'

Mum just sat back in her chair with a quiet smile, as though confident it was her arrival that had precipitated this miracle.

When Jonathan and I came down with temperatures and vomiting during the night, it was Mum who stepped up to the role of Christmas co-ordinator extraordinaire. She dressed Sophie up in her reindeer outfit and ears, and videoed her 'opening her presents' (though she was actually attempting to eat a three-dimensional noughts and crosses game at the time). She put the turkey on to roast, and set Dita up at the kitchen table peeling vast quantities of vegetables, because she was sure Jonathan and I could 'manage a parsnip or two.'

In the week that followed, she took charge of Sophie's care and entertainment, taking her out to the Botanic Gardens each morning, and then to a museum, gallery or soft play centre each afternoon. She cooked homemade, organic meals, played string quartets continuously, and never once switched on CBeebies.

'She's showing us how it's done,' muttered Jonathan one afternoon, peeking through the curtains as Mum marched off towards the Water of Leith with Sophie. We'd both been sent to bed with hot water bottles. (Dita had been sent to bed with a hot water bottle, too, even though there was nothing wrong with her. She'd made the mistake of mentioning a slight tickle in her throat.)

'Well, let her,' I said. I was getting some proper sleep, for the first time in months. And it was almost enjoyable to feel ill for a *normal* reason. The doctor, when I'd been to see her that morning, had been delighted to write a prescription for antibiotics for my sore throat – I think she'd thought I'd booked the appointment to discuss my dizziness again, even though the blood tests had shown up nothing.

'It feels like we're teenagers,' sniggered Jonathan. 'And she's just flown in and discovered we've been attempting to look after a baby all this time.'

'I know.' I shook my head.

'Unbelievable.'

'I just can't believe we got away with it this long.'

*

Jonathan and I were up and about again by Hogmanay, but we hadn't made any plans to celebrate. Not that we would have wanted to venture out anyway – sheets of rain had been moving in from the north all day, wind shaking the house in rattling gusts.

In fact it was a pleasant change to have some time to ourselves. Dita was spending the night with her friends in Linlithgow, and my mother had gone to bed early with a headache. So Jonathan and I saw in the New Year together, slumped on the sofa in front of the television. We watched, glassy-eyed, as four fiddle players convulsed on a low stage and some elderly, bewildered-looking people attempted an Eightsome Reel. After the bells, Jonathan went into the kitchen to open a bottle of champagne, and I followed him in there. We drank standing up at the kitchen counter, giggling a little.

'It doesn't matter that we didn't go out,' I said. 'It's nice to stay in. I wouldn't want to be standing around in Princes Street Gardens in this weather. They said on the radio that there'd been flooding. I hope Dita's train got to Linlithgow okay.'

'Was it Linlithgow again? God. She was there only last week. She seems to be spending more time with Norm and Barbara than she does with us.'

'How does she know them? From some church committee back in the 1980s, wasn't it? They must be scintillating company. Maybe they're all up on their feet in the living room doing the Gay Gordons. Oh *no*, Jonathan, listen. Those wretched fireworks.'

The noise had woken Sophie; we could hear her screaming through the monitor, tinny and desperate.

When I got upstairs and lifted her she was trembling, her face hot with tears. The front of her sleeping bag was covered with purple vomit and half-digested blueberries.

'Uh-oh,' said Jonathan, who'd followed me into the room. 'Here we go again. I'll take her. You go and get the stuff.'

I went to the linen cupboard to fetch fresh bedding, then down to the kitchen to get a beaker of water for her to sip. As I stood with my finger under the tap, waiting for the water to cool, I thought about the first Hogmanay I'd spent with Jonathan. We'd gone to the big party at the Assembly Rooms. We had a photo from that night in an unsteady frame that kept falling down the back of the chest of drawers in our bedroom: Jonathan in a dinner suit, looking red-faced and a bit overwhelmed; me wearing a dark green dress that didn't fit properly, and a brittle self-conscious expression.

The following Hogmanay, we'd queued for hours to go to the top of the Empire State Building, where Jonathan had proposed under a slate grey sky. Then in the evening, suddenly homesick, we'd got drunk in our hotel room and sung Auld Lang Syne over and over again, crying and dancing round and round in circles until we fell down.

There had been some other good ones since then, although last year's had been a bit of a washout. We'd toasted one another with cans of Sprite from a vending machine, me strapped up to a foetal monitor in a triage room at the Edinburgh Royal Infirmary. When we finally stepped out through sliding doors into the dawn of the New Year, worries about a low-lying placenta having been put to rest with an ultrasound scan, we hugged one another with relief then drove home, bleary-eyed, to sleep the day away.

Smiling at the memory, I took Sophie's beaker upstairs and together we got her out of her sleeping bag and pyjamas. Jonathan pulled off his sick-covered jumper and dropped it in a pile with all the other sick-covered things. Then, after I had given Sophie a spoonful of Calpol and a sip of water, he rocked her while I stripped off the cot sheet and replaced it with the fresh one. Gradually, she stopped crying. I picked up the dirty things to take down to the washing machine, then stopped and knelt down beside them. Still rocking, he began to half-whisper, half-sing:

> *Should auld acquaintance be forgot,*
> *and never brought to mind?*
> *Should auld acquaintance be forgot,*
> *and auld lang syne?*

'Oops,' he said, breaking off just as Sophie pulled herself upright and vomited the watery Calpol over her fresh sleeping bag.

'Poor love. Mama's here,' I murmured, rubbing her back until she stopped crying. I went back to the linen cupboard to search for another sleeping bag, but couldn't find one.

'Let's just take her to bed with us,' I suggested from the doorway. 'It'll be easier to keep an eye on her, anyway.'

'Okay,' he agreed, moving to get up. Sophie's bottom lip stretched into a line in preparation for another bout of crying. 'Shhh-shhh now, little one,' he whispered. 'I'm not putting you back, you're coming with us.'

I laid towels out on our bed in case she was sick again, and we all settled down. Sophie lay nestled in the crook of my arm, watching me solemnly until her eyelids drooped and then closed. A change came over her in sleep; her features looked soft and unformed, like those of an unborn baby photographed in the womb. She seemed for a moment like the little traveller that she was; on a private, unknowable journey to places I couldn't follow. Watching her sleep was the richest of luxuries. There was a certain number of times that I would do it. Maybe not fixed, yet, but not infinite, either.

Jonathan had fallen asleep too, his breathing deep and steady, his arm heavy over my waist.

I couldn't move without waking them. And in that moment I was more than just me; I was the atomic heart of this small family, its forces and energies spinning and bending around me. So I lay awake as the night crept on, listening to the distant bursts of fireworks all around the city and the sound of the rain, soft now, against the bedroom window.

23

'Cassie!' Jonathan called me through to the living room where I found him clicking through the programme guide on the television. 'That *Workplace Phantoms* is on tonight at eleven and I think it's your episode. "The team investigates a funeral home in Edinburgh." There you go!'

I cursed inwardly. I had known that the episode was due to be shown tonight and had been hoping that he wouldn't notice. I didn't want to revisit that night – and certainly not in the company of my husband and both our mothers.

'Hey MUM!' he shouted. 'PAM!'

'Jonathan, shush,' I said. 'They're upstairs fighting over Sophie. Just leave them.'

'Let's go up and tell them.'

Dita was sitting on the edge of the bath drying Sophie while Mum stood to the side, arms crossed, holding a second towel.

'Here,' said Mum, as Dita finished off with a little dab of the towel on Sophie's button nose. 'I'll take her.' She carried Sophie into the nursery, where she sat down on the rocking chair and proceeded to dry between each of Sophie's toes. Dita took a nappy from under the changer and stood hovering. Mum pressed her lips together and dried even more vigorously. She hadn't forgiven Dita for whisking Sophie off to the Botanic Gardens earlier that day while she, Mum, had been occupied ironing baby clothes.

'Cassie's on television tonight!' announced Jonathan. '*Workplace Phantoms* is on.'

Mum raised an eyebrow. 'It'll have been edited right down. I wouldn't get your hopes up.'

Sophie woke up for the third time at quarter to eleven, raising my hopes that we might have to miss the programme. But as the opening credits rolled, Dita appeared in the doorway with Sophie, who stopped crying as soon as she saw that the television was on and gave a beaming smile. Mum tutted oh-so-softly, but for once didn't attempt to take over.

I was a little alarmed when, interspersed with shots of the Victorian house silhouetted against the darkening sky, the camera panned on to Malkie and me, arriving in his car.

'Cassie! It's you!' cried Dita.

But thankfully, the film quickly cut to the goings-on inside the house. I had to admit, it was cleverly done. A narrative had been constructed around the flimsiest of events – a sudden draught prompting everyone to put their coats on, an unexplained blob of light caught on one of the night vision cameras. The failing of the night vision camera was a climactic point in itself. But just before the second advert break, the voice-over cut in: 'Coming up in part three, events in the funeral home take an unexpected turn.'

'Huh?' I said, as the adverts came on and Mum got up to go and make tea. 'I wonder what that's all about? I didn't think they'd got much in the way of evidence. Maybe they made something up.'

The first ten minutes of the next part lulled me into a false sense of security. Sophie was drawing all eyes in the room anyway, playing peekaboo. She only covered one eye when she was hiding behind her hands, keeping the other wide open so she could monitor the reactions of her audience.

I almost missed the voice-over moving in for the kill:

212

'But then Cassie, the Braid Hills lawyer, shares a shocking revelation.'

And there I was, standing in the little room off the reception area, talking to Elliot.

'Is there a child on the premises? Have any of the investigators brought a child?'

Of course, I realised with a slam. Cameras had been left in all the hotspots. One of the grievance statements had even mentioned the room behind the reception area, saying the lights used to go on and off in there.

I watched myself on film, stooped over with urgency and tension as I spoke to Elliot, worrying at the bracelet around my left wrist.

The next shot showed Elliot heading for the meeting room to check it as I'd asked, brushing aside the ghost investigators, claiming that he had to check something unrelated to the filming. The camera didn't follow him along the corridor, but showed him, in silhouette, entering the meeting room, then coming out again a minute later. Then it panned on to his face as he approached the reception area again, focusing on the beads of sweat that had appeared on his brow.

Dita transferred Sophie to Mum, and came over to sit beside me on the sofa.

'Cassie?' She put a hand on my knee. 'What did you see?'

I gave a halting description of what had happened, as the film moved on to some supposedly meaningful readings on the EMF meters. But then, horror of horrors, a wash of lurid green filled the screen. Something was being filmed in the car park, something caught by the night vision camera.

Dita must have seen my face. She pulled up close beside me and put a firm arm around my shoulders.

The shot moved closer in . . . closer in on Malkie and me,

caught in the moment of our embrace. Caught with our bodies held seamlessly against one another; cheek to shoulder, chest to chest, hip to hip. Glowing green, white-hot and dangerous.

The voice-over stepped in with a helpful observation: 'Emotions run high for the Braid Hills lawyers as the vigil draws to a close.'

Mum gasped. 'Cassie! That's not you?'

Dita tightened her grip around me.

Jonathan left the room.

★

After giving him a while to cool down, I went to look for him and found him in the kitchen going through Sophie's changing bag. He had taken out a couple of yellow-crusted bibs and a scrunched-up empty milk carton, and was adding fresh nappies and an extra change of clothes. We were supposed to be going on a trip to Hopetoun House with the Babycraft crew the next day. It was reassuring to see that he was still making preparations, with the inherent suggestion that things were, in some ways at least, to go on as normal.

'Jonathan? I'm really sorry about the programme. I'm sorry you had to see that.'

'I know, I know – you did tell me at the time. So I've no reason to complain, is that it?'

'I'm not saying that. I'm just saying I had no idea they were filming any of that stuff.'

'Grow up, Cassie,' said Jonathan lightly. 'It's entertainment. A gibbering idiot of a lawyer will be perfect, as far as they're concerned, to make up for the fact that they didn't see any ghosts.'

A gibbering idiot. That's what I'd looked like, going to Elliot with my concerns. That's the kind of lawyer I'd been – the kind of person I'd been – since becoming a mother.

'Sorry,' I said again, turning to leave the room. If I was going to break down, I didn't want to do it in front of him.

'Cassie.'

There was something urgent in his voice. He was pulling something out of the bag. A slip of white paper. He looked at it and gave a deep throaty groan.

'Oh for FUCK's sake, Cassie, what's going on?'

He handed it to me.

Tell Jonathan, or I will. I have a right to see my own child.

A rush of blood fizzed through my head.

'Jonathan, I have no idea.'

'Still saying that this is Bobby Spencer, are you?'

'I don't think so. No, it can't be. I have no idea who it is.'

'You have no idea,' he repeated, under his breath.

'Jonathan, you can't believe for a second that—' I broke off in shock when I looked up at him. He was shaking, his face contorted with distress. In a sudden flash, he was that keening, dark shape again, the one who'd wept over Sophie's cot in the middle of the night.

With a deep breath, I took hold of myself.

'Now come on, Jonathan. You can't believe that this is true. It's some nutter, that's all. Hey, come here. Don't be upset.'

I made a move towards him but he stepped back sharply. Then, with a single broad sweep he knocked the changing bag, and all its contents, off the table onto the floor. He didn't even look at me as he turned and left the room, slamming the door behind him.

24

When I emerged from the bathroom after my shower the next morning, Jonathan was on his knees searching through the chest of drawers. For a horrible moment, I thought he might be packing up his things; leaving.

'A-are you looking for something?'

'I'm looking for those swimming trunks.'

I gave an awkward laugh. 'The ones you got for the birthing pool? Why?'

'That was Jody on the phone. Apparently Hopetoun House is closed for the winter, so we're all going *swimming* instead.'

'You don't need to come,' I said immediately. 'I'll take Sophie. I'll say you're . . . still getting over the flu.'

'I've told her we'll go,' said Jonathan, his voice flat and calm. 'So we'll go.'

'But—'

'But nothing.'

Great. What could be better than an afternoon with the Babycraft crew, sporting a pre-pregnancy swimming costume two sizes too small, and pretending that my husband wasn't (a) irrationally afraid of swimming pools, and (b) in all likelihood, considering divorce after the events of last night.

In the car, I tried to get through to him.

'We need to talk about the note, Jonathan.'

A deep sigh, and an unnecessarily sharp jerk of the gearstick.

'We should tell the police about it.'

'Yes – you should.'

'This stuff about Sophie being . . . you know . . . his child. He's obviously delusional.'

Silence.

'He *is* delusional, Jonathan.'

'Yes – you said.'

★

'Sooo pleased you could make it,' said Jody, as we met her, Tom and Vichard emerging from the disinfectant footbath. 'Shona and Paul aren't coming, by the way. Apparently Shona has to prepare for a case, and Paul has a phobia of the water.'

I shot a glance at Jonathan, shivering in his trunks. He looked away.

'This is actually Sophie's first time swimming,' I said, pulling her close against me. I could feel the warmth of her compact little body through the fabric of her swimsuit – a Fifi and the Flowertots one with a frilly skirt over the hips.

'Is it really?' said Molly, emerging from the footbath now, followed by Dave, who was carrying Cameron. 'How fabulous.'

I turned to Jonathan, anxious to make this as easy as possible for him. 'Shall we start off in the toddlers' pool over—'

There was a movement in my peripheral vision and I turned to see Cameron drop like a stone under the surface of the water.

'Oh my God!' I thrust Sophie at Jonathan, preparing to jump in after him, but Molly had already plopped into the water.

'Hey,' said Dave. 'It's cool, don't worry. Cam likes swimming under water. He's been doing Fishy Fun classes since he was six weeks old.'

'Did you just . . . *drop him in?*'

'He's cool with it.' And Dave jumped in too, joining his family under the water, his long hair floating together with Molly's like blonde and brown seaweed.

I climbed carefully down the steel ladder into the pool, and Jonathan handed Sophie to me before climbing in himself, his face white and pinched.

'Woooo!' said Molly, bringing Cameron to the surface. 'How was that, big boy?'

Dave emerged in a great whoosh of water, back arched, face lifted towards the ceiling.

'It's so amazing that you can teach babies to do that,' I said, trying to compensate for my earlier expression of horror.

'Oh, it's not about teaching him,' said Molly. 'If anything, *he* teaches *us* about moving naturally through the water. Humans are descended from fish, you know – we spend a lot of time reflecting on that, in the classes.'

I pretended to reflect for a moment, and bobbed with Sophie over to Jonathan, who was crouched against the wall of the shallow end, knees bent so that he was immersed in the water up to his mid-chest. Tom and Vichard were getting into the pool now, followed by Jody, who was carrying an armful of plastic toys she'd lifted from the toddlers' pool.

'So Cassie,' she said. 'Are you coming to my fabulous girls' day out?'

'What's this?'

'Tom and I are staying overnight at Glenallan House Hotel on the twenty-fourth, to go to the Burns Supper. But boring old Tom's going to be playing golf all day' – she poked him on his white hairless chest – 'so I thought we should have a Babycraft spa day! Shona's coming!'

'I can't,' Molly called over, her face twisted into a pained expression. 'I'm doing a shift at our community café.'

'Er . . . well, if Jonathan doesn't mind looking after Sophie for the afternoon?'

He assented with a slow blink.

'Great!' said Jody. 'And it was so nice that we could all get together today! We're trying to build up Vichard's water confidence.'

She picked up one of the plastic ducks she'd taken from the toddlers' pool, and squirted it at Vichard's face. He screamed and grabbed Tom tightly around the neck.

'Time for another submersion, little fella?' said Dave, taking Cam from Molly.

Cam eyed his father balefully, but made no protest. Presumably he'd learnt that there was no point. Under they went.

'Ah yes,' said Jody. 'Soooo nice.' She scooped some water into a red plastic watering can with a flower-shaped nozzle, lifted it over Jonathan's head and poured.

'Oh – !' I cried.

'We all love the water, see Vichard?' said Jody.

Jonathan didn't move, or even attempt to brush the water from his eyes – he just stood there, his hair flattened in a wet slick against his forehead, his face a picture of abject misery.

Sophie threw back her head, revealing her two new sharp milk teeth, and laughed as though it was the funniest thing she'd ever seen.

She pointed, quite clearly, at Jonathan, and said, for the first time: 'Dada!'

'Yes!' I said. 'Dada! Say it again, Soph.'

'Dada,' she said, dissolving into chuckles again.

Jonathan, his face streaming, his expression unreadable, reached over and stroked her head. Then he hauled himself out of the pool and walked off to the changing room.

★

219

'Jody didn't know,' I said in the car. 'She didn't know you had a thing about swimming pools. You know what they're like.'

Nothing from him.

Through the car window, Edinburgh looked grey and tired, far from the magical city it had seemed at Christmas time, with its sparkling lights and shop windows. But he could have redeemed the cold January day in a second, if only he'd say something that would let us move beyond last night's note, and the green-glowing image of Malkie and me in the car park at Braid Hills. I wanted him to crow in delight over Sophie's first proper word, and the fact she'd said Dada rather than Mama. I wanted him to make a disparaging comment about Dave and his Fishy Fun branded swimming trunks, or Molly and her loud rendition of 'Five Little Ducks Went Swimming One Day' (sung in English first, and then in French) in the café afterwards.

Without Jonathan's poking fun, without our sweet, sly, shared references to the antenatal classes and the various disastrous get-togethers, the Babycraft crew were just a bunch of wearisome people who didn't really have anything to do with us.

I thought, for a few bleak moments, about how life might be without him, and I remembered Dita's words about the last few months of her marriage, and the aftermath of Frank's death.

She'd said that love was twisted into the fabric of everyday life. And that you didn't always realise it until it was gone.

25

It would be too much to say that I enjoyed the drive up to Glenallan House Hotel, sitting alongside Shona, who was giving me a lift. But it was a change of scenery, and she was easy company – for once her legal stories were a welcome distraction.

It wasn't just the fact that Jonathan was still barely talking to me, two weeks after the *Workplace Phantoms* fiasco. Murray Radcliffe was furious with me, too. He'd appeared, incandescent, at my desk, going on about the firm being shown up in a bad light because of me and my actions. If it hadn't been for Elliot McCabe's low-key reaction to the programme (he'd admitted – apologetically – that he'd been relieved that the focus had moved away from the employees and their unhappiness, and on to me), Radcliffe would have probably dismissed me there and then. As it was, he'd set a date for the meeting to discuss the findings of my competency review, which would now encompass my handling of the Braid Hills affair, as well as Jean Forrester's grievance hearing.

I thought about whether I should confide any of this to Shona – whether there was any chance she might be able to help in some way – but decided I couldn't face the look of shock that would inevitably appear on her face when she heard about the threatened demise of my legal career. It was easier just to let her talk.

We turned into the impressive driveway of the hotel at about half past one. It was a dark, drizzly day, but the hotel was lit up like a Christmas tree, all the windows blazing. And all the trees in the grounds were strung with fairy lights. The gleaming Bentley in front of us pulled into the circular courtyard area at the front of the hotel, to be met by two uniformed doormen, but we cut left to go into the main car park.

'Jody wanted us to text her when we arrived at the car park,' said Shona.

She appeared in five minutes, with her usual shrieks of delight.

'Isn't it amazing to have a girls' day out! Absolute BLISS! You should see the room, it's stunning.'

I didn't really register, at the time, that she took us round to a back entrance of the hotel, near the swimming pool. She kept talking all the way up to the room, a small but nicely appointed double.

'So what's the plan?' I asked as Jody poured us each a drink from the minibar. 'You said we were going to have lunch, and then go to the spa? I looked on the website to see if I could arrange day passes for the spa but there wasn't any information about how to do that.'

'A-ha! It's all in hand, girlies, all in hand. Because it's Burns Night, there's a fantastic buffet lunch for residents. And our room comes with free use of the spa!'

She imparted this with such delight that it seemed churlish to enquire further, so I just gave an anxious smile. Shona, however, had no such qualms.

'But Jody, we're not residents, are we? We're not staying here.'

'Oh, come on,' said Jody. 'We'll just wing it. I'm a golf widow today. My dearly beloved won't be back until at least six, so I need my girlies with me! And anyway, I have a plan.'

She disappeared into the bathroom for a second and came out with three fluffy white bathrobes.

'Ta-da! I was a bit sneaky earlier and pretended there was a bathrobe missing, so they brought another one up and now we have THREE!'

I smiled again, completely in the dark as to why this should be such a triumph.

'If we're all wearing bathrobes, the staff will just assume we are ALL staying! Come on girls, strip off.'

Reluctantly, I began to peel off my clothes, and put my swimsuit on, followed by the bathrobe. And indeed, Jody's bathrobe theory seemed to hold up; as we walked down to lunch, we passed several staff who all smiled benignly at us as if we had every right in the world to be there. Jody even asked one of them the way to the buffet, and he took us there in person, finding a table for us, and pulling back the seats for us as we sat down.

The lunch was superb: asparagus soup with poached quail's eggs, strips of filet mignon wrapped in bacon, lobster tempura ... all washed down with champagne, glasses of which were being liberally distributed by white-gloved waiters.

Our table was set by a large bay window that overlooked the golf course and the purple moorland rising up to the mountains in the distance. By the time we'd finished eating it was getting darker outside, and the clouds were gathering in low around the hills.

Nobody questioned us when we walked into the spa. Jody signed the book at reception, the two of us trailing behind her.

We walked through to find ourselves in a softly lit, limestone-tiled area, scented with peppermint. Whale song emanated mournfully from hidden speakers. We drifted on, past steam rooms and crystal rooms, saunas and light therapy cabins. We came to an area with heated, curved stone beds next to a trickling fountain, and we lay down. For the first time in days, a feeling of calm crept through me as I felt the heat radiating into my back and legs.

A girl appeared at our side offering us drinks. Jody took a herbal 'tisane', in a little curved glass with silver handles. Shona and I took iced water, served in crystal glasses with slices of cucumber and lime.

When we'd finished our drinks, we made our way up a stairway to an outdoor terrace, and the rooftop hydrotherapy pool. I lay back on an underwater bed, bubble jets battering against my neck and back muscles, easing tension I hadn't realised was there. We spent a good long time there, and I was quite in a daze when we emerged.

'Oh golly, is that half past three? I'll need to check in with work,' said Shona, heading towards the locker room. 'Could you give me the room key, Jody? I'll just make a quick call and then come back down again.'

'Oh, I'll come up too. I've got another swimsuit I might change into. Cassie – see you at the stone beds in ten minutes?'

I found my way back there and settled down on the warm stone. Flicking through a couple of magazines, I couldn't keep my eyes open. I let my mind drift, soothed by the sound of the water.

*

An hour and a half later, the calm feeling had evaporated completely. Jody and Shona hadn't returned. One of the members of staff had walked past four times, so I'd moved away from the heated beds into a small, dark steam room. It was empty, and at least I could wait there for a bit, without arousing suspicion by loitering for too long on the heated beds.

But as I sat, enveloped by the jasmine-scented steam, my mind began to race. Where had Jody and Shona gone? I'd kept my phone with me, in my bathrobe pocket, but Shona's was going straight on to voicemail and Jody's was ringing out. What if they'd left without me? What if I was discovered by the hotel staff? Could they call the police; could I actually be charged with theft? The lobster tempura and champagne surely didn't come cheap. Could they actually prove what we had eaten? God, I thought with a sinking feeling, just the use of the spa facilities alone could run into hundreds of pounds.

I racked my brains, trying to remember my criminal law lectures – was there a legal basis for a theft charge? I tried to recall some ancient cases involving stolen cows and bottles of ginger beer; I could visualise the pictures I had drawn in my revision notes. A decomposing snail seemed to feature heavily too, for some reason. The images spun around in my mind in a macabre kaleidoscope. Then – *oh Christ* – I realised what I'd done.

Not theft, but fraud. A false representation of a matter of fact, calculated so as to gain an advantage. I had falsely represented myself as a hotel guest, so as to gain an advantage, in the form of spa use, lobster tempura and champagne. And even if I wasn't prosecuted, what if the hotel staff contacted the Law Society? I could be struck off.

But first things first. I had to leave the steam room before I rendered myself unconscious. And then try to find Jody's room and see if anyone was there. I couldn't remember the number, but knew it was the third floor.

It was a relief to come out into the cool air after the scented fug of the spa, and I'd left just in time – by the looks of it, I was the last guest to leave, and they were about to close up for the evening. I wandered around until I found the lift we'd come down in earlier. When its doors opened, they revealed a party of guests in full Highland dress, caught in mid-laugh at somebody's hilarious joke, and clearly half-cut already. The drinks reception for the Burns Supper must be about to start. I concentrated on imagining, very hard, that I was in fact a hotel resident, and smiled as I stood aside in my bathrobe to let them pass.

I found my way to the third floor and the corridor where Jody's room was. I recognised the outside of the room when I saw it, two doors down from the lift. Unfortunately, judging from the noise that was coming from inside, it was very much occupied: gasps, shrieks, and a rhythmic thumping noise.

Was that *Jody and Tom*? Oh God. I couldn't go downstairs again; I would just have to wander around the corridors until they'd stopped. I turned and started walking, and almost collided with someone just coming out of the lift.

'Oh! Sorry!' I drew back, instinctively pulling my bathrobe closer around me.

It took me a second or two to remember his name, to dredge it up from the old student days. But of course – he was Kevin Hartley, ex-boyfriend of Jo the psychology student, and near-victim of her sleep deprivation experiment. No such problem placing the man coming out of the lift behind him . . . Malkie.

'Oh my God! Cassie! What the hell are you doing here?' Kevin's loose, easy grin spread across his fleshy face.

'Hi . . . hi.'

'Look, Malks. It's Cassie!' He threw a glance over his shoulder. 'Your ex-bird,' he added, *sotto voce*.

I wasn't best pleased about being called anybody's ex-bird, or indeed about bumping into Malkie in these circumstances, with my face as red as a tomato from the hour spent in the steam room.

'Bloody fantastic to see you!' Kevin went on expansively, drawing me into a bear hug and releasing alcohol fumes around me. 'We're just up for Burns Night ... I've brought some clients with me to entertain – give them a bit of the old Kev-ster treatment! I'm with Devalio's – y'know, the PR firm? What are you up to these days?'

'I'm a solicitor at McKeith's. Malkie and I work together – didn't he mention it?' I shot what I hoped was a disdainful look in Malkie's direction.

'Hey – that's brilliant! And how's Helen these days? I heard she moved to New Zealand.'

'She's great,' I said. In truth, we'd barely been in touch for weeks. We'd exchanged Christmas cards, and I'd commented on some of her Facebook updates, saying things like, 'Wow!' when yet another sunset photograph appeared. But we hadn't spoken since I'd emailed her a very belated, and not entirely accurate account of the Braid Hills vigil, saying that it had passed without event, and that Malkie and I had behaved impeccably. I was now hoping that *Workplace Phantoms* wouldn't be aired in New Zealand.

'Well, say hi to her from me. Right! Time to get the old kilt on. Lots of drinking to get through! Might see you later?'

'I'll catch up with you in a sec,' called Malkie to Kevin's departing back. He turned to me with a smile playing round his lips.

'Well-well-well, Ms Carlisle. So what are you doing here anyway?' To my relief, there was no trace of the clammy, panicky Malkie who'd bared his soul in Bar Twenty-Nine.

'What are *you* doing here? Since when do you qualify as a client of Devalio's? I didn't know they did PR for junior litigation lawyers.'

'He just sort of snuck me in, you know. A business contact,

rather than a client as such. In fact, Kevin's firm is paying for me to spend the night in none other than the Fairview Suite! Are you staying for the Burns Supper?'

'No, I'm not. My friend Jody is staying here and she invited Shona and me to spend the day with her, but the hotel is strictly residents-only today. And a couple of hours ago they said they were just going to the room for a few minutes but they disappeared and neither of them are answering their phones. All my clothes are in Jody's room, but I can't get them because somebody's shagging in there. Which is a bugger, because if I'm caught I think I might get arrested or even reported to the Law Society.'

He gave a little laugh.

'You can come up to the suite if you want,' he said in a sort of resigned way, as if it was a minor inconvenience – certainly not a proposition. 'I'm going to have to go up there soon anyway, to change.'

Reviewing my options, this did seem like the most promising one. Perhaps Malkie could even lend me some clothes. And if I stuck with him, I could always say that I was staying with him in the Fairview Suite. The danger of prosecution would be temporarily lifted, at any rate.

26

We made our way along to the suite, my slippered feet padding on the thick carpet, Malkie's boots trudging purposively. As we walked I quickly keyed a text to Jody telling her where I would be, assuming she'd ever bother to try and find me. When we arrived, Malkie used his key card to unlock the door and flung it open to reveal the most beautiful suite I'd ever seen. There was an enormous canopied bed, a sitting area with armchairs and an elegant chaise longue positioned around a real log fire lit in the grate.

The room had been 'turned down' and the long, thick curtains drawn against the evening. The bedspread had been folded back to reveal crisp white linen sheets, and a pair of white towelling slippers waited by the bed. There was a decanter of whisky on the table in front of the fire, and a plate of handmade shortbread.

I sat down carefully, anxious not to make any squeaking or squelching noises in my swimsuit, still wet from the steam room. Malkie poured me a drink. A cashmere throw in smoky grey and blue tartan lay folded over the arm of the chaise longue; I held it against my cheek for a moment, as soft and warm as kitten fur.

'Look, do you think I could borrow a t-shirt, Malkie? And maybe some trousers or something if you have any?' I was beginning to feel chilled and shivery under the bathrobe.

Malkie pulled open the wardrobe and rummaged around in

a sports bag. Then, over his shoulder, he flung a white cotton t-shirt followed shortly by a pair of tartan boxer shorts.

'Sorry, I don't have any other trousers. I'm wearing my kilt tonight.'

I went into the bathroom to change. I dried myself off on one of the thick fluffy towels, then held the t-shirt up to my face and breathed in, curious to see if it smelt of him. Then I pulled it on, sat down on the edge of the bath and hid my face in my hands.

'Here you go,' he said when I re-emerged into the bedroom, offering me a glass with an inch or so of whisky in the bottom. 'I think you need this.'

'You know, I never asked you,' I began. 'When we did the psychology experiment. The guys that took part ... were those all your t-shirts that Jo stuffed into those jars?'

'Yeah,' said Malkie, finishing a mouthful of shortbread. 'And I take it that those were your tights?'

'What?'

'Uh-ohhhhh,' said Malkie, a smile spreading across his face. 'You never realised, did you?' His voice squeaked up in characteristic 'Malkie excited' style.

I shook my head. When Malkie had finished splitting his sides laughing, or rather, when he was able to draw occasional breaths between paroxysms, he continued.

'When Jo came round to my flat to ask me if I would be in the experiment, I noticed afterwards that one of my t-shirts had disappeared – it had been lying on my bedroom floor. Kevin admitted later that Jo had nicked it as part of the experiment, that she was nicking everybody's stuff. That's why she had to give up her Masters – because her tutor found out. Did you never know?'

'No. So let me get this right, all of the guys who were doing the experiment had to go into a room beforehand and sniff . . . oh God.' I covered my face in my hands.

'Mmm-hmm,' said Malkie, trying to look apologetic but unable to conceal the cheeky delight in his eyes at having been the one to break the news.

I sat there, unable to think of anything to say. I hoped my cheeks were still red from the steam room, so that my flush of humiliation might be less noticeable.

'Were any of the tights . . . did they smell nice?' I finally asked in a tiny voice.

'Mmmmmm-hmm,' said Malkie wiggling his eyebrows in a ridiculous manner.

I threw my shortbread across the room, hitting him on the shoulder. He squealed and dived behind the sofa, from where, a moment later, another piece of shortbread appeared, flying in a perfect arc towards me.

I had an inkling of where this might be leading – probably a tickling match on the floor, if history was anything to go by – and decided not to retaliate.

A moment later, Malkie popped up from behind the sofa. 'Ms Headley,' he said in a low, stern voice, using my maiden name. 'Are you trying to get us evicted from the Fairview Suite?' When I ignored him, he threw another piece of shortbread at me, then laughed gruffly. 'Look, I need to go and get a bath and get changed.'

He poured himself another whisky and went into the bathroom. I heard whistling and running bathwater. I sat and leafed through one of the *Scottish Life* magazines on the table, and tried to concentrate on the snapping and hissing of the fire, rather than the sound of Malkie's ablutions in the next room.

Finally, he came out, wearing nothing but a white towel

231

wrapped around his waist. He poured himself another whisky, and turned on the television, flicking through the channels until he found a football game to watch. He sat down, leaning far back in his chair, knees stretched apart underneath the towel, feet planted firmly on the floor. Just as he'd always used to.

The buzz of the commentary became almost hypnotic. The luxurious surroundings seemed to melt away, and it was as if we were in his musty flat again on a dark wintry Saturday afternoon. I could even imagine a vat of Secret Recipe Bolognese bubbling on the stove, and the ping of the timer he used to set to remind us to stir it every five minutes.

He roared, as one of the strikers on his team scored a much-anticipated goal. My phone beeped, announcing a text message. It was from Jody:

SORRY! Shona got called into office. Tom came back from golf and we got a little bit carried away in the room! Hope U have been enjoying the facilities? Where are U? Want 2 hav drink B4 U go? Then Tom will drive U to station if U like?

'Right,' I said. 'It's okay, Jody and Tom's shag-a-thon is over. Tom's going to give me a lift to the station. I'll get going – you need to get ready for the Burns Supper anyway.'

Malkie didn't seem to absorb any of this. 'God, I'm actually drunk,' he declared. 'Come and sit next to me.'

'I can't Malkie,' I said, in a tight voice. I didn't get up to leave, though.

'I know. I'm sorry,' he said with a sigh, dragging his hands down the sides of his freshly shaved face. 'I just find it difficult to be around you without . . . I don't know. I just keep expecting something else to happen. It just seems such a waste, that's all.'

'Malkie, you're the one that dumped me. Four times. You feel bad that you can't have me now, but I felt bad for years, and in fact am still feeling bad. So just . . . *shut up.*'

'Cassie, you've got to understand. I had to end it because you scared the life out of me.'

'Why? Why did I scare you? That's ridiculous. I'm the least scary person in the whole world!'

'You were so intense. I felt like you were always wishing I would recite poetry or something.'

'No. When I was with you I felt like I was *living* poetry. It was like living life at another level. I felt like there should be a soundtrack playing, wherever we went.'

It had been a long time since Jonathan and I had had a soundtrack moment, I realised, with a hollow feeling. Lots of happy times, yes, but no soundtrack moments.

Malkie looked at me strangely.

'It felt like a story,' I went on, suddenly realising I had put my finger on it. 'I felt like it was my story – our story – about to happen. And when you dumped me, and nothing happened, not ever again, well . . . it was just emptiness, I suppose. It was – I don't know – hard to bear.'

A story without an ending. Could I make the ending be now, I wondered. Could I? Malkie came over and sat next to me on the sofa, snatching *Scottish Life* out of my hands and thumping it down on the coffee table.

'Cassie. Look, we never had a chance back then. And I know we don't really have a chance now, but what I'm saying is . . . we need to finish this properly.'

Yes, we needed to finish it. But to hear him say it – how bleak that made me feel.

'How about you just . . .' He paused and looked at me with pleading eyes.

'What?' I shook my head.

'How about you just give me one more day.' He mumbled it in the direction of the floor, as though he didn't want to see my reaction.

'What do you mean?'

'Remember the time we went to St Andrews for the day?'

I laughed. 'The coldest day of my life.'

'I know,' he smiled. 'I know. But let's have just one more day. I'm not asking you to be unfaithful here. I just want to spend the day with you. We could go to the beach, look at the shops, have some lunch. Then I would drive you home and that would be it.'

'And how exactly would we engineer this? I don't think Jonathan would be too pleased if I just announced I was going off to spend the day with you in St Andrews.'

'I have a client there,' he said softly. 'I go up there from time to time. They've talked before about needing employment advice. It wouldn't be difficult to arrange.'

I thought about wandering along the beach, our hair getting whipped about in the wind, or clambering over the old weathered stones at the cathedral ruins. I thought about going back to that greasy little café and ordering bacon rolls, warming our hands around mugs of strong coffee. I pictured how we would linger over the walk back to the car park on the outskirts of the town, how it would feel as we drove home in the failing light. Would it somehow be easier to say goodbye this way? Would it be easier to get all this longing wrapped up in a little ball, squeeze it into one short day, and then throw it away?

'He will have you *every day* for the rest of your life.' His voice was gravelly with emotion. 'Can't I have you for just one? You and me, one more time, for one more day. One more day in this life.'

234

I gathered myself together, looked him in the eye. Having a day together wouldn't do, of course it wouldn't, and I would have to tell him so. But . . . his hand. I could take his hand, and have just a few seconds. I could kiss his fingers, one by one, and then say goodbye. Surely that would hurt nobody.

I began to reach for him, but then stopped. I couldn't let my life – not to mention Jonathan and Sophie's lives – be tossed around on these waves of helpless emotion. I had to navigate these waters with a steady hand, even if I didn't have a steady heart.

'No,' I said. 'No. It's not going to happen.'

There was a knock at the door.

'That'll be my shirt,' said Malkie. 'I sent it for pressing. Hang on.' He strode over to the door and opened it.

It was Jonathan.

*

He took one look at Malkie, then turned to me.

'Who is this?' he asked.

'It's Malkie.' There was no other possible answer.

'Ahhh yes. Malkie. Hello. Sorry, I couldn't place you for a second there. But of course, how could I forget you after *Workplace Phantoms*? And would you care to enlighten me, Cassie, as to what you are doing here with Malkie?'

'I'm stranded!' I appealed, dramatically. 'But how did you know I was here anyway?'

Jonathan took his mobile phone out of his pocket, pressed a couple of buttons and then tossed it at me. A text message was displayed on the screen:

I'm in the Fairview Suite, rather tired of waiting around in this bathrobe. Come and get me!!!

I gasped. 'This was meant for Jody!'

Jonathan raised his eyebrows sharply. 'And I'm supposed to be relieved about that? Good God, woman.'

'I'll . . . leave you to it,' said Malkie, slipping out of the room.

'Are those . . . his *boxer shorts* you're wearing?' asked Jonathan, pulling back one side of the bathrobe and letting it fall in disgust.

'Yes, but I . . . Nothing happened.'

'I just cannot believe this. It's fucking unbelievable.'

'Honey, honey,' I said. 'Listen. You need to *listen* to me.'

Suddenly I felt sheer panic, impossible grief, at the prospect of losing him. I looked up at him, tears in my eyes. I wanted to hold him. But his face was a brick wall.

'I'm not listening to anything,' he said. 'I'm tired and I'm going home.'

★

Jonathan drove. We purred along dark country roads, through woodland and moorland, past farmhouses with lights glowing in the windows, and holiday cottages empty for the winter.

'Nothing happened,' I said again, scanning his face for a reaction.

There was a T-junction up ahead, and he nudged the indicator on. The ticking was loud in the small space of the car, in the silence where his response should have been.

'But I know that's not the point. I'm sorry. I'm so sorry about it all.'

A few moments passed, and I thought he'd chosen to ignore me.

But then, when he'd checked the traffic and moved out onto the main road, he spoke, his voice soft: 'These things happen.'

Then he turned on Radio 4, and asked if I wanted the heater on higher.

I realised, then, the enormity of this and felt sick to my stomach. It wasn't that there was tension between us – rather the opposite. We should have been pulling against each other, twisting and tugging over what had happened, what I'd done and hadn't done, and what it might all mean. But Jonathan, instead of pulling, had simply loosened his hands and let go.

27

The venue for Jean's grievance hearing was a meeting room in a travel lodge not far from Edinburgh Zoo. She was full of conspiracy theories about this and interrogated me in the taxi as to what I thought it could mean.

'Maybe they don't have a big enough meeting room at Brand New You?'

'No, dear,' she cried. 'It's designed to intimidate us!' She leaned forward in her seat, and her plump, powdery face seemed to fill my field of vision. Gerry was with us, so I was perched on one of the fold-down seats facing the rear of the taxi, feeling nauseous and buzzy-headed.

I'd clocked up only two hours' sleep the previous night, what with Sophie's antics, and my worries about this hearing. Jonathan had left our bed at about two a.m. and had gone to sleep in the spare room. I'd followed him, thinking it might be another sleepwalking episode, but he'd stepped away from me when I tried to take his arm, and said I should get back to bed.

In the week that had passed since the Glenallan House episode, Jonathan hadn't so much as mentioned it again, not even when he'd found me in the kitchen the next day parcelling up the bathrobe in brown paper to send back to the hotel (anonymously, of course). I wished he would say *something*, wished he'd have a go at me, fight with me. Fight for us.

'Are you all right, dear?' asked Jean. 'You look a bit peaky.'

'I'm fine. Just thinking about the case.'

When we arrived at the travel lodge, a girl from reception

showed us in to the meeting room. At the far end of the room was a long desk, behind which sat 'the panel' and Chantal-Marie, the HR Manager.

I recognised Wilf from Jean's description; he had a long thin face and a wispy goatee. He wore a black waistcoat over a loose, beige and brown striped shirt. Chantal-Marie was dressed in a red power-suit, with a bright slash of lipstick.

The second panel member was an elderly Japanese gentleman. 'Who's that?' I whispered to Jean.

'Oh, goodness, that's Mr Kishimoto. He's Wilf's business partner – owns sixty per cent of the business, actually. I've only seen him once before.'

She narrowed her eyes, as if to check that it was really him, and not an impersonator.

'He doesn't have any day-to-day involvement, but keeps up to speed with the financials, and all that. And I suppose Wilf involves him in some of the bigger strategic decisions. I'm surprised they've brought him into this ... oh, my! Look who it is!'

A young woman had entered the room and was walking towards us; a tiny, thin woman with short dark hair and wide eyes, just as Jean had described her. I stood up and held out my hand.

'Nina Deneuve? Thanks so much for coming.'

'Hello, dear!' said Jean, then turned to me. 'Now, Cassie, why didn't you tell me you'd found Miss Deneuve?'

'I didn't know I had until about an hour ago. She's not an easy lady to get hold of.'

'I've been away travelling,' said Nina by way of explanation to Jean. 'I just flew in from the States last night, and came back to a dozen answer-phone messages from Cassie. When she explained the situation, I was only too pleased to come along and ... well, offer some damage limitation, if I can.'

239

At the front of the room, Chantal-Marie stood up and cleared her throat.

'Ladies and gentlemen. Thank you for attending our hearing today. Before we start I'm just going to run through the procedure. Mr Weeks, Managing Director, and Mr Kishimoto, our Non-Executive Director, will be deciding the outcome of the grievance hearing today. My role is to help set out the facts of the case as I see them, for the benefit of Mr Weeks and Mr Kishimoto, and provide background as to the legal position, and best practice.'

The door opened again, and in walked Murray Radcliffe. Without acknowledging me, he sat down on a chair at the back.

'First of all,' went on Chantal-Marie, 'we will give Mrs Forrester the opportunity to state her case, giving us full details of the facts and circumstances surrounding her grievance, and the reasons why she feels she has been treated unfairly by the Company. Thank you. Mrs Forrester – over to you.'

Jean looked at me. I gave her an encouraging nod.

'Do I have to stand up?' she whispered.

'Not if you don't want to,' I said. I wasn't going to let this set-up intimidate her. 'Just read out the letter we wrote to them, if you like.'

She did so, while Gerry sat with his arms crossed, adding the odd 'hmmph' for emphasis.

As she spoke, a calm feeling settled over me despite the presence of Radcliffe in the room. It was a sort of confidence – a readiness. I'd felt it before, on occasions when my own convictions had fallen into alignment with what I was trying to achieve professionally. And now, with Jean faltering through her statement, and Gerry sitting so trustingly at my side, it was combined with an almost maternal ferocity.

'Thank you, Mrs Forrester,' said Chantal-Marie. 'Mr Weeks, Mr Kishimoto, if I could just set out for you the reasons why a decision was taken that, regrettably, it would no longer be possible to accommodate Mr Forrester on the premises. First of all, there are health and safety issues . . .'

She bleated on through her list of reasons. Then she paused, a cruel gleam creeping into her eyes. 'However, the most serious example of Mr Forrester's unsuitability was when he accosted one of our customers, causing her to cancel a treatment regime, an outcome which cost the business thousands of pounds of lost revenue.'

Jean gave a loud, huffy breath.

I put a hand on her arm, and stood up.

'May I presume you are talking about Miss Nina Deneuve?'

'Indeed.' Chantal-Marie's voice was grave.

'Have you ever met Miss Nina Deneuve?'

'Er . . . not in person, no.'

'So that'll be why you haven't noticed that she's sitting next to me?'

'Em—'

'I'd like to ask Miss Deneuve to explain her position – to call her as a witness, if you like. Your disciplinary procedure provides for this at Paragraph 5.3(b).'

'Miss Carlisle,' said Chantal-Marie, with a deathly, apologetic smile. 'As you will know yourself, while an employee is permitted to bring a representative along to a grievance hearing, that representative is not allowed to address the panel. If anyone is to question this witness, it will be myself, the grievance hearing fact-finder and facilitator.'

I shrugged. 'Fine.'

'*Mrs Forrester* will have an opportunity to ask any supplementary questions afterwards, in accordance with the applicable procedures and best practice,' went on Chantal-Marie, barely disguising her glee.

'Miss Deneuve, would you be kind enough to step up here? Thank you so much. Thank you for coming today. Can I ask you to state your full name and address for the record?'

You had to hand it to Chantal-Marie: she had some nerve, acting for all the world as though this was a witness *she* had pulled out of the hat. Out of the corner of my eye, I saw Radcliffe glance over at me.

'Miss Nina Charlotte Deneuve, 91 West Links Avenue, Edinburgh.' Her voice was soft with a neutral accent.

'Thank you. And can you tell us in your own words why you first contacted Brand New You?'

'I booked in for "The Works". It was advertised as: *A complete mind and body overhaul, guaranteed to reduce your perceived age by a minimum of six years, or your money back.*'

'And can I ask why you decided to book in for "The Works"?'

'Because my husband left me for a girl of twenty-two.'

'Oh, I'm sincerely sorry about that, Miss Deneuve. Please accept my condolences. Can you describe your experience on the day you came into the clinic to start your treatment?'

'Yes. I arrived about ten minutes early. I gave my name to the receptionist, and sat in the waiting area.'

'And did anybody approach you whilst you were in the waiting area?'

'An elderly gentleman in a wheelchair approached me.'

'Thank you. Can you see that gentleman anywhere in this room today?'

For God's sake. Was Chantal-Marie some kind of would-be Perry Mason?

Nina pointed at Gerry and said, 'That's him.'

'Am I right in thinking that Mr Forrester engaged you in discussion about . . .' – here she made a show of checking the notes on her clipboard – '. . . incontinence pants?'

'Yes.'

'Thank you. Sorry, Miss Denueve, I realise that this must be difficult and embarrassing for you.'

'Not really, no.'

'And at the end of your discussions with Mr Forrester, did you proceed with your scheduled appointment?'

'I did not.'

'No. I understand that you approached Mrs Forrester and asked to cancel your appointment, indeed, the entire course of treatment. You paid the cancellation fee, and then left the premises. Is that correct?'

'It is, yes.'

'Thank you.' Chantal-Marie strutted round to the front of the panel's table and perched her bum on the edge of it, crossing her legs. 'And can you state for the benefit of the panel, in your own words, your reasons for doing so?'

'Yes. Mr Forrester told me that I reminded him of a young Audrey Hepburn.'

'What?' A scarlet flush began to creep up Chantal-Marie's neck.

I sat back in my seat with a big smile. Even I knew the first rule of questioning a witness – never ask a question to which you don't already know the answer.

I glanced across at Gerry and Jean. She gave him a sharp poke in the ribs, looking rather peeved. He simply raised his eyebrows and shrugged, in a bewildered sort of a way.

'And . . . you found this . . . offensive?' Chantal-Marie was floundering, looking at her notes again.

'Far from it. Would you?'

'But you were . . . alarmed . . . to find yourself accosted by somebody who was clearly not of sound mind . . .'

Keep digging, Chantal-Marie, I thought. Keep digging.

'I didn't consider Mr Forrester to be of unsound mind. I thought he was the most genuine person I had met in a long time. He had a spark about him, a charm, even when he was joking about incontinence pants. Age didn't come into it. And I cancelled the treatment because he had achieved in ten minutes what your crew were going to charge me £2,435 for.'

Gerry nodded sagely.

Chantal-Marie stood for a minute, biting her lip and tapping her pen on her clipboard. Eventually, she turned her head round to Wilf and Mr Kishimoto, and hissed, 'You see! He's bad for business!' and she scuttled back to her seat.

We were asked to leave the room while the panel made their decision on the grievance. I went to order some coffees, but when I came back to the lounge area I saw that Jean had accosted Radcliffe and seemed to be delivering some sort of extended monologue. So I made myself scarce.

When we returned to the meeting room, it was Mr Kishimoto who addressed us.

'We recognise,' he said in his heavily accented voice, 'that Mr Forrester has been an integral part of the set-up at Brand New You and its predecessor, Healthy Mind, Healthy Feet, for many years. We recognise that it would be difficult for Mrs Forrester to attend work without Mr Forrester being accommodated. The conversion of the staff room must go ahead, in accordance with our business plan. However, we propose that one of the other smaller treatment rooms will be allocated as a staff room. Mr Forrester will be free to make use of this during Mrs Forrester's working hours, if he desires. Will this arrangement be acceptable?'

Jean nodded, her mouth falling open.

'Will this room have access to the garden area?' I demanded, ignoring the fact that I was forbidden to address the panel. I remembered that Gerry liked to wander around the garden and sit on the bench, and I could envisage problems ensuing if the only route to the garden, for the absent-minded Gerry, was through the midst of a live sex-therapy session.

Mr Kishimoto leaned over and spoke to Wilf for a moment.

'If we can obtain planning consent, we will knock a door through from the staff room into the garden. Will that be acceptable?'

I nudged Jean.

'Yes, it will indeed,' she said. 'Thank you, Mr Kishimoto.'

She turned and enfolded me in a hug. Gerry shook my hand; he looked as though he wanted to say something but couldn't get any words out. Out of the corner of my eye, I saw Radcliffe hurrying away.

On the way out, after we'd thanked Nina and said goodbye, I asked Gerry why he hadn't mentioned the Audrey Hepburn angle when initially questioned by Wilf.

He looked sad, and old, for a moment. 'It just slipped my mind, my dear. I just don't know . . .'

Jean took his old gnarled hand in her neat, gloved one. It was a protective gesture, and something about it made me uneasy.

'Now don't you be worrying, love. We'll get this sorted. We'll get this appointment over and then we'll see.'

'Yes, Jeanie. I know.'

It was a private exchange, and I gazed into the middle distance, as though I hadn't been listening. When Jean turned to me, the usual smile was back on her face. And we set off back to their flat for afternoon tea, since there was to be raspberry sponge today.

28

Sophie's first birthday came round in February. She'd spent most of the night in bed beside me, and I woke to find her half on top of me, hands propped on my chest, her wide eyes inches from my own. She pressed her open mouth against my face for a moment – she hadn't yet learned to kiss but this was her approximation of it. I pulled her on top of me and covered her face in noisy kisses until she was helpless with giggles.

'Happy birthday, my little love.'

'La-d'la-d'la. Dada.'

'Yes – shall we go and find him? He must be in the spare room.'

'Here I am!' He strode into the room in his dressing gown and seized Sophie, lifting her high in the air till she squealed. 'Happy birthday to you, happy birthday to you, happy birthday to Sophie, happy birthday to you! Hooray! Daddy's taken the day off work and we're going to do lovely things. Yes we are.'

I got up and peeped through the curtains. It was a bright morning, pale sunlight casting long shadows on the lawn. The day of the birth itself had been bitterly cold, I recalled as I opened the window to let in some fresh air. Going down to the kitchen to get Sophie's milk, my mind flashed back to those interminable hours of early labour: kneeling over the stairs, body twisted in pain, night slowly leaching into a drizzly grey morning. It had been about nine o'clock when the midwife, speaking on the phone from the hospital, finally agreed that we could go in.

'Don't cry,' Jonathan kept saying, as he drove us to the maternity unit. 'You'll soon have something for the pain.' But I wasn't crying because of the pain – it was fear. Terror. My whole life closed in, contracting to a short dark space. And as the labour intensified in the stark hospital room, I seemed to feel echoes of the day – far into the future – when I would die. Dim images flickered through from another, too-close reality, like one reel of film stuck on top of another; unimaginable pain, acrid animal fear, people waiting and watching, whispering, 'Not long now . . .' as though I couldn't hear. And most of all, the feeling that wherever I was going, I was going there utterly alone.

Jonathan sat, white-faced, on a chair on the other side of the room as I screamed and wept, while a young midwife held my hands, rubbed my back and intoned calm words. Only when the epidural had finally been administered – hours later – did he creep to my side and hold one of my fingers – I suppose he was afraid to take my hand because of the needle attaching me to the drip. I smiled as the numbness spread through my lower body, and he smiled back.

He interrupted my train of thought, now, as he came into the kitchen with Sophie.

'Is that your birthday milk, Soph? Oh yummy.'

'Here,' I said. 'Do you want to give it to her?'

'Will Daddy give it to you? Ooh yes, please.'

This was our default mode of communication now – I would speak, and he would respond through Sophie.

'Happy birthday, little one,' said Dita, coming into the kitchen in her dressing gown. 'One year already!' She tickled

247

Sophie under the chin, eliciting a throaty chuckle. 'You should see the cake I'm going to make for your little birthday tea – yes you should! I know it's just going to be the four of us, but we've got to do something special for a one-year-old girl. Is she allowed chocolate buttons, Cassie?'

'Oh, I should think so, just this once. It is her birthday, after all.'

For Vichard's recent birthday celebration, Jody had prepared a 'birthday cake' made up entirely of salt-and-sugar-free rice crackers, piled up on an ornamental cake stand. I'd felt so sorry for the babies – they didn't know they should be disappointed, and that almost made it worse.

'We'll have a lovely day,' said Jonathan to Sophie. 'A walk to the swing park this morning, a nice nap after lunch, and then cake and presents.'

★

It was almost uncannily quiet as we set off on our walk along Ravelston Dykes. The only sounds were the gentle squeak of the buggy wheels, and a blackbird singing in somebody's garden, its tune spilling through the bare branches.

'Feels like spring's coming,' I said shyly.

'La-d'la-d'la,' said a little voice from the buggy.

'What do you think, Soph?' said Jonathan. 'This is your *second* spring now – what a big girl.'

We walked on until, suddenly, I realised that I could hear the clop of horses' hooves coming from somewhere nearby. I unbuckled Sophie's straps and hauled her out of the buggy.

'Sophie, listen, can you hear the horsies?' Beneath the woolly hat, her solemn eyes surveyed the street.

Round the corner they came, looming up through the

sunlight like a dream. The clip-clopping grew louder, echoing round the empty street. I thought at first it must be a wedding party – two horses pulling a plain white carriage. The carriage was overflowing with flowers, so much that they almost obscured the long, low white box in the midst of them all.

Sophie was pointing at the horses, attempting to click her tongue against the roof of her mouth.

'They're lovely, aren't they Soph,' I murmured into her ear. They really were. No finery or feathers, no plumes or drapes. Simply two white horses. But as I looked more closely, I could see that someone had haphazardly woven a few narrow lengths of pink ribbon through their manes.

A stately white car crawled along behind the carriage. A diminutive figure stared out of the window, red curls pulled back from her porcelain face. On impulse, I lifted my hand and waved. Nestling against me, secured in my other arm, Sophie copied me, squeezing her fingers into a dimpled fist. After a short pause, there came a hesitant little wave in reply.

And just like that, it can happen, I thought, as I watched Jonathan strap Sophie back in her buggy. A door swings open through the back of a sunny day.

This time I was just a passer-by. I only had to glimpse through to that other world, that world Milly now inhabited, where everything is finished, because everything that matters is lost. But I knew that the door could open anywhere, at any time, and I was as powerless as Milly to stop it. It was a certainty that made me dizzy and weak; I thought my legs were going to buckle under me.

'Oh . . . *God.*'

Jonathan glanced at the carriage, then back at me, nervously.

I reached for him, then. I hung my arms around his neck, and sobbed silently into the collar of his jacket, closing my eyes against the world as it spun round about me.

★

When we got back to the house, Jonathan parked the buggy in the hall – Sophie had fallen asleep – and followed me into the kitchen.

'What's the matter?' he asked. 'Please tell me.'

'I knew that little girl,' I offered after a long pause.

'What little girl?'

'In the funeral car. I met her and her mum at Braid Hills Funeral Home.'

'Poor Cassie,' he said. 'You must have got a shock. Sit down and I'll make you some tea.'

'No. That's really not it, Jonathan. That's not it at all.'

'Well . . .' I heard him swallow. 'What, then?'

I was quiet for a long time, trying to formulate the words.

'How are you supposed to live in a world when that kind of thing happens?' I hated the sound of my voice, thin and melodramatic. 'I mean, how are you supposed to be strong enough? When a little girl has to be told she will never see Mummy again. When everything can be lost. Just gone in the blink of an eye.'

I expected him to change the subject, to offer tea again or to say that Sophie needed waking up, but he came over and stood in front of me.

'Cassie, I don't think I can help you with any of this. This is beyond me, I'm afraid. But I'm concerned.'

'Concerned?'

He waited for several moments until I raised my eyes to his.

250

'Yes. I'm fucking concerned.' His gaze seemed to burn into me. 'It's like you're somewhere else half the time. I feel like you've slipped out of my reach.'

I looked down at my feet.

'Maybe you should make an appointment with the doctor. Just tell them how you're feeling. Tell them you're crying a lot. Tell them you're not sleeping.'

So he had noticed. He'd never mentioned it before.

'Please,' he said. 'I want you back.' Then his mobile went.

He disappeared off into the hall. 'Charles, my boy! What can I do for you?'

I stood in the kitchen for several minutes, trying to put a name to the feelings swirling around inside me. Something had fizzed between us in that moment of eye contact. It had felt like love, and it had felt like fear. Maybe it was both.

29

To my horror, the doctor referred me to a 'Discussion Group'. Chaired by a psychotherapist, the group offered a 'safe place' for new mums – and dads – to get together and discuss their feelings about parenthood and its challenges. Seeing, perhaps, the scepticism on my face, the doctor had assured me that this approach had been shown to be just as effective as medication or one-to-one counselling, in combating symptoms associated with mild post-natal depression. Although, of course, it wasn't just for people with post-natal depression – oh no, anyone could go. Lots of people went just to meet other parents and chat. Yeah right.

The first session was at nine a.m. on Wednesday morning. Jonathan walked with Sophie and me as far as Randolph Place, before heading towards his office. He'd offered to come to the Group too – the whole family was welcome! – but I had shuddered in response and he had shrugged, as if to say it was all the same to him.

The first problem was getting Sophie and myself into the venue – a Georgian townhouse with steep steps up to the front door. I thought of leaving the pram at the bottom of the steps, but didn't have anything with which to fix it to the wrought-iron railings, and was worried it might get stolen. So I had to yank the pram up the steps at a hair-raising angle, Sophie squealing in her seat, hanging from the straps.

Once inside, I did abandon the pram at the bottom of the huge, curved stairway. It would have been a beautiful hallway, light flooding down from the ornamental cupola two floors above, but it had been rather spoiled by the brown hairy carpet and yellowish walls, replete with posters about breastfeeding, contraceptive implants and smoking cessation.

Following the signs for the crèche, we arrived at a small room at the back of the building. A large woman in a green apron held out a hand to welcome Sophie in, prompting her to start screaming. She clung to my body, digging her fingernails into my arms, scrabbling at my waist with her feet, hot tears rolling down her face.

Eventually she calmed down, after several minutes of shushing and cuddling by me, and deep, shuddering gasps from her. I was just detaching her and preparing to leave when another mum came into the room.

'Oh hello, Mabel. Here's Rory. He was sick five times in the night but he seems okay now. Just give me a shout if there's any problem. I've put a couple of spare changes of clothes in his bag just in case . . . you know . . . diarrhoea.'

I stared, open-mouthed in astonishment. So to reap the promised benefits of the Group, I was expected to leave my daughter in a disease-ridden crèche. How, exactly, was it going to help me, in my struggles with motherhood, anxiety and exhaustion, if I had to spend the next week nursing poor Sophie through a vomiting bug before then, in all likelihood, succumbing to it myself?

I hauled Sophie back onto my hip, and went next door to explain that I wouldn't be able to attend the session. It wasn't due to start for another ten minutes and the room was empty apart from one short figure standing by the window.

It took me a second to place him – it was Bobby Spencer, the undertaker's assistant and possible stalker.

He took a step towards me, a look of mild amusement

on his face. And somehow, in that moment, I knew he wasn't the culprit. He didn't look threatening at all, or even very interested in me. And I could see, now, that he was far too distinctive-looking to be an effective stalker, with his diminutive proportions and marmalade hair.

But why was he here? I could see that he might be an ideal candidate for therapy – the childhood bullying issues, and the death of his father for starters – but surely he had the wrong room . . . he didn't have kids, did he?

'Cassie Carlisle? Welcome. It *is* you. I saw your name on the list but wasn't sure if it was you.'

I remembered in a rush of horror that he had trained as a counsellor and that his ambition had been to set up a combined funeral parlour-come-counselling practice.

'Bobby. Are you . . .'

'Have a seat, Cassie,' he said in a low, compassionate voice, gesturing towards the circle of brown plastic chairs. 'I'm co-facilitating today. Liz Collins, the key facilitator, is one of my supervisors. I'm doing a training module on group therapy.'

'Bobby. I'm sorry; I was going to have to cancel anyway because there's a problem with the crèche. But I'm going to have to ask to be reassigned to another group.' I spoke matter-of-factly, snapping into lawyer mode. 'To be frank, I'm not comfortable discussing my personal issues with you. There's a clear conflict of interests.'

With this dubious assertion, I mentally pulled myself back onto comfortable ground. And, God, it felt good to be a lawyer again, rather than a struggling 'first-time mum'.

'You mean because I threatened to report you to the Law Society? Yes – sorry about that. I was just trying to put a little pressure to bear on the situation. Nothing personal, you understand.'

Pressure to bear? Sophie, still wriggling in my arms, grabbed my hair and shrieked into my ear.

'I can assure you,' I said as I disentangled Sophie's fingers, 'that your complaints about me had nothing to do with Elliot's decision to offer you a settlement. The complaints were without foundation, and I'm confident the Law Society would have thought so too.'

'Really? So it didn't make you extra keen to wrap up the settlement quickly?'

'No. Goodbye.' I turned, and made for the door.

'Bye-eee!' said Sophie, with a hundred-watt smile.

'It was a load of nonsense,' Bobby called out after me. 'In case you hadn't figured it out.'

'What was?'

'The ghost thing. I made it all up – didn't you realise?'

'That's not my concern.'

'Don't you want to know what I was doing, going into the preparation room in the middle of the night?'

'No.'

'I was trying to get caught,' he said. 'I knew that if I was caught on CCTV doing anything like that, I'd be out the door like a shot. Old McCabe's got a real thing about anything supernatural – he sacked the receptionist, last year, for claiming to have seen a ghost waiting in the lobby. Apparently when she approached it, it said it had an appointment with McCabe, and then disappeared right in front of her eyes.'

Bobby seemed delighted by this, and paused for my reaction. I raised an eyebrow. He went on.

'So I knew how he would react to my little story. But I was planning to play the driven-mad-by-grief-over-the-death-of-my-father card and take him to a tribunal, or at least threaten to do that, and I knew he'd have to pay up. I needed the extra

255

money to pay for the final part of my psychotherapy training.'

And he'd got his way – Elliot had paid him £2,000 as part of the compromise agreement.

'What about the bit about running away from home with the Ritz crackers and the bananas?'

Bobby fell into a paroxysm of silent laughter, unable to speak for several moments. 'It was brilliant, wasn't it? The little poignant touches. I thought it up very carefully.'

I spoke in my most severe voice. 'This is extremely serious, Bobby. Do you realise that you may have perpetrated a fraud?' I was hoping he wouldn't ask for my case law authority. But at that moment, the mother from the crèche, having successfully offloaded her vomiting child, appeared in the doorway.

'Welcome!' said Bobby. 'Take a seat, Sandra. Why don't you sit next to Cassie? She's new to the Group.'

'I'm going to go now,' I said.

'Do see about joining another group, though, won't you?' urged Bobby. 'I would hate to think you weren't getting the help you needed.'

The cold air was wonderful against my hot face, as I manoeuvred the buggy out of the front door and prepared to tackle the steps down to the pavement.

And then – joy broke over me like a shaft of sunshine. Jonathan was standing there waiting for me. He came up the steps and helped me down with the buggy.

'I had a feeling you might not go through with it,' he said. 'I thought I'd better wait for you.'

'But you'll never guess *why* I didn't go through with it! You'll never guess who was there.' I told him the story, and was rewarded with a small smile, a roll of the eyes reminiscent of the old Jonathan.

Maybe he didn't understand how I was feeling. Maybe he couldn't get inside my head; couldn't feel, as if they were his own, the heft and tangle of my anxieties. But he was there, just outside. He was waiting for me.

30

I went to see Elliot McCabe a few days later.

'Cassie!' he exclaimed when he walked into the reception area and saw me waiting. 'Well, this is a surprise.'

'I hope you don't mind me calling in. I was just passing by and thought I would drop off these employment policies. There's quite a good new one on pandemic flu. A few others, too. They're just templates, but they can be adapted for any business.'

'Oh I see,' he said. 'Thank you. How useful. I'll take a careful look through these. Would you like a coffee while you're here?'

'That would be great, thanks.'

He nodded to the receptionist, and led me along the corridor and into the back garden.

'It's just about warm enough to sit outside, wouldn't you say? Nice to enjoy the sun while we can.' He dragged the garden bench slightly out from the wall and gestured to me to sit down.

'Just about.' I was glad I was still wearing my winter coat.

The receptionist came out and fussed around, pulling up a little ironwork table and setting out cups and plates.

'Elliot, I ran into Bobby Spencer the other day,' I began. 'He admitted that he'd lied about the whole ghost scenario. I just thought you'd want to know. I feel rather awkward . . . you know, that you offered him a settlement, when that was clearly what he was angling for. I feel that I should have been able to secure a better outcome for you.'

'Oh, no, don't worry,' said Elliot, frowning and shaking his head. 'The settlement was worth it, to get shot of him. It was my own fault for taking him on in the first place. That boy was never right for the funeral business. He could put on an act, undoubtedly. He could practically drip with sympathy, when he felt like it. But that isn't what our clients need or want.'

'No?'

'No. What they need, to be quite honest, is someone who can take the drama out of it. Who can quietly get on with all the arrangements and merge into the background. The thing is to try and make it seem as though everything has organised itself. Bobby was far too much of a drama queen for that, always wanted to be the centre of attention.'

The tea arrived, with a plate of chocolate biscuits. I cradled my cup in my hands, watching the steam race off into the cool air.

'What about Milly Watkinson's mother? That funeral certainly didn't organise itself.'

Elliot gave me a long look.

'I saw the carriage,' I explained. 'The white horses. They passed along my street. To be honest, I haven't been able to stop thinking about it.'

He gave a brief nod. 'So these employment policies . . . Do I need to take any immediate action, or can I just file them away?'

'Oh, just file them away . . .' I began, and then remembered that wasn't what I was supposed to say. 'Well, I suppose you should really read them and decide if they are appropriate for you as a business. You never know – they might come in handy.'

'Well, I'm not sure about this one here,' said Elliot, leafing through them. 'We don't really have any breastfeeding mothers. All our employees are men, except for Julia the receptionist, and she's quite old.'

'Well, just bin that one then.'

'And this one on carbon off-setting . . . well, I'm not sure about all that.'

'Yes. Well, just bin that one too, then. Or recycle it. Whatever.'

'Was there something else that you wanted to talk to me about?' Elliot asked.

'No, no,' I said brightly. 'I'd better be getting on.'

But Elliot didn't move. He sighed, and looked up towards the sky, squinting in the weak sunlight. When he spoke, he sounded soft, a little awkward. The blustery corporate act was gone completely now.

'Her name isn't Watkinson, Lord love her. Watkinson is the family dog. Her name is Milly McCabe. She's my granddaughter.'

'What?' I exclaimed, unable to keep the horror out of my voice.

'Her mother, Ann, was my daughter-in-law.' He said nothing for a few moments, shifting slightly on the bench. The sun slipped behind a bank of cloud and the air seemed to grow even colder.

'Euan's wife. My son's wife. My *boy's* wife.' His voice plunged an octave or so onto those last two devastating words.

'How . . .' I began. I wanted to ask how they had coped, how they had got through it. But of course, none of them had. They were still in the middle of it.

'He's doing his best. He knows she wanted him to be strong, but he's still reeling from it all. It wasn't easy, towards the end. They had the pain more or less under control, but she couldn't see properly. The wretched thing had got into her brain, you see.'

He shook his head, and scuffed at a stone on the path with

his shoe. I wondered how it must have felt for her . . . to witness her own senses beginning to shut down. Knowing she'd seen her daughter's face for the last time.

'She used to tell him that all those things would pass . . . hanging around hospitals, waiting for test results, the limbo of not being able to plan anything, the rawness of it all. She said they would forget those things, just as they would have done if she'd been able to recover and go home. And that, some way down the line, they would just be left with her. As she was. She told them not to be scared of the grief – that it was just another form of love, at the end of the day.'

He made this last statement with almost no expression in his voice – no bitterness, but no warmth either, no conviction. There was only, perhaps, a sense that there might be a question behind it, thrown out into the space between us.

But if there was a question, it was one that I couldn't answer. There was no getting away from the fact that she was leaving behind a small child. She would never be able to put her to bed again, or make her favourite meal. She would never be able to go to her school plays or carol services, or stay up with her in the night if she wasn't feeling well.

'You don't look convinced,' smiled Elliot, a tiny quiver in his voice.

'She sounds incredibly brave,' I said.

'Oh, she was,' said Elliot. 'There's no doubt she was brave. She made everyone else brave too, or so it seemed at the time.'

But what about Milly now, I thought – a seven-year-old for goodness' sake. What about the rage, the confusion, the abandonment? The sheer hollow longing for someone who had gone and would never come back. How could that ever be made right? All the bravery or beautiful words in the world could not make that right.

Elliot opened his jacket and took a photograph from the inside pocket. 'Here's a picture of the three of them. It was taken at New Year.'

It showed Milly and her parents piled up on top of each other on the sofa, each wearing pyjamas and a pair of reindeer ears.

'Ann blacked out in the kitchen a couple of days later, would you believe it. That was when she went into the hospice.'

'What a lovely photo,' I said woodenly.

'I'll need to give it to Euan. He's collecting a few final bits together for Milly's memory box.'

The thought hovered there in front of us for a moment, and then vanished into the blank white sky.

'I'm so sorry.' Caught up in a wave of sadness, I put my hand over his and held it there for a minute. And then, because there was nothing else to say or do, I gathered my things together, said my goodbyes, and left.

★

There was a note waiting on my desk when I got back to the office; Radcliffe wanted to see me. Somehow I didn't feel nervous as I climbed the stairs to the top floor. I had cried all the way back from Braid Hills and was exhausted beyond the point of nerves.

'Ah, Cassie, thanks for dropping by,' said Radcliffe. I noticed that his tone was different today – almost, perhaps, conciliatory.

'I've just had an email from Elliot McCabe,' he went on. 'I'd asked him for feedback about you as part of the competency review.'

'Oh?'

'Yes. Oh indeed. Do you want to read his response?' He pushed a sheet of paper across the desk towards me.

> *Murray,*
>
> *You asked my opinion of Cassie as a lawyer representing your firm. I find this hard, because she has never seemed like a lawyer to me. She seems to me to be something else entirely ... a human being, perhaps. She is, however, the only person I would ever consider instructing, in relation to employment matters.*
>
> *Kind regards,*
> *Elliot McCabe*

I said nothing. Perhaps the dig about human beings and lawyers would annoy Radcliffe. I wasn't sure. And I wasn't sure I cared, either.

'So,' said Radcliffe. 'In light of this rather ... *odd* ... but positive report, and the extremely favourable feedback I've had from Jean Forrester, I think we can let the competency review drop for the time being.'

I pulled my face into a smile.

'And I would like you to set up a social event: you, me, Elliot and his wife Lorna. You know she's—'

'On the Board of Turley Sturrock. I know.'

'Invite a couple of others, too – Malkie Hamilton, maybe. Organise whatever you like. A dinner, a concert, tickets to the rugby. Something fun.'

I gave a deep sigh. 'Sorry Murray, but I can't do that just now.'

'Can't do it? Why?'

'They've recently lost a daughter-in-law. To cancer. The funeral was only a couple of weeks ago. I don't think they'll feel like attending a social event with us. His wife certainly won't want to be ambushed for business.'

Murray raised his eyebrows at the word 'ambushed'.

'A daughter-in-law, you say? Well, give it another week or two, then,' he said. 'But don't wait too long. We need to strike while the iron's hot. Move in for the kill.'

My insides heaved with contempt. Thoughts of trying to find a new job, and having to put Sophie in full-time nursery, flitted across the back of my mind; all the reasons I'd turned myself inside out trying to please Radcliffe since coming back from maternity leave. But here it was now: the line I wasn't prepared to cross.

'No,' I said in a quiet voice. 'I won't do it.'

Radcliffe stared at me for the longest time. I couldn't read his expression. It could have been frustration, annoyance – there might even have been a hint of amusement.

'Okey-dokey,' he said finally. 'It's your call. I suppose Lorna knows where to find us, if she's looking for representation. Maybe we'll arrange an event for later in the year.'

'Thank you,' I said, nodding. 'I think that's best.' I got up and left the room.

31

I was on my way to the supermarket the following Sunday afternoon when the text arrived. Jonathan and Dita were looking after Sophie at home – it was a heavy, grey day and it looked as though a downpour might begin at any moment. The phone chirped in my pocket while I was waiting in a long queue at traffic lights on Queensferry Road.

Leaving today for job in London. Packing up the flat. Drop by if you have a chance. I'll be here till four. Malkie.

Leaving. The word slammed into my chest, making it hard to breathe. I'd done so well, pushing him to the back of my thoughts the last few weeks. Seeing him would undo all that effort in an instant. But if I wanted to say goodbye, it would have to be now. Did I want to? My hand seemed to think I did, since it moved up and flicked the indicator from left to right.

In minutes I was there, outside Malkie's flat. I double-parked behind a white van which had its flashers on and its back doors wide open. There were piles of boxes inside, and an old sofa which I recognised as Malkie's.

How many times over the years had I imagined doing this again – ringing the buzzer, walking up the tenement stairs, softly knocking at the black door on the top floor. But it was the small details that got me now. I'd forgotten the tangle of dusty spider plants at the door of the neighbouring flat. I'd forgotten the view from the stairwell window onto the back of the next tenement, the patches of green blooming around the downpipes, the row of narrow bathroom windows with their dingy net curtains.

'Hey,' he said as he opened the door. Scruffy, in fraying jeans and a grey university t-shirt, he stood aside to let me in. My insides lurched with unequivocal desire. But as I walked into the hall and breathed in the musty, damp stone smell – the same smell from all those years ago – the desire dissolved into a sadness so heavy I could hardly move.

'Well, come in, then!' He gave me a playful shove and closed the door behind us. 'Cup of tea? Actually, sorry, the kettle's gone. Can of Irn Bru? Sandwich from Greggs?'

'No, it's okay. Thanks.'

He led me through the hallway towards the bedroom-sitting room. It was empty, the bay window and the ugly stone fireplace standing out as the only features. Even the grey velvet curtains had gone. The rucked up navy carpet – an offcut that Malkie had fitted himself – showed a darker, deeper-piled square against the wall where the bed had stood.

This room. It had been the stage for so many scenes played out between us. A drawn-out drama of intense highs and lows, cut off from the ordinary life going on outside. I remembered how everyday things – chatting about our days, watching television, settling down to sleep, getting dressed in the morning – had all been oddly charged with unreality. There had been a sense that we were acting it out, that we couldn't quite get inside the relationship we were supposed to be having.

And the room had stayed tucked away in my mind for years afterwards, the same scenes playing in endless loops in an attempt to understand it all – what went wrong, what could have been. It was strange to think that it had been here all along, looking the same, smelling the same, in a solid world outside of my imagination. Where had it been most real, I wondered, in the world or in my head?

I sat down cross-legged on the fluffy square of carpet, on what would have been my side of the bed. He sat down next to me.

'So . . . you're going to London? That was quick.'

'Yeah. Ach well, they offered me my old job back. McKeith's weren't keen on me working my notice. In fact, Radcliffe pretty much turfed me out on the spot. It's fine though. No point in hanging about. There's nothing for me in Edinburgh now.'

'So you're selling the flat?'

'Yup. Had an offer the day it went on the market.'

'Why didn't you say anything? Why didn't you tell me you were leaving?'

'I didn't want to make a fuss. Didn't want you to try and stop me. You'd made your feelings clear.'

I nodded. I'd come across more resolute than I'd felt, obviously. A good thing, all things considered.

'So this is it,' he said, with a lift of his eyebrow. 'The end of Cassie and Malkie.'

There was a wry, self-deprecating note to his voice. He was trying to take the edge off the goodbye. But I knew I needed to speak straight and true.

'It is the end, isn't it. And I've loved you for such a long time.'

He looked awkwardly at his trainers, biting his lip and fiddling with the Velcro straps. It reminded me of how he'd looked after our first night together, when we'd sat on the grass in the summer heat of Princes Street Gardens, overwhelmed with feelings neither of us knew what to do with.

The thought seemed to take all the energy out of me. I

uncurled my body and lay down on my side, on the carpet. He lay down too, facing me, close enough to breathe each other in.

'You'll always be part of me. In here.' I held my hand to my throat, which felt tight with tears. 'But in the real world ... well, there's nothing left for us.'

There was no reply, other than the look in his eyes. I committed his face to memory for the last time. The freckle above his lip; the two tiny white spots under the lower lashes of his right eye; his eyebrows, too dark against waxy skin; the blue eyes, too close together. Flawed, perfect, part of me. But not part of my life, not any more.

He squeezed his eyes tight for a second, then rolled on to his front, his face buried in his hands.

'Goodbye, Malkie.' I gathered myself into a sitting position, rested my hand on his shoulder briefly, then stood up and walked away. The hurt was physical – I felt as though I was leaving a part of myself lying next to him on that patchy carpet.

As I walked out, I breathed in the musty stone smell again, and knew, now, why it had made me so sad. It was the smell of the quiet despair of those wintry Saturdays, those cold, bright Sunday mornings, shot through with longing, and the knowledge, held deep down inside me, that I would never really be his. It was despair that belonged to then, not now ... and it was time to leave it behind in this empty flat, with all the other ghosts.

*

I was paying for my groceries when I felt a hand on my arm.

'Hello, Cassie dear.'

It was Jean Forrester, and Gerry behind her pushing the trolley. I was shocked to see that Jean looked older, paler, the lines etched more deeply on her face, her usually stiff white curls somewhat wilted. And Gerry looked just plain miserable.

We went to the café. We talked about Brand New You for a while. Jean confirmed that everything was fine, that she was taking Gerry into work with her again. She described the new arrangements at some length, but it almost seemed like she didn't care about any of it any more. And Gerry, instead of adding his usual nods of concurrence, just stared down at his teacup throughout Jean's monologue, seemingly lost in his own thoughts.

'Is something wrong, Jean?' I asked finally. 'You don't seem yourself today.'

Jean sighed. She shot a glance at Gerry and then fixed her gaze on me. 'Gerry has Alzheimer's. We'd been hoping it was something else, a temporary thing. A thyroid problem, Marjory Parkinson from next door had said. But no – now the doctors say they're pretty sure.'

So this was to be the end of Jean and Gerry's story. The blankest, the emptiest of fates. I had witnessed my grandmother's slow, relentless descent into the abyss of dementia – Granny Woods, I used to call her, to distinguish her from Granny Britt. Until I saw it happening, I used to think it was almost just a natural part of growing old, a gentle, creeping fuzziness. I didn't appreciate how it could gnaw its way through your brain like a cancer, slowly stripping you of not only your memory, your faculties, your dignity, but ultimately your personality, perhaps your very soul itself.

To see Granny Woods, who had been a kind, dignified person, become paranoid, aggressive, even violent, had been hard for me as a young teenager, but for my mother, it had caused unthinkable pain. She told me once that the guilt was the worst thing; wishing her own mother dead, praying for that final release.

'Oh no,' I breathed, my voice catching. 'Not that.'

Gerry, sitting opposite me across the Formica table, stirring his tea with a white plastic stirrer, didn't say anything. But I could see the look in his eyes. He knew what his fate would be. What could be worse than knowing that everything that made you you would be mercilessly unraveled and emptied out of you?

'What are you going to do?'

'Well, we're going to take this one step at a time.' Her voice was strong and level. 'He's going to take part in a drug trial which may hopefully slow the disease down. And it varies a lot from one individual to another . . . sometimes people can stay relatively stable for years.'

'I've made her promise to pack me off to a home as soon as she's had enough of me,' said Gerry. 'Or arsenic in the soup, perhaps,' he added thoughtfully.

We finished our tea and cake. As Jean and Gerry gathered their things up to go, I felt a rush of sadness at the idea that I might never see them again, now that the case was fully resolved.

'You know, Jean,' I said. 'That cake was really dreadful, wasn't it. Mass-produced, I would think. I must say, I don't think I've ever tasted a cake as good as that raspberry sponge. What did you say the name of that baker was?'

'Well, dear,' Jean said, 'I think his order book's full, for the raspberry sponge. I don't think you would be able to get it. Oh dear, I don't know what to suggest. Why don't you come round next week, for a bit of tea and cake? The whole sponge is really too large for just the two of us.'

'I'd love to,' I said.

★

When I got back home, I gathered up my courage and emailed Helen, filling her in on the events of the past few months, saying I was sorry for not confiding in her. I asked if we could establish a regular time to talk – because life was too short, and altogether too tricky, to try and manage without your friends.

And then I spent the rest of the afternoon making Malkie's Secret Recipe Bolognese (the secret being four tins of tomatoes for every pound of mince). It was dark outside – the rain that had been threatening all day had finally begun to fall – but the kitchen was bright and warm. Sophie played with crayons at the table while Dita rolled pastry and peeled the apples for a blackberry and apple pie. Jonathan browsed the internet looking for villas in Italy, for a much-dreamed-about summer holiday. This was good; it was life, it was growing, it was making plans. I pictured Malkie, powering down the motorway to London, and his flat, empty and dark now, rain battering against blank windows.

I stood by the cooker, leaning on the work surface and flicking through recipe books, stirring the Bolognese every few minutes. I stirred all my sadness into it – for Milly and her mother, for Jean and Gerry, for the damage I'd inflicted on my marriage these past few months, for the time I would never spend with Malkie in this lifetime.

But it was happiness and satisfaction – not loss and longing – that I felt when we sat down to eat later. Jonathan opened a bottle of red wine we'd been saving, poured a glass for Dita and me. Happily oblivious to the origins of the recipe, he appeared to enjoy the food, making appreciative noises as he twirled spaghetti round his fork. And Sophie, who hadn't been eating well recently, pressed it into her mouth with her hands, her little, pink-socked feet swinging vigorously under the seat of her high chair. Intent on watching her, I almost forgot to eat. Because it was a tiny miracle – my history, the richness of my experience, being converted into the very cells of my daughter's body. And finding itself all the way up my kitchen walls, too, spaghetti, and toddlers, being what they are.

As I cleaned up afterwards, while Jonathan bathed Sophie upstairs, and their singing drifted through the house, I felt fine. Maybe I will always think of Malkie when the light falls in a certain way on September afternoons. But I will smile, and go on with my life.

32

That night, I decided to take Jonathan away for the weekend. If our marriage was going to turn a corner, if we were going to start talking, then now was the time.

Practically speaking, it was our last opportunity to do it for a while – Dita was leaving on Monday, to attend to some matters in Holland. She'd assured me that she'd be delighted to take care of Sophie for a couple of days, and I booked a bed and breakfast at Glen Eddle, a remote corner in the south-eastern Grampians – a quiet place where we could do some walking and clear our heads.

Jonathan finished work early on the Friday afternoon, and we hurriedly packed the car and left, waving to Dita, who was standing at the front door with a bemused Sophie in her arms. My stomach was turning over at the thought of leaving my baby overnight, some dark (but by now very familiar) part of my mind wondering if she would still be alive by the time I got back.

'It feels strange leaving her, doesn't it?' I said as we made our way towards the Forth Road Bridge.

'Yes – it's ages since we've been anywhere. Did you check whether they do a full Scottish breakfast?'

I shrugged. I wasn't going to be waylaid by discussion of breakfasts.

'I've been thinking a lot about Elliot McCabe, and his daughter-in-law.'

He grunted.

'Yes, I've been thinking about them a lot. It makes every ordinary moment with Sophie seem more precious.' I didn't add that my anxieties had quietly climbed to full pitch since hearing the details of Ann's illness. I didn't add that I felt disgusted with myself at this, when other people had real problems to contend with. And I didn't add that the dizzy spells were coming on so frequently that I was scared to drive. I needed a cue from him first.

'Did you remember to put my walking socks in?' he asked. 'They were on the dryer in the kitchen.'

We drove on, eventually leaving the motorway and taking a complicated route through a network of narrow country roads. The landscape changed, the flat agricultural land ending abruptly as we entered the Angus Glens and the foothills of the Grampians. The last part of the journey, into Glen Eddle itself, was along a single-track road, which wound along the side of a scree-covered slope. Mountains rose sharply on either side of us, dark against a fading violet sky.

The farmhouse where we were taking bed and breakfast was, quite literally, at the end of the road – or at least the point where the road turned into a forest track. Jonathan brought the bags in from the car, and the farmer's wife, Mrs Petrie, showed us to our room. She led us up a narrow, steep stairway, with a treacherously worn orange carpet.

Our room was basic and didn't seem to have been updated since the 1950s. The bed was a squashy double, covered in a white candlewick bedspread. The furniture comprised a bedside table and a tall dresser, both in dark wood, and a single high-backed chair.

Mrs Petrie wished us a pleasant night, and left. The old-fashioned room seemed forgiving, gentle, like returning to a grandparents' house once visited as a child. Something unwound a fraction inside me, and a deep shuddery sigh escaped me as I fell back onto the lumpy bed.

We slept for nine soothing, uninterrupted hours that night. In the morning, Mrs Petrie made us an enormous cooked breakfast that satisfied even Jonathan, and we put on our walking things and set off to climb the highest of the mountains surrounding the glen.

The route took us through the forest to begin with. Liquid, early morning light played through the branches, falling in pools on the forest floor; and it was quiet in there, even the noise of the river was hushed. The track climbed steadily until we reached the deer fence, crossing a wooden stile that brought us out onto bare, open hills. We picked our way along the hillside, crunching over streams that trickled over the path at intervals, gravel sparkling under the surface.

We reached the summit at lunchtime. We huddled together in the shelter of a rocky outcrop and ate the cheese sandwiches Mrs Petrie had made for us. I studied the view across the glen, and far down the valley to the south, where the river meandered as the plain widened.

On the way down we took a different route, and scrambled down a stony gully into a wide corrie, a hollow scoured out of the mountainside by glaciers in unimaginable years gone by. We could see a waterfall, a thin white ribbon twisting down the rock, and I wanted to see it up close so we set off across the heather. It was further than it looked, and to see the larger cascades we had to clamber up the steep rocks for some way, before pulling ourselves up on to a shelf of boulder that would pass for a viewing platform.

I stood, lost in the water as it tumbled over the rocks, pounding into a black swirling pool at the bottom. Every so often the breeze lifted the spray onto our faces. The beauty of it, the way it filled all my senses, made my throat ache. When Jonathan turned to go, I could hardly bear to follow him.

We got back to the farm at four-ish, as the light was starting to fade. The wind was icy now, and the sheep were huddling together in clumps near the river. When I peeled my boots and walking socks off, flexing battered, exhausted feet, my body seemed to glow. We climbed the orange stairs to our bedroom and slept for an hour.

Later that night, I suggested we go for a walk; it was a clear night and there was a viewpoint up behind the farmhouse. The farmer's wife lent us her torch, and we set off.

We let our eyes adjust to the dark, agreeing we would only use the torch if we got lost. Sound and touch became everything: the roar of the river, the crack of twigs under our feet, Jonathan's strong, warm hand taking mine. It was the first time he'd touched me since Glenallan House. After ten minutes' steep climb we came out of the trees at the viewpoint.

There was a narrow bench and we sat down. The coal black mountains were just traceable against the sky. They seemed to have a presence in the darkness, waiting, perhaps, to see how this was going to play out.

I searched for the right words, words that would spark a connection. But the longer I sat twisting my fingers in my lap, the more uncertain I became. The outcome of all this seemed inevitable. This space between us was just too wide. Even if I could find the words and throw them out there into the darkness, I sensed that their meaning would dissipate before they made it across to him. Misinterpreted, misunderstood, they would simply disappear into the void. So we would sit here for five or ten minutes, and walk back to the house. Then tomorrow morning we would pack up our things and drive back to Edinburgh, slot back into normal life, and go on as before.

It wasn't going to be a cinematic sort of heartbreak, this. It wasn't as though I was facing the end of our relationship; I wasn't going to let that happen. But I felt as though I was at the beginning of a slow, sad process of acceptance. Our relationship seemed to be settling into something different than I'd hoped it would be. Not the shining love of my life, but a lesser thing; a partnership, an alliance, a friendship, perhaps.

I sighed and let my head fall back, wanting to lose my gaze, to let it drift in the darkness. But the sky was an astonishing sweep of stars in every direction.

'Look at the stars!'

'The darkness ... that's how they know the universe is expanding,' said Jonathan. 'If it wasn't, there would be no space between the stars, and the sky would be white.'

It was something he'd referred to many times before; he loved to expound on subjects such as this.

'It always amazes me,' he went on, 'how the light left some of those stars millions of years ago, and is only just reaching earth now.'

'And the light has come all that way, has travelled for millions of years, just to fall on the back of our eyes, and be detected by our little human brains.'

'Well, that would be assuming the light had a purpose in mind, that it was thinking, "Oh yes, I'll just leave now, and travel for ten million years and that will time it nicely for landing on Cassie Carlisle's retinas in the early twenty-first century." It's just physics, Cass.' He snapped a twig and chucked it into the darkness. 'There is no purpose.'

'Not a purpose, maybe, but it's quite something, isn't it? That we're here, and conscious, to detect it at all.'

'Yes,' said Jonathan. 'I suppose that's true. How does a

bunch of atoms and molecules turn itself into something that can see, and think, and feel—'

'—and *talk* . . .' I added. 'To other bunches of atoms and molecules.'

In that moment, I seemed to see it for the miracle it was.

Maybe there is no 'meant to be', I thought. Maybe the best you can do, with another person, is try to *see* them, ignoring the chatter in your mind, putting aside your own agenda. And at the same time be brave enough to allow them to see you.

'I worry about things.' I resisted the urge to lapse into a childish voice, to give Jonathan the cue to respond like a reassuring parent. 'My worrying is really very bad.'

'What things? What things do you worry about?'

'I worry that something awful is going to happen. Since Sophie was born, I've been convinced I'm going to die.' I paused. Could I say it? 'Or that something will happen to Sophie. Some days, it's getting to the point where I can barely function. And I get dizzy, and I get worried about being dizzy, and I think I might be about to have a seizure or a stroke or something, and who will look after Sophie, and I might fall down the stairs and be lying at the bottom of the stairs with her at the top, and how will she get down, because she can't climb down the stairs herself, and who will get her lunch and dinner for her and—'

I had to stop to breathe. 'I've got a theory,' Jonathan said. 'We evaluate risk, all the time, without even knowing it. Like the risk of walking out the door and getting run over by a bus, the risk of marrying someone who turns out to be an axe-wielding maniac, the risk of getting ill or losing your job. At some level, you're aware of these things, these possibilities, but you have to put them to one side. Otherwise you couldn't function.'

Was he about to tell me to pull myself together? I couldn't see his face in the darkness.

'And I think that maybe – and actually, Cassie, I've felt this too – when you have a child, all that gets stripped back. Your whole risk-assessment thing falls away, and you have to build it again from scratch. Maybe it's an evolutionary thing – designed to make parents protect their kids. I don't know.'

It was an interesting idea. 'So, you don't think I'm nuts?'

'I certainly do think you're nuts. I wouldn't have you any other way.'

'I'm sorry I've been so . . .' What was it he'd said? 'So out of reach.'

'I've hardly been much better. It's been a crazy old year, hasn't it?'

'And I'm sorry about the whole . . . Malkie thing.' I winced, wondering if this was the point where he would change the subject.

But he let the words settle, and then spoke carefully. 'Well, you loved him once, didn't you. Sometimes it's easier to see love from a distance than when you're standing right in the middle of it.'

There it was again – he had taken me utterly by surprise. And his arms went round me and he held me now, this man who I still had so much to learn about. Looking up, I traced the patterns of the constellations, some of which I'd never seen before, but remembered from school textbooks or trips to the planetarium.

Amazing, to think that all this was up here in the sky all the time, but was visible only on the darkest of dark nights. The rest of the time, you just had to take it on trust.

33

We got home just after five o'clock on the Sunday. Jonathan pulled up in the driveway and turned off the engine. But he didn't move to get out of the car.

'Cassie.' His voice was heavy. God, was he about to say he was leaving me or something? But he was opening his hand, showing me something.

'I took this stone from the stream,' he went on, his cheeks faintly pink. 'You know, on our walk yesterday. I think we should make it a worry stone.'

'What do you mean?' This was so unlike Jonathan.

'Well, I read about it in one of your magazines. Both of you have to sit down, and whoever is holding the stone gets to speak. The other one has to listen. The listening person is not allowed to say anything at all until they've got the stone in their hand.'

'You've been reading my magazines?'

'I was racking my brains, darling. I couldn't think how to make things better. You just seem so . . . I don't know. Weighed down. Bothered by things. I just wondered if I could help at all, with any of it.'

'I'm not sure,' I twisted my wedding ring round my finger. 'I'm not sure I could say any of it out loud.'

'Shall we start now?' He handed me the stone – a cool, smooth weight in the palm of my hand, flecks of mica sparkling amidst the greys.

I swallowed. It was one thing to have a deep and meaningful discussion halfway up a mountainside, in almost total darkness. Quite another to turn and face your husband, at five o'clock on a Sunday afternoon, parked up in your front drive, and tell him all the things you didn't want anyone to know. But could it be all that difficult? All I had to do was open my mouth, and speak.

So I took a deep breath, and jumped off into the unknown.

I told him about the dizziness first, how I worried about brain tumours and about how Sophie would feel growing up without a mother.

Jonathan gave a deep nod once I had exhausted the subject of neurological diseases, so I moved on to the next item. I was halfway through telling him about my possible impending blindness when he suddenly shouted out.

'Mr Caravaggio!'

'Jonathan, shut up! You're not holding the stone!'

'No. There's Mr Caravaggio!'

Dita's old lover . . . what would he be doing here? I looked, and saw a slight, grey-haired man walking up the steps to the front door. He slipped something through the letterbox, and squatted down to peer after it.

'Hang on,' said Jonathan. 'There's something not right about this.' He launched himself out of the car and reached the man in a couple of strides. I followed a few steps behind.

'Would you mind telling me what you are doing?'

The man turned towards us with a look of surprise. It wasn't a threatening sort of face. But still, there was something odd about it, something that pulled my gaze. I couldn't quite think what.

'Jonathan! Don't you remember me . . . I'm Tony . . . ah . . . a friend of your mother's!'

'I know who you are. I'm more interested in why . . .'

The door swung open to reveal Dita. Sophie was peeping out from behind her legs.

'Mama!' she cried, holding out one arm – the other remained entwined around Dita's knee. I edged past Jonathan and Mr Caravaggio and stooped to pick her up. There was a little slip of white paper lying by her left foot, where it had fallen through the letterbox.

You have ruined my life but I will always love you.

Dita's stalker then, not mine. I handed her the note.

Sophie patted my face with damp, exploratory hands. She was covered in strawberry juice and moist crumbs of scrambled egg. Through her splayed fingers I regarded Mr Caravaggio once more. To think that *this* was the face behind my imaginings – this old man with his beige trousers and mushroom-coloured polo neck. This was the evil mastermind, the shadow in the corner, the creak on the stairs, the almost-heard whisper in my ear.

'Dita!' he moaned. 'I only want to talk to you. Just hear me out. Dita.'

'I *thought* it was him that day in B&Q,' said Jonathan. 'Mum, did you speak to him in B&Q when we went to look at mixer taps?'

'Yes, we passed the time of day, but . . .' She turned to face the man again. 'Was that when you started this . . . this watching business?'

'It was long before that,' said Mr Caravaggio. 'I was driving the taxi. The one you and Jonathan took home from the airport. Sophie was five weeks old. You were going to visit her for the first time. You didn't recognise me.'

A flicker of a chill went down my back. I wasn't sure whether it was the casual use of my daughter's name, or the hollowness in his voice.

'Oh, but Tony!' cried Dita. 'Why didn't you say anything? We couldn't see you, sitting with your back to us, behind the glass. We didn't know it was you. Oh Tony, we didn't know . . .'

But something didn't add up. I recalled the last note, tucked into Sophie's changing bag on the day that *Workplace Phantoms* had been shown (of course – Dita had taken her to the Botanic Gardens that afternoon). Mr Caravaggio, mad as he might be, could surely not think himself to be Sophie's father?

But Sophie's name hadn't been mentioned in the note. The only name mentioned had been . . .

'Jonathan? What . . . do you think . . . Jonathan . . . is your *son*?' I could barely frame the question.

'Well isn't he?' He was still addressing Dita. 'Come on now, be straight with me for once. The timing speaks for itself.'

I glanced at Dita. She caught my eye and gave an almost imperceptible shake of her head.

'No, no, Tony. You've got mixed up. Our . . . affair . . . was later, *much* later.' She spoke gently, as though addressing an overwrought child. Or perhaps an old person who was losing the plot. I almost expected her to ask if he'd been remembering to take his pills.

'Oh, Dita,' he said. 'We need to sit down and talk it over. There's so much we need to sort out. And Jonathan and I need to have a chat.'

'Tony, listen . . .' began Dita, in a 'let's all be reasonable' sort of voice.

Jonathan simply stood there. For once in his life, he seemed unsure what to do next.

With a sigh, I walked inside with Sophie. I took her upstairs and lowered her into her cot with a firm kiss, ignoring her outraged cries as I left the room. Mr Caravaggio was clearly one sandwich short of a picnic, and one had to take that into account, when considering the harassment campaign. But now he had committed an offence that seemed to me, at that moment, to be a hundred times worse. It was his assumption that, now he'd been discovered, we would all stand around and pay attention, all jump to his pathetic little agenda and go inside for 'sorting out' and 'chats'. After all these years of pissing around, I had finally found the guts to look my husband in the eye and risk a proper conversation. And he had finally found the guts to look me in the eye and listen. Well, if this pitiful grey streak of a man thought he could just walk up to my front door and *interrupt* . . .

I strode downstairs and through the hall to the front door, with a short diversion to the bookcase and *Animal Farm*.

I stood in the doorway and steadied myself, feeling the weight of my body transfer through the soles of my feet onto the ground. I raised up the wasp spray can so that it was aimed directly into his eyes.

'If you come near my family again, I'll rip your fucking head off.'

He jerked back in surprise. He shot a shifty glance at Dita, then at Jonathan. Then he turned and half walked, half ran, down the front path and off down the street. My hands only trembled a little as I handed the can to Jonathan and ran upstairs to respond to my baby's cries.

★

'So what did he say to you in B&Q that time?' I asked Dita later, while we all had tea in the kitchen. I sat holding Sophie on my knee – I hadn't let her go since our visitor had departed.

'Oh well . . . he was quite charming. Said how delightful it was to bump into each other again. He asked if I would meet him for a drink, for old times' sake, but I fobbed him off with an excuse, said I was only in Edinburgh for a short time. I guess that must have made him angry – if he had been watching the house, he'd have known that wasn't true.'

'I feel stupid,' I said. 'Just assuming the notes and everything were all meant for me.'

'Don't feel stupid, Cass,' said Jonathan. 'Maybe he was deliberately vague about who he was targeting. I wouldn't be surprised if he was trying to intimidate the whole family. I think he saw us as a cosy little unit and he just wanted to poke us and see what happened.' It was a Jonathan-like thing to say, assessing events, fixing his interpretation on them. But his voice was oddly flat.

'You're right, Jonathan,' agreed Dita. 'He would have been jealous. He never had a family of his own.'

I pictured our house, the way the lights peeped from behind the curtains as you approached it on a dark night. I wondered how that might make someone feel, if he was out driving the cold streets of Edinburgh in a taxi, nursing a shattered heart from twenty years before.

'It's not a logical thing to do,' I mused. 'Stalk somebody, I mean. I guess we'll never really know what it was all about. What he hoped to achieve from it all.'

'Oh, I wouldn't read too much into it,' said Dita. 'He was always highly strung. A bit unpredictable. A little bit crazy!' She gave a light laugh, and stood up to clear away the cups and plates.

'There was something odd about his face, too,' I said. 'Something unnerving. I can't quite put my finger on it.'

'Do you think?' said Dita, 'Hmm. Anyway, I'd better get on with my packing. Leaving tomorrow!'

She suddenly seemed in a hurry to leave the room.

'I'll get your cases down,' Jonathan said, following her out.

That was when I realised what had been odd about Mr

285

Caravaggio's face. It was his nose. His nose and the shape of his eyebrows. They looked really quite like Jonathan's.

★

Later on, as we were getting ready for bed, I raised the subject.

'You don't think there's any chance that Mr Caravaggio could be your biological father?' Then, to take the edge off the question, I answered it myself. 'No, probably not.'

I was sitting at the dressing table, taking off my make-up with cotton wool pads. I couldn't see Jonathan's face, but I heard a deep, exaggerated sigh.

'If my father is a delusional taxi driver who leaves anonymous notes and rearranges people's rockeries in the hope of getting a reaction, then to be honest, I'd really rather not know.'

'But Jonathan—'

'Okay, okay. I'll speak to Mum about it again when she's next here. Maybe.'

'But I don't get it. If her ... affair ... was much later, I mean, many years after you were born ...'

'I'm not so sure about that. As much as Mum would like us to think he's nuts, he didn't seem that way to me.'

'You'll need to talk to her about it.'

'I can't, Cassie, all right? I don't want to.'

I realised then that, for all Dita's openness with me, she and Jonathan had never had that kind of relationship. They had never quite connected, not to the point where negative feelings could be safely aired, difficult topics discussed. I wondered whether his angry outbursts and childish hurts had always been squashed with a matter of fact, sensible, school nurse-ish response, just as mine had been.

'But Jonathan,' I said. 'Don't you want to know?'

'Cassie, I've always known.' He pulled his shirt off and flung it across the room. 'I've always known, deep down. That's what the *bloody* argument was about with my dad.'

'What?'

'Do you really want to know, Cassie? I'm warning you it's not pleasant.'

I nodded. He'd gone white, as white as I'd ever seen him.

'Okay then, Cassie, if you must know, this is what I said.' His chin trembled as he took a breath in. 'Okay? Ready? This is what I said: "Who are you to say I can't go to the rugby weekend anyway? You're not even my real dad. You're just a great big sad fucking fake. Don't try and deny it, I know somebody else knocked her up, and actually, I'm relieved. I couldn't stand to be related to you. Because I hate you, you fat, balding, freckly, old arsehole." '

Bloody hell. How utterly miserable for both of them.

'Okay, Cassie? Are you glad you know now?' His voice cracked. 'Oh God, don't cry. Please don't cry.'

'Jonathan, he loved you. Even if he wasn't your biological father, he loved you and he'd have forgiven you straight away. He must have been prepared that you might find out some day, that you might react badly. He'd have understood why you were angry.'

'But what if that was the first he knew of it? What if it was the shock that killed him?'

He'd been carrying this guilt around for twenty years. My love.

'Well, what were the reasons that made you suspect? Surely if it was that obvious, he'd have known, too.'

'I'm not sure. I can't explain it. I didn't know it was Mr Caravaggio. It's just that I knew, in my bones, from sometime before I can even remember, that I wasn't really Dad's.'

'Darling. If it is true, I think it's very likely that he did know. And even if he didn't, I think it's not at all likely that he died from the shock of being told by you. But you should speak to Dita, if you can.'

'One day, maybe, Cassie. It's not going to change anything now. He loved me, looked after me, made God knows what kind of sacrifices for me, day after day, for fifteen years, and I destroyed it all in one clumsy, vicious swipe.'

And then, here it came. The Jonathan Special. The pulling up by the bootstraps, the assertion of a position, the stepping over his emotions.

'Look, either he died because of what I said or he didn't, but we'll never know. Either way, it won't bring him back. I've gotten along fine for twenty years by not dwelling on it, and I don't intend to start now.'

★

We all saw Dita off at the airport the next day. Jonathan had taken the day off work and he drove us there, Sophie wailing the whole journey, trying to squeeze her arms out of the straps of her childseat.

While he parked the car, Dita and I got her bags checked in, and then took the escalator up to the food court. I bought some tea for us both and a couple of claggy muffins wrapped in cellophane.

'Thanks so much, Dita – for everything. I don't know what I would've done without you these past few months.'

Dita tore a bit of her muffin off and gave it to Sophie, who partially dissolved it in her mouth before rubbing it into her pink flowery top.

'Oh, I don't feel I've been much use. Tony harassing us – that was all my fault. Ah, what a mess.'

'Don't be silly,' I said. 'It wasn't your fault. And we're really going to miss you.'

'You know,' she continued, eyeing me carefully. 'I've got a little confession to make.'

Oh God, this was it. I felt like putting my hands over my ears, running away. She should be telling Jonathan – and where had he got to, anyway?

'Well,' she continued. 'I didn't say anything before, because I wasn't sure of my plans. But I'm actually coming back to Scotland in June, to stay for a while.'

'Really?'

'Yes, I'll be staying at Linlithgow.'

'Linlithgow? You mean with Norm and Barbara?'

'Well.' There was a pause. 'Not so much Barbara. She . . . ah, well she died.'

'Oh no! God, I'm sorry.'

'She . . . she died about five years ago actually.'

'I'm so sorry, Dita, I didn't realise. Jonathan never said. I'm not sure he even . . .'

She poured herself another cup of tea, and stirred a sachet of sugar into it. 'He may not have picked up on it, no.'

'So the trips to Linlithgow . . .'

Her cheeks reddened. 'Norm and I have become quite close.'

Alongside the sincere relief that we had bypassed all discussion of Jonathan's paternity, I felt a rush of affection for her. However messy her past with Frank and Tony, she deserved the chance of some happiness after all these years of widowhood.

'That's *fabulous*, Dita. I couldn't be more pleased. You'll have to introduce me.'

'We're hoping it's going to be a long-term thing, but I guess we'll just need to see if it works out. In any case, while I'm here I'd be happy to come over . . . maybe one day a week or something? To look after Sophie? Or I could babysit in the evenings so you and Jonathan could go out.'

'That would be great.'

'And you know, Cassie, there's something else I wanted to say to you.'

'Oh?'

'I love being Nana Dita. I love that you and I have got so close. I'm grateful that you and Jonathan have let me into your life, so kindly and beautifully. But you've got a mother too. I just wanted to say that . . . well, your mother is a good woman. A bit tense perhaps. Slightly overbearing. Very controlling.' She gave a little frown, a twist of the mouth, which made me want to laugh. 'But she's a good woman, nonetheless.'

'Hmm. Yes, I know.'

'I just think that . . . well, you and your mum might benefit from a good long talk.'

'I've tried to talk to her about things . . . she just refuses to—'

'You'll have to make her, Cassie. You can do it. You managed to do it with Jonathan. The two of you are talking now, no?'

'Yes, but—'

'It takes so many different kinds of courage to love a person, Cassie. Nobody said it was easy. But you're stronger than you think you are.'

I leaned over and hugged her, holding her close against me for a few seconds. Sophie smacked her crumby hands on the high chair tray.

'Ah Sophie, you want a cuddle too? Come to Nana Dita.'

290

34

'Aaaaa-choooo!'

It was the following week and I was attempting to attend another session of the New Parents Discussion Group (the Friday morning session – with a different facilitator). However, Mabel, green-aproned supervisor of the crèche, was clearly not one hundred per cent well.

'Oh, don't worry, love,' she said after depositing the contents of her nose into a tissue. 'It's just a touch of hayfever.'

March seemed early for hayfever. But I had psyched myself up for the session and was reluctant to miss it. And two other little boys were already there in the crèche, playing with a young blonde girl who seemed in good health. So I extricated myself from Sophie, said goodbye with a cheerful smile, and went next door to the Group.

Two women were already there, chatting. I chose a chair on the other side of the circle and sat down.

'Well, I did comb tea tree oil through his hair,' one of them was saying. 'But I didn't like to use any of those harsh chemicals.'

'Will that kill them, though?' asked the other. 'I've heard they're a bugger to get rid of.'

'Well, I had a quick look this morning. I couldn't see anything crawling, certainly. Though he was still scratching quite a lot in the car, on the way here.'

Quietly, I rose from my seat and returned to the crèche. I swooped up Sophie and left, with a wave to Mabel, who was busy blowing her nose again.

Coming out of the front door, I nearly collided with someone who was on their way in.

'Cassie!'

'Paul!'

It was *River City* Paul, Shona's husband from the Babycraft group. He was carrying Elgin against his chest.

'Are you . . . ?' he began, glancing through the door.

'Oh. I was going to the New Parents Discussion Group. But unfortunately there's a lice infestation at the crèche.'

'Oh, crikey. I think we'll steer clear then.'

We walked out onto the steps.

'I'll help you,' said Paul. He strapped Elgin into his buggy, which was at the bottom of the steps, chained to the railings, and helped me carry Sophie's buggy down.

'Hang on,' said Paul, 'I think I'll just give Elgin some milk. He's starving.' He sat down on the step beside the buggy and pulled a carton of baby milk and a bottle out of the bag he was carrying. Holding the opened sterilised bottle between his knees, he cut open the milk carton with a small pair of scissors and poured the contents in. Elgin's hands waved for the bottle, and he grabbed it and sucked greedily.

The street seemed to spin round a little. Dizziness again. I sat down next to Paul.

'So has Shona stopped breastfeeding altogether now, then?' I asked, with a nod towards the empty carton.

'Oh God, yes,' said Paul. 'Breastfeeding was destroying her – it was the reason she was referred to the Group.'

'So Shona was referred to the Group . . . not . . . you?'

'Oh yes. Except she can never go, because she's usually in court in the mornings. So I go instead. I pick up any leaflets, tell her what topics they've discussed.'

'Goodness. Is she okay?'

'Yes. But she's been on antidepressants since November. She just pushed herself far too hard. She was working full time, obviously, and up several times through the night feeding Elgin. Because he wouldn't take a bottle from me during the day, he was always really hungry at night. And she just kept feeding him, because it was the only time she got to spend with him. On top of that, she was still expressing milk at work, three times a day, to keep up her supply, even though that milk ended up being thrown away, because Elgin wouldn't drink it from a bottle. And she had to make up that time at the end of the day to keep up her billable hours, so she was working later and later. Eventually, she went to pieces. Just went to bed and didn't get up for three days. Didn't even call into the office. I had to phone in for her, didn't know what to say.'

'Paul, why on earth didn't she say anything? I feel terrible. I was up at Glenallan House with her in January, and she didn't say a word.'

'She was a bit better by January – by that time she'd stopped the feeding, and had been on the antidepressants for a while. What could you have done, though, anyway? And don't take this the wrong way, but I don't think she would have wanted to talk to you about it. She thought she was such a bad mother compared to you. The way you stepped back, with your career, working part time so you could still spend lots of time with Sophie.'

'Well, listen. Tell her I'll give her a call. We'll meet up for coffee or something.'

'That would be nice, she'd like that. But she's back working full time now, of course, so it would really need to be at the weekend. And she's got that court case coming up – the one about the woman with the alien tumour thing. So she won't be around much.'

Sophie had fallen asleep in her buggy. I reached across to pull the fleecy pram cover over her. Elgin continued to suck noisily at his nearly empty bottle.

'And what about you?' I asked. 'How are you getting on?'

'Actually, I'm fine. Things are going quite well for me. You know my blog, *Dads Aloud*? Well, I've expanded into a social networking website. For dads rather than mums, and particularly those who take on the main childcaring role. In fact, I'm going to be on a radio programme next week, talking about the whole breastfeeding/bottle feeding debate – giving the other side of the story, so to speak.'

'Wow, that's amazing.' It was wonderful to hear him speak with such confidence. I thought back to the Babycraft classes in Colinton, with the hippy-ish teacher and her flip charts, all of us too scared to speak. 'I hope our Babycraft teacher doesn't find out you've become an anti-breastfeeding campaigner.'

'I wouldn't call it that,' laughed Paul. 'At least not out loud. Listen, do you want to go and get a coffee? We spend all day in town on Fridays so we can get a lift home with Shona.'

'Great.' I stood up, and the ground seemed to swim underneath me. I fell backwards onto the steps. 'Ow,' I said, rubbing my hip, where I'd bashed it against the stone edge.

'You okay?'

'Yes. I just went dizzy there for a second. I get that sometimes.'

'Oh, I used to get that,' he said, unconcerned. 'Are you stressed? You might be overbreathing. That's what it was with me.'

'What?'

'Breathing too quickly and shallowly. From the chest rather than the diaphragm.' He placed one hand on his chest and the other on his tummy, and breathed slowly in and out.

'Happens when you get stressed . . . Too much oxygen . . . Too little carbon dioxide . . . Can cause all sorts of symptoms.'

'What sort of symptoms?'

He turned to face me. 'Dizziness, tingling, chest pain. Christ, I can't even remember them all. Feeling sort of strange and outside of yourself . . . even seeing things that aren't there. The problem is, you can get so anxious about the symptoms that you actually overbreathe even more. I used to get it as a teenager.'

'Really?'

'Bullying at school,' he said matter-of-factly.

'That's awful.'

He shrugged a shoulder.

'So what should you do?' I asked. 'Take deep breaths?'

'No, that makes it worse. You need to breathe slowly and quietly. Here.' He reached for my hand and placed it so that it was covering my mouth and one of my nostrils. 'Sit quietly. Breathe from your tummy and not your chest.'

I sat breathing like that for several minutes, Paul doing the same beside me. At first I wanted to giggle – we did attract a few curious glances from passers-by. But the dizziness passed. My head cleared. I felt tentatively hopeful, but also scared of being hopeful. For what if I really was ill? If I put down my worries, I might not be strong enough to take them back again, if I needed to.

'Shh,' said Paul. 'You're speeding up again. Just think slow thoughts.'

But Elgin started crying, so we abandoned our slow thoughts and made our way down to Stockbridge. After a visit to the swing park and a trip to feed the ducks at Inverleith Pond, Paul and Elgin came back to ours for lunch and a play in the garden.

It was easy to spend time with Paul. We talked when we

felt like it, lapsed into long, companionable silences when we didn't. He dropped more information about overbreathing into the conversation as he remembered it, and we practised the exercises during the rare moments when the babies were playing happily and independently. We covered other topics, too. We swapped tips about feeding babies, helping them to sleep and dealing with tantrums. Paul told me how he managed to get Elgin's toenails cut, and gave me a recipe for pasta sauce with eight different hidden vegetables. I demonstrated the headlock technique I used to brush Sophie's teeth, and gave him a list of three child-friendly restaurants.

It almost felt like being with Helen – but different. Discussions between Helen and me had tended to centre around relationships and work, with a smattering of self-help-book psychological analysis, both of ourselves and other cases who merited analysis from afar. She wouldn't have appreciated the finer points of baby nutrition, or the merits of baby art classes, which Paul and Elgin did every Tuesday, versus the (very optimistically named) 'music' classes Sophie and I had attended a couple of times.

When it was time for them to leave – they were getting the bus up to Shona's office – I suggested we should meet up the following Friday, too. Paul smiled shyly, and said that would be lovely. We stood waving at the door. Sophie's body shoogled against me as she flapped her arms vigorously and shouted, 'Byyyyyyye! Byyyyyye!'

It occurred to me then that, for all the ridicule Jonathan and I had heaped upon it, Babycraft might have served its purpose after all. After all these months of struggle, and worry, and not measuring up, I might just have found a friend. And maybe, if we were very lucky indeed, we could struggle, and worry, and not measure up together.

35

I went to see Jean and Gerry the following Monday after work. I'd worried about how they might be coping, in the aftermath of Gerry's Alzheimer's diagnosis, but Jean ushered me in to the sitting room cheerfully, whisking my coat and my briefcase away and handing me a cup and saucer. Gerry was there, sitting in his usual chair by the fire.

'We've started a list together – of things we think Gerry will still be able to enjoy, whatever the state of his mental faculties may be.'

She waggled over to the bureau, then handed me a piece of paper with a beaming smile. This is what it said:

'My Fair Lady'
Bacon sandwiches

I looked up, wondering what reaction was expected of me.

'It's not exhaustive, of course,' said Jean apologetically.

'What about sitting in the garden?' I suggested.

'Bubble baths . . .' went on Jean.

'And that raspberry sponge, wherever it's got to,' said Gerry. 'I expect to be waited on hand and foot, you know, woman.'

By the time Jean had come back into the sitting room with a tray bearing tea and cake, I had tired Gerry out with observations about the weather, and he had slumped back against the cushions, asleep.

I gave Jean a desperate look. Now that she'd broached the subject of Alzheimer's, I wanted to ask her a question but didn't know how.

'What's the matter, love?' she asked gently. 'He's an old man. These things happen. If it wasn't this it would've been something else.'

'But Jean.' I paused as I tried to find the words. 'How are you going to save your marriage?'

She smiled and let me continue.

'How are you going to keep loving him, when he's not even ... him ... anymore?' From my experience with Granny Woods, I knew what would happen. With each tiny thread of memory that was lost, another piece of Gerry would disappear. Until there was nothing left but a body.

'The end of your life, darling, that's not really the point. It's not as if we have to wait until the end of the story to find out how it all turned out. Me and Gerry, we already know.'

She crossed over to the couch where Gerry lay and kissed the tip of her right index finger, before touching it gently to his lips.

'There's always going to be a goodbye at the end, whenever you love someone. There's no easy way, whether you're young or old.'

That's what I had been running from all these months – the shadow of that goodbye. I felt it every time I looked at Sophie's sleeping face; it was there in every moment that I loved her. But, even as I feared it, I knew that it held the moment down, stopped it from floating away with no consequence, like a wisp of a dream.

'I'll keep Gerry going as long as I can; I'll be his memory, as far as I'm able. The list's only a bit of fun, but it's important, really. I'll play him his favourite music when he can't remember what it's called. I'll sit him in the garden among the flowers, with the sun on his face, so he can smell the lavender and hear the bees. I'll keep him together, as long as there's anything of me left.'

There was a determination on her face that made me understand that her love encompassed all roles. It was the love of a wife, and a best friend. It was a maternal love.

'Think about it, dear. Think about all the things you did for Sophie when she was tiny. Babies don't know what's going on, they can't understand what's being said to them. But we read stories to them, we sing to them, we dress them in nice clothes. We talk to them even though they don't understand. Just because Gerry's at the end of his life rather than the beginning, why should that make any difference?'

I thought about pushing Sophie round the park in her pram, pointing out the flowers, the pond, the ducks, and the pigeons for the thousandth time, as her gaze drifted upwards to the trees and the sky. Jean was right; we have faith that it sinks in somehow, that they can feel love in the air all around them even if they can't give it a name.

And now Sophie was bigger, it was the same but different. I thought about the picture books I had to read ten times over each night, the interminable games of peekaboo which were only allowed to end when she got bored. I thought about how I'd learned to make her laugh when she was pouting, by tickling the corner of her mouth; the way I had to remember to take her sippy cup everywhere, and her favourite grey bunny. In a few years there would be homework to help with, and swimming lessons to drive her to, worries to be listened to. And so it would go on throughout a lifetime together – small, everyday acts, fixing the love in place, again and again and again.

Jean sat down next to me on the sofa and picked up a photograph album from the coffee table. 'Have a look at this. Gerry bought this yesterday, and he's been going through the old photographs, finding the ones he wants to put in.'

I turned to the first photograph, and she leaned over me, pointing.

'Here, see . . . now this is the church where we got married. Beautiful, isn't it? A draughty old place in the middle of nowhere.'

'But this isn't . . .' The picture showed Jean, wearing her raincoat and a headscarf over her white curls, standing smiling by the door of the church.

'No, not our wedding day, no! Gerry and I pop back from time to time. This was last summer – we were driving home from visiting friends one evening, and we stopped by as we were passing. There was nobody about and we just took a wander around the churchyard.'

She turned the page before I could say anything.

'And here's Robert's first day of school. Our son, you know. Lives in London now. See his uniform? So smart. The toes were out of those shoes in a matter of weeks, though. We didn't go back to that shop. Oh, and here's a picture of that snowman we built on Christmas morning . . . that Christmas back in the Eighties when it actually snowed, do you remember?'

'Yes. I do . . .' An image flashed into my mind – my mother taking me sledging near Corstorphine Hill.

'Oh my, look at these sunflowers! I'd forgotten about them . . . the ones that grew so tall that very hot summer . . . when was that, now? See how small I look standing next to them? And Robert just a wee baby.'

She turned the page as if to move on, but the rest of the pages in the album were blank.

'Ah, that's as far as he's got then. He wanted to do more this afternoon, but he'll probably sleep till tea time now, bless him.'

'It's . . . lovely.'

'Oh, have I forgotten the sugar? I'll just go and get it. Have a look at the inside cover. It's T.S. Eliot, Gerry said.'

She disappeared off to the kitchen with a shuddery breath, her hand squirrelling in her pocket for a tissue. I wondered if I should go after her, but then . . . I found the place where Gerry had written his inscription.

It was just a few lines in shaky handwriting.

> *There is a time for the evening under starlight,*
> *A time for the evening under lamplight*
> *(The evening with the photograph album).*
> *Love is most nearly itself*
> *When here and now cease to matter.*

It was from *Four Quartets*. I'd studied it for my final-year dissertation, but the words had never hit home like this. Something was falling into place, at the back of my mind, just out of reach. I closed my eyes and seemed to see Jean sitting with Gerry, on this very sofa, in a few years' time. She was going through the album with him, coaxing him to remember names and places that were slipping into the relentless swirl of the past. And I realised that the act of remembering these moments – fiercely reclaiming them, with love – was as valid as the lived experiences themselves. Reworking the past into the present, like kneading dough, so that each could help make sense of the other. Layer upon layer of love, over the years.

And the bravery needed to do it, to feel that love, in the shadow of a goodbye that was so close now . . .

Hearing a voice, I opened my eyes. It was Gerry. He was

looking across at me. At first, I thought he was halfway between sleep and waking. He spoke as if through a dream, low and toneless, sounding somehow very far away. I realised that he was quoting from the poem.

> *. . . Not the intense moment*
> *Isolated, with no before and after,*
> *But a lifetime burning in every moment*

And that was it. The lines of my world shifted and refigured themselves in a different pattern.

Relief flowed through me, as profound as anything I'd experienced. I didn't need to dread what I didn't know, didn't need to know the end of the story. I already had what I was looking for, and nothing could take it away from me.

And there we sat, Gerry and I, with tears streaming down our faces, all in silence except for the hiss of the gas fire. Overwhelmed by the appallingness, the beauty of it all.

36

Jonathan and I sat down with the worry stone every night that week. I kept pretending to forget, but my husband, once he has decided on a course of action, can be very stubborn.

I learned some new things about him. I found out that one of his greatest fears was that he would drop down dead one day, like his dad, leaving me and Sophie to fend for ourselves. I found out that Stephen had a tendency to depression, and that Jonathan worried constantly about him. I found out that he feared I would eventually become bored with his work commitments and long hours, and leave him. I found out that I had damn nearly broken his heart, with the business over Malkie.

I squirmed with embarrassment when it was my turn. He had a notepad, and made bullet points as I listed my anxieties. He made me list each thing, first rating its severity out of ten, secondly articulating what made it so worrying, and thirdly speculating as to what might help resolve it. And he didn't say a word.

It was hard going to begin with. Even with the dizziness question tentatively resolved, there were a host of other intractable worries. They all sounded so shameful, so shocking, out loud. But after a few days, something strange happened. I began to get a little bored.

'Do you mind if we just miss out motor neurone disease tonight?' I said.

'Fine,' said Jonathan, looking at his list. 'Shall we downgrade that one to "inactive" status? That means that we don't need to discuss it again unless there are any further developments, for example new symptoms.'

'Or, maybe, if I've seen a particularly scary documentary on TV.'

'Exactly,' said Jonathan with characteristic enthusiasm, drawing a big arrow across his page, and creating a new column. 'And you *could* downgrade your worry that I'll murder the whole family in my sleep.' He shrugged. 'Only if you want to.'

I nodded. 'Okay – fair enough. You have been sleeping much better recently.'

He glanced up at me with just a glimmer of insecurity in his eyes. 'You know, I think I'll downgrade my Malkie one, too. No new developments expected there.'

I leant over the table and gave him a kiss.

★

On Sunday evening we sat down for another worry stone session. I'd just got Sophie off to bed while Jonathan spoke to his mother on the phone. Fortified by a small glass of wine over dinner, he'd finally screwed up the courage and asked the question he'd been running away from all these years.

'Well?' I asked, handing him the stone. 'What did she say?'

'She doesn't know,' he said, his voice shaking. 'She said that she had a "one-time thing" with Mr C. around about the time she got pregnant with me. So there's a chance that he is my father. She doesn't know whether Dad knew about it or not. But she thinks he guessed about the later affair, the one that took place the year before he died. So maybe, at that point, he noticed the similarity between us and put two and two together. I don't know.'

I put my hand over his.

'I'm sure he knew, Cassie. I've been trying to remember it, you know, that final argument. The look on his face, it wasn't shock. It was more like anger. But I don't think it was anger at me. It was kind of a protective look. A tigress with her cubs sort of look.'

I nodded and we sat in silence for a minute.

Then it was time. 'I've got you something, Jonathan.'

'A book?' he said, taking it from me and tearing off the wrapping.

'A book, yes, and a sort of idea . . . something I want to try and pass on. Something that I'd never dreamed of trying to talk about before we got the stone.' I wouldn't have been brave enough, I'd have feared a swift change of subject or a belittling laugh.

He nodded and passed the stone to me, signaling that he wouldn't interrupt.

I felt my face redden as I took the risk and opened my heart.

'You see, Jonathan, real love, the kind that lasts a lifetime . . . it comes from ordinary things, tiny acts of love, moments that pass by and you barely register them. It builds up in layers over days and weeks and years. And while you're not noticing, it turns into something else, something way beyond those things, something that can't be touched. I know, because I saw it – Jean and Gerry have that kind of love. And from what I've heard about your dad, I'm sure he had it for you. Jonathan, don't you see? That's why one argument on one miserable rainy school morning couldn't possibly have mattered.'

I opened the book at the bookmark I'd left, and let Jonathan read the page, and the lines I'd marked.

> . . . *Not the intense moment*
> *Isolated, with no before and after,*
> *But a lifetime burning in every moment*

He stared at the page, his face blank until his mouth twisted into a line and his forehead crumpled. His face fell into his hands and his shoulders heaved with silent sobs.

*

It took an hour for him to cry it all out. I held him and shushed him, the way I'd learned to do with Sophie in those dark lonely hours of the night.

Finally I felt his body go quiet.

'Jonathan?' I whispered.

He gave a deep, shuddering sigh and looked up at me, looked me straight in the eye.

'You and me, Cassie. We're going to have that kind of love.'

37

Three weeks later, Jonathan, Sophie and I were waiting to board a flight, comfortably ensconced in seats by the window in Edinburgh Airport's departure lounge.

Jonathan had bought fruit pastilles, three packets each, to help our ears with the ascents and descents. And he had six tiny packets of raisins for Sophie.

'So,' he said, checking the tickets and boarding passes. 'We should get to Granny Britt's at about half past eight. Are you sure we've got enough food for Sophie? I could go to Boots if you're not sure.'

'No, I think it'll be fine,' I said. 'I'm sure we could pick up some baby food somewhere if we're delayed. Or yoghurt, at least.' Sophie was going through a yoghurt craze.

'We should think of this as a test trip,' said Jonathan. 'If we manage the flights okay, we could think about visiting Stephen and Moira later in the year. Or even Helen – she's been pestering us to go and stay, hasn't she?'

'We could do all sorts of things,' I agreed, feeling a little flutter rise in my stomach. 'Let's see if the raisins work.'

It was a warm day, for April, and the sun was streaming in through the windows. Being the Easter holidays, there were lots of families there. The kids looked as if they'd been wound up, running around in circles, pressing their noses up against the windows to look at the planes.

Sophie toddled over to the windows with Jonathan, and eyed the planes seriously for a minute. She pointed her finger at the nearest plane, looked up into her daddy's adoring face, and said, 'Duck'. Then, satisfied with this categorisation, she toddled back over to me and climbed up into my lap.

I settled her on to my knee, my arms securely round her, and imagined my grandmother's house: wooden, dark and a little cold inside. I pictured the rickety wooden gate into her rambling overgrown garden, with its gnarled, stunted apple trees and climbing roses. I pictured myself climbing the wooden stairs up to the spare attic bedroom, which always made me feel like Heidi climbing up to her hayloft to sleep.

I imagined the room itself, light and sunny at the top of the house, the window looking over the garden and on, out to the sea in the distance. The bed with its white sheets and pillows, the crochet bedspread which had once been my father's.

And now Sophie would see all this too – it would be set down deep in the layers of her memory, as it had been mine.

A boarding call came over the tannoy, making me jump.

'It's okay,' said Jonathan. 'It's for the next gate along, not us. Look, that queue at Costa has gone down. I'll go and get you some hot chocolate.'

I nodded happily, then glanced over towards the neighbouring gate. To my surprise, I saw the small, duffel-coated figure of Milly Watkinson (or, I suppose, more prosaically, Milly McCabe) hopping on one leg towards the desk to have her ticket checked. A tall man in a dark coat was scrambling up from his seat and calling out, 'Milly, wait, there's a queue!'

Milly darted between the legs of the other passengers to get to the front. For once, nobody seemed to mind, and they smiled indulgently. The tall man followed her to the desk, shaking his head and apologising to the crowd as he went.

'Ma-ma?' said Sophie pulling a lock of my hair. I turned my head round and kissed her cheek. When I looked back a moment later the crowd had drawn round them and I couldn't see any more. But then I heard the pounding of small feet running down the walkway towards the plane and the man shouting, 'Milly, wait!' Then they were gone.

It would be too much to say that Milly looked happy. I suppose she looked kind of neutral. All I could say was that she was there, she was being looked after, she was on her way somewhere; a little girl hopping through an airport lounge.

And it would be too much to say that I felt, as I sat there, a warmth, a pressure in the air, something watchful, surveying the same scene from the empty seat just to the left of me. Probably it was my brain skipping ahead of my senses for a moment, noticing that it would be easy to imagine such a thing, playing with the idea of how it would feel. Or perhaps it was my imagination working hard to tell me that a scene can always be seen from another perspective, from somewhere outside of myself.

But suddenly, in that bustling airport lounge, with everyone around us heading off to different places, for purposes and reasons known only to them, to see people that I would never meet and never know, I was overcome, for a moment, with an intoxicating sense of embarking on a journey.

Jonathan appeared at my side with my cup of hot chocolate. He carefully took Sophie on to his knee so that I could drink it. I looked at the two of them, the way she melted against the shape of him, the way his arm curved protectively round her.

'I like airports,' said Jonathan happily.

'Ducks,' added Sophie.

'Yes, Sophie. I like those too. Isn't it exciting?'

'Ma-ma-ma-ma!' she chirped, holding out her arms to me

with a big wide smile, her one-year-old self bursting with a desire to feel more, see more, know more.

I put down my drink, picked her up, and carried her over to the window.

Epilogue

So that's the end. I say 'the end', but who really knows what will happen? Jonathan might lose his job tomorrow and slide into depression like his brother. One of my suspicious symptoms might turn out to be something after all. Sophie might grow up to become a teenage goth, or move to Australia.

And what about now? I still worry, of course I do. But I've learned to step back a little, to trace my anxieties back to their roots.

I've realised that part of it comes from the fear that I'm not good enough, not grown-up enough, to function in this world; that I will someday be caught out and discovered. But now, if I catch myself worrying about such things, I close my eyes and imagine what I would say to Sophie if she told me, as a young woman, that she felt that way. And the tremendous tide of my belief in her, my faith in her and everything she is, would surely sweep those concerns away in an instant.

The other worries: about Sophie, about dying and disaster, about whether my marriage is safe, are tributaries that can be traced back to a single source – that I will somehow be wrenched from those people who make up the core of me. Sometimes these fears rush at me, threatening to sweep me away; but sometimes they're just a background trickle, barely detectable on a sunny day. Either way, I now respect them for what they are. They mark the place of love, are inextricably linked with it.

But I can't let them overwhelm me, can't let them get in the way of the day-to-day business of love: the plump, splashy ritual of Sophie's bath time; the distracting songs necessary to facilitate toothbrushing, hair washing, and long car journeys; making banana sandwiches with the crusts cut off; winter evenings in front of the television; afternoon tea at the bookshop café on a Saturday afternoon.

I have to be brave. Brave enough to allow myself not to know how it all turns out. Brave enough to love them nonetheless.

I don't know, can't know, everything that will happen. But what I have learnt is that the end of the story is there, implicit, in every moment. It's the catch in your voice as you say goodnight to your child, it's the extra moment you hug your mother on the doorstep. It's when you stop, on a walk through the park in autumn, caught short by the surge in your heart when you see the flaming leaves against a crisp blue sky.

And in every moment, with every heartbeat, I hold Jonathan and Sophie close inside me. When everything around me falls quiet, I feel the words that my heart beats out.

At least for now, at this moment where our lifetimes cross, for the duration of this infinitesimal blip in the face of eternity: 'You're mine, you're mine, you're mine.'

The End